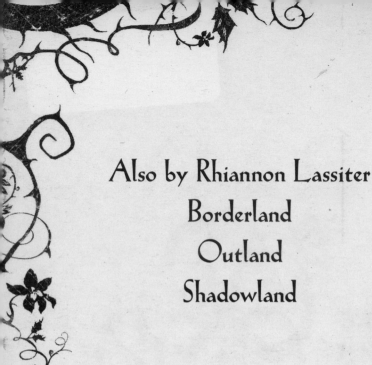

Also by Rhiannon Lassiter

Borderland

Outland

Shadowland

BAD BLOOD

Rhiannon Lassiter

OXFORD
UNIVERSITY PRESS

OXFORD
UNIVERSITY PRESS

Great Clarendon Street, Oxford OX2 6DP

Oxford University Press is a department of the University of Oxford.
It furthers the University's objective of excellence in research,
scholarship, and education by publishing worldwide in

Oxford New York

Auckland Cape Town Dar es Salaam Hong Kong Karachi
Kuala Lumpur Madrid Melbourne Mexico City Nairobi
New Delhi Shanghai Taipei Toronto

With offices in

Argentina Austria Brazil Chile Czech Republic France Greece
Guatemala Hungary Italy Japan Poland Portugal Singapore
South Korea Switzerland Thailand Turkey Ukraine Vietnam

Oxford is a registered trade mark of Oxford University Press in
the UK and in certain other countries

Text © Rhiannon Lassiter 2007

Cover and inside artwork © Christopher Gibbs 2007

The moral rights of the author have been asserted

Database right Oxford University Press (maker)

First published 2007

British Library Cataloguing in Publication Data

Data available

ISBN: 978-0-19-275473-8

3 5 7 9 10 8 6 4 2

Printed in Great Britain by Cox and Wyman Ltd, Reading, Berkshire

Paper used in the production of this book is a natural, recyclable product
made from wood grown in sustainable forests. The manufacturing process
conforms to the environmental regulations of the country of origin.

For Farah Mendlesohn,
who reads between the lines.

Contents

The Beginning 1

1. A Waste of a Name 3

2. Slightly Foxed 20

3. A Rag and a Bone and a Hank of Hair 35

4. Rotten Wood 50

5. Who is Alice? 64

6. The Make-Believe Game 73

7. Whispers in the Walls 91

8. The Hanging Tree 101

9. Fractured Light 112

10. Fox Brush 129

11. What's in a Name? 141

12. Ghost Hunt 154

13. Sticks and Stones 170

14. Things that Sting 185

15. Crossed Out 201

16. Deep Water 218

17. Shadows Beneath the Skin 237

18. Then There Was One 250

19. Ready or Not 263

20. The Waiting Game 284

21. Nameless Fears 301

The End 313

The Beginning

Above a densely forested hillside black bird-shapes wheel and turn over a weed-clogged tarn. It is winter and the bare branches reach like stunted arms up into the leaden sky. Beneath them, the landscape looks bleak and barren. Leaf litter lies in great drifts between the trees and clogs the streams, massing with rustles and whispers behind the lone house on the side of the fell.

It is a decaying house of shuttered windows, overlooking a tangled garden where strangling weeds are fighting the flowerbeds and winning. Winged reflections tremble briefly in the stagnant water of a garden pond and vanish into the grey distance. The woods rustle with animal movements and, inside the house, there's a scratching noise from behind the walls and under the floorboards.

The landscape is sleeping, beneath its blanket of dead leaves, waiting for a cruel April to rip the earth open and bring the barren world to life. But spring is not all that it is waiting for. This landscape has hibernated for sixteen winters, waiting for more than the shifting seasons. Now a change is coming and beneath the earth something stirs, a nightmare waking from its deep sleep.

1
A Waste of a Name

It began with an amusing coincidence. When Peter Brown met Harriet Wilde at a London art gallery they had each mentioned their children in the course of their conversation and been struck by the similarity of names.

'Is your Kat a Katherine as well?' Peter had asked.

'She's Catriona, Cat with a C,' Harriet explained, adding for good measure, 'My ex-husband chose it.'

'Katherine was my wife's middle name,' Peter replied, using the past tense rather self-consciously.

'We cat people should stick together.' Harriet smiled, and they'd chinked their glasses with a feeling of camaraderie.

Their children had felt rather differently about it. When Harriet confessed to them that she was seeing Peter seriously Roley and Cat had been appalled. Their mother's new boyfriend had seemed like such a dull and boring person on his occasional visits to the house that neither of them had really paid him much attention. It had come as an unpleasant surprise that Harriet wanted them to get to know his family 'because it would be nice for the two families to do things together'.

'She means because she might marry him and we'll have to live with them,' Cat had said, suspending her usual state of hostilities with her older brother to enlist his support.

'And they're bound to be awful and dull, just like him. Mum says they have good manners—you know what that means.'

'We'll have to be nice to them because their mother is dead,' Roley predicted dolefully. 'Mum says we're lucky we've still got a dad.'

'And their *names*.' Cat had pulled a face. 'John and Katherine? Could you be more boring than that?'

'Might as well be called Child A and Child B,' Roley agreed.

That remark was one he'd regretted later. He hadn't imagined that Cat would remember it or that she'd say it to anyone's face. That first lunch at Peter's flat had degenerated into a screaming row. Roley had been grateful when John asked him very politely if Roley would like to see his dinosaur collection. Afterwards they'd spent a soothing hour together building a spider robot out of John's mechanical Lego.

'I've got some dinosaur Lego at home,' Roley had said, not knowing what else to say to the younger boy. They were both pretending to ignore the noise from the living room.

'That sounds good,' John said, looking up from his part of the robot with a considering expression. He was thinking that going to tea at Harriet's house next week might not be so bad if there was going to be dinosaur Lego.

Roley had seemed enormous in the living room but scrunched up half underneath John's desk he seemed smaller and his eyes behind his thick glasses screwed up with alarm whenever the noise from the other room got louder.

'It's a pity, isn't it,' John said thoughtfully. 'About both of our sisters having the same name.'

'Mum said her name was Katherine.' Roley shifted awkwardly and fiddled with the robot's arm. 'I didn't know you called her Kat.'

'She's always called Kat,' John explained. 'That's why she didn't like it when your sister said she should be Kathy instead.'

'Catriona's always Cat as well,' Roley said glumly. 'Just like I'm always Roley instead of Roland.'

'There isn't anything John can be shortened to,' John said, thinking about it. 'It is a dull sort of thing to be called. I suppose that's what your sister meant when she said it was a waste of a name.'

'At least it can't be turned into anything embarrassing,' Roley said, trying to offer some compensation. 'My mum sometimes calls me Roley Poley.'

'All the same, I think your sister was right,' John said, snapping the last batteries into place and setting the robot upright with small careful movements. 'It is a waste of a name.' He looked at Roley, watching the bigger boy's eyes screw up again behind his glasses. 'If we were both called it, I wouldn't mind changing to something else. I expect I'd get used to it eventually.'

They'd had two and a half years to get used to it but the problem had never been solved. They'd tried calling the two girls 'Katherine Kat' and 'Catriona Cat'. They'd tried calling them 'my cat' and 'your cat' and 'cat with a Cee' and 'cat with a Kay'. Nothing had worked.

Katherine still called Catriona 'her' or 'Harriet's daughter'.

Catriona had been ordered to stop calling Katherine 'Kathy' or 'Jennyennydots' but she still did it when the adults weren't listening. Under the circumstances Roley had felt too guilty to ask his mother if he could be called Roland now he was sixteen. And John had celebrated his tenth birthday by inventing a secret name for himself and writing it in invisible ink on a piece of paper he kept in his sock drawer.

It was the kind of thing that couldn't be helped. But it seemed to make every conversation just a bit more difficult. And people always noticed and pointed it out and said how awkward it must be. At the wedding the best man had told the story of how Peter and Harriet met and there had been an awkward silence as the guests wondered if either of them had thought it might be much simpler to marry someone else instead.

Roley had got used to living in a war zone. Since the wedding he'd found Catriona easier to get on with. She used to criticize him all the time, calling him a 'great lummox', 'clumsy oaf', or 'cave bear'—all criticisms she'd copied from their mother. By the time he was sixteen Roley had got used to feeling as if he was a shambling ape-like creature, incapable of entering a room without knocking something over, unable to express himself except in grunts.

But after Peter had sold his flat and moved in with his children, Catriona had focused her hostility on Katherine and John. She hadn't wanted to share a house with them at all, had refused to even discuss the plans, and then been furious all over again when Harriet had spent that year's holiday fund on decorating rooms for Katherine and John. It had meant losing the upstairs living room with the 'children's TV' which Cat had appropriated anyway, and Harriet giving up her study.

'We all have to make sacrifices,' she'd said, getting Roley to help move her desk to a corner of the dining room. 'And the books about reconstituted families all say it's better if each child has their own room.' Harriet was amassing a collection of these books, coming home with a new one after each row, as if the new book might have the answer to all their problems.

Roley had read a few of those books himself. Cat had been so bitter and angry and resentful that Harriet spent most of her time having long careful talks with her and Roley had wanted to sort out his own feelings. He had noticed that any time he might have been inclined to object to something, Cat made a huge scene and he ended up being less on her side than before. He wished his mother would appreciate he was making an effort but, in a house constantly seething with resentment, where doors slammed and voices were raised to a headache-inducing pitch, he ended up lurking in his room more often than not.

He was secretly lifting weights, a birthday present from his father he'd not told anyone about. Harriet and Cat were naturally skinny and they both looked at him with a sort of amazed pity when he finished his first course and looked around for seconds. At least Peter had supplied another man-sized appetite, and an enthusiasm for puddings. He made these himself and Roley found it difficult to keep his new resolution to lose weight when another mouth-watering concoction of brown sugar and baked apples was served up. However, a lot of meals never made it to pudding, ending when Katherine left the table in tears and locked herself in the bathroom.

It was John who Roley really felt sorry for. He felt it was rough lines on someone who'd obviously been used to peace and quiet, to have to live in such perpetual uproar. The worst thing about it was that Harriet had been right when she said the Brown children had very good manners. At least, they had had. Nowadays Katherine seemed to spend most of her time on the verge of tears and Roley inwardly groaned every time she locked herself in the family bathroom, since she had a perfectly good room of her own to go and sob in. John was still quiet and polite, saying please and thank you even when people didn't seem to notice him, and quietly playing in his room when the grown-ups didn't have time for him. Sometimes he would knock on Roley's door, the only person who ever did: Harriet would shout up the stairs when she wanted him and Cat walked in and out without asking. But John knocked so quietly you could barely hear him and would ask as politely as always if Roley minded him being there.

Roley wasn't ever sure what to talk about, but John seemed to be happy to watch whatever he was doing, and was actually getting quite good at computer games. Roley thought that when money was less tight he might suggest that they got John a computer of his own. But that would lead to another fight. After the room redecoration Peter and Harriet had spent their free money on a new family sized car, a vast Toyota Previa that Cat claimed was an embarrassment to be seen in, although Roley was grateful that he didn't have to sit with his arms between his knees any more.

The car was so they could go places together but it looked as if for a third year running there'd be no family holiday, when the letter arrived.

It was a lumpy brown envelope with Peter's name on it in wavering handwriting. When he'd opened it with the butter knife three pieces of almost transparent paper had fallen out, covered with crabbed densely-written italic script, wrapped around a heavy iron key.

'It's from Thomas Stone,' Peter said in surprise, as he tried to decipher the black spikes of words, apparently written with a poker. 'Anne's uncle. I rather thought he'd passed away years ago.'

The others hadn't paid much attention. Harriet was busy with her usual morning rush and Cat and Kat were hissing insults at each other behind the cornflakes packet. Roley was trying to decide whether, if he didn't have another piece of toast now, he would need a chocolate bar to sustain him through break later on. But John picked up the key.

'What's it for?' he asked, turning it over in his hands.

'It's the key to a house in the Lake District,' Peter said, holding the transparent paper up to the light and squinting at the writing. 'Anne grew up there. Her parents moved away when she went to university and the house was rented out for a long time but now it's empty again. Thomas writes that he intends to sell it in the summer but he's offering us the use of it for a holiday. If we'd like to go.'

'Mum lived there?' Kat looked up at that. 'I'd like to see the house she grew up in.'

'I've already been to the Lake District,' Cat said coolly, using the last of the milk on her cereal. 'I went with Josie from school. Her parents have a house and a boat.'

Harriet was looking interested now and leant over Peter's shoulder as he read the rest of the letter.

'This would be different,' she said seriously. 'This would be our first holiday as a family.'

Roley had needed a second and a third piece of toast to cheer him up during the rest of breakfast. Doing Things as a Family was quickly becoming his least favourite activity. It seemed to act as a cover for trips to places that no one wanted to go to and conversations about things that no one wanted to talk about. It meant Cat shouting and Kat sulking and Roley and John having a strained conversation about marmosets, or Beethoven, or whatever it was they were supposed to be appreciating, while their parents tried to calm the girls down.

All the same, being a family seemed to mean that Roley didn't get a vote. No one asked him if he'd rather spend the holiday doing something else. Catriona had said she'd been invited to stay at a friend's house but their mother hadn't listened. Katherine said she wouldn't come if she had to share a room but her father had said he was sure they could work something out and had started telling John about the Lakes. 'It's a perfect holiday spot. Lots of beautiful walks. Heavenly scenery. And we can go sailing on the Lakes.

Arthur Ransome wrote stories set there about the Swallows and Amazon children having adventures in boats. Perhaps the four of you will learn to sail.'

'I can sail already,' Catriona said flatly. 'I've been with friends from school heaps of times.'

'That's terrific,' Peter said cheerfully. 'Then you'll be able to show the rest of us what to do.'

'The Swallows and Amazons had different boats,' Katherine muttered under her breath. 'And they had a war, not an adventure.'

Roley thought glumly that a war sounded only too likely. Especially since a cottage in the Lake District probably wouldn't have enough bedrooms for all of them to have their own. He'd made plans to sign up to a gym this summer and go to the swimming pool and try to get a tan. He was sick of the pale podgy face he saw in the mirror, which seemed to be stuck as a 'Roley', and he had a vision of coming back to school next year as someone who you'd take seriously as Roland. He'd even thought he might meet girls at the swimming pool, pretty *quiet* girls who wouldn't be swept up by lads like Mark who did karate or Julian who had tanned good looks from summers spent windsurfing in the Med.

But the Lake District holiday moved ahead with the same inevitability as Peter and Harriet's wedding. Two weeks later they had loaded up the car and set off up the M6 in a car packed so tightly with luggage that Roley was as cramped as ever. Thomas Stone had written directions in his letter but Harriet had printed out a precise route from the internet, saying that she never trusted directions unless they were real ones with road numbers.

The only problem was that once they got to the Lake District the roads didn't seem to have any numbers. The directions had been fine until they left the A road and things suddenly went from bad to worse. The atmosphere of forced jollity emanating from the front of the car had been replaced by the exaggerated politeness of an imminent argument.

The Toyota Previa rumbled along the narrow lanes between walls of slate-like stones overgrown with moss. The fields beyond rose and fell lumpily every which way until they eventually heaved themselves up into the smoother curves of the fells. Afternoon was shading into evening and the scenery seemed muted, a watercolour palette of greens, yellows, greys, and browns rising up to the pale sky bruised with grey purple clouds.

Roley, sitting in the middle row of seats in the seven-person car, squashed his nose against the window, trying to conjure up one of the signs from the old man's letter: the sharp turn right, the five-barred gate, and the narrow entrance between stone walls. The only trouble was the Lake District seemed to be full of sharp turns, wooden gates, and stone walls and each mistake resulted in the car having to reverse, or mount a lumbering turn like the beast of burden it seemed to be.

Beside him the tish-tish-tish of Catriona's MP3 player leaked out from her in-the-ear headphones with irritating repetitiveness. His mother had made him turn off the sound on his Game Boy but she'd let Cat be. His sister had spent almost the whole journey slumped in her seat, head hunched forward into the fluffy collar of her coat, eyes hidden behind dark glasses, and the fact that she didn't want to be here written in every line of her body. During the journey she had eaten KitKats with painful slowness, unwrapping and eating each piece in small neat bites before finally swallowing the last segment and licking the chocolate from her fingers.

In the third row of seats Peter's children were squashed up with luggage that had spilled over from the boot. The hierarchy of the car seats had required that the two youngest take the smallest space and any conversation with their father had to happen past the backs of the others' heads.

John had spent the journey reading the *Spotters' Guide to the Lake District* his father had given him, carefully looking up the long words in the dictionary he had packed in his new rucksack. Harriet, his stepmother, had given it to him with instructions to pack anything he needed for the journey and when she discovered it still virtually empty had seemed oddly apologetic. When John had opened it in the car he'd been pleased and surprised to discover that she had added four chocolate Tracker bars, a puzzle game that fitted neatly into a polished wooden box, and a pair of shiny new binoculars in their own special case.

In her uncomfortable seat, Katherine stared at the back of Catriona's head and thought of new reasons for hating her. The smooth conker-like shine of dark brown hair irritated her with its too-perfect advert glossiness. She was annoyed at her father's acceptance of each piece of KitKat wrapping that Catriona peremptorily held out for him to dispose of. She was cross about everything and each new twist of irritation rubbed salt into the raw wound of the fact that her stepsister had stolen her name.

She'd never thought much about her name until the infamous row at that first lunch. 'You can't be Kat,' Catriona had said. '*I'm* Cat and I'm older. You'll have to be Kathy. That's fair, isn't it?' The terrible thing was that it had seemed for a moment as if everyone would just agree. Harriet had smiled nervously and Peter had looked uncomfortable, but he hadn't said no. Sitting at the table, looking at the meal she'd helped to make beginning to congeal on her plate into something she couldn't imagine eating, she'd felt as if someone had taken a cloth and just wiped her out, like a whiteboard. And even though afterwards, when she'd been sobbing in her room and Peter had promised her that she'd always be Kat, that Katherine had been her mother's second name and was doubly precious to him, things had never been the same again.

Deep down, she thought all the others felt she was making a fuss about nothing. And Catriona had said in a sweetly reasonable voice later on that no one had said she couldn't be Katherine but everyone knew Katherines were Kathys and Catrionas were Cats, implying that Kat had never had any right to the name in the first place.

In her lap, Kat's book sat unregarded. She'd brought *Swallows and Amazons*, which she'd read twice before, but she didn't think she could bear to read it now. She'd started it but she'd got to the part where the children's mother was coming to meet them and had felt the tears start to well up in her eyes. She hadn't wanted the others to see her cry. She hated the look of bored contempt that slid across Catriona's face like a mask and Roley rolling his eyes heavenwards again, and John looking small and pinched and worried as he did so often these days. Instead she'd watched the scenery go past, weak and watery in the blurred view through the window and her own wet eyes, wishing herself anywhere but here.

Harriet had just manoeuvred the car around another hairpin turn when John sat up in the back seat, swivelling around to look through the window. It was getting dark now and he frowned into the shadows at the roadside.

'Did you see something?' Kat asked quietly, turning to look.

'I thought I did,' he said. 'I thought I saw a face.'

'What kind of face?' she asked, dropping her voice to whisper.

'A foxy sort of face,' he said. 'With shiny eyes.'

'Oh.' Kat glanced over at him, seeming to come out of a daydream, and her eyes focused on John's wildlife book. 'Good going. We've only been here half an hour and you've already seen a fox.'

'No.' John shook his head. 'That's not what I meant.' He looked up at his sister, surprised that she hadn't understood him, and tried again to explain. 'It wasn't a real fox . . . ' he began.

'I see a gate!' Roley called out, causing Harriet to stall the car as she looked around in all directions for any sign of it. 'Over there, the road swings right and just round the corner . . . '

Roley was winding down his window as he spoke, staring into the dusk, as if trying to fix the gate in place by staring at it.

'That could be it,' Peter said cheerfully. 'Well done, old chap.'

The engine juddered as Harriet turned it back on and edged the car around the turn. There she stopped so Peter could get out and open the gate. Roley continued to hang out of his window, trying to see ahead, and Cat straightened up out of her hunched position to look over her shades with a cool expression.

Peter got back in and shut the door with a firm thump and Harriet began to creep the car forward. The stone walls on either side had climbed up high banks where they jostled against the slanted trunks of trees and the view ahead was obscured by drooping branches. None of them could see any sign of the house until the walls came to an abrupt end, opening out on the right to reveal an expanse of mossy lawn and flowerbeds tangled with greenery, stretching into the dim distance.

On the left-hand side was the house. Its dark bulk merged into the grey and brown shadows of the wooded hill behind it so that at first it was difficult to make out anything except how large it was.

'This can't be right,' Harriet said, uncertainly, pulling the car to a crunching stop on the gravel drive. 'It's too large, surely?'

'The gate and the stone walls fit the directions,' Peter replied, but he was also looking doubtful. 'This should be Fell Scar House. Perhaps there's a sign somewhere?'

Roley was on the wrong side of the car to look properly, but craning his neck he saw a row of six windows on the ground floor alone, a second row above and then a third, hooded by grey slate eaves.

'There aren't any lights on inside,' he said. 'Perhaps this is the place.'

'Well, if it isn't, they're probably wondering if we're casing the joint,' Catriona pointed out. Releasing her seat belt and dumping her rucksack in the minute fraction of space left between her and Roley, she reached out and opened the door.

'Cat . . . wait!' her mother said and Catriona stopped halfway out of the car with a contemptuous look.

'Why don't we just see if the key works?' she asked. 'Who's got it, anyway?'

'Here.' Peter took it out of the glove compartment and wound down his window to hand it to her. Catriona took it without comment. As she turned to walk up the broad stone steps, John unsnapped his seat belt as well.

'I want to come too,' he said, and pressed the release for his side of the middle seats, wriggling through the gap to follow Catriona out into the dusk.

Roley was already getting out of his own door, wanting to get a better look at the house, even if it wasn't the right place. Harriet and Peter followed, watching Catriona as she reached the top of the steps. But Katherine remained in the car, shivering in the chill from the open doors. The house was huge, more like a stately home than a holiday cottage, looming out of the side of the hill. She didn't believe for a second this could be the right place and was crossing her fingers for an irate householder to come out and yell at Catriona for trespassing.

John caught up with Catriona at the top of the steps and she paused before trying to put the key in the lock.

'I'm going to knock first,' she said.

'With that?' John asked, staring at the door knocker. It was in the shape of a mask: a cruel mask with a long curved nose like a bird's beak.

'Urggh,' Catriona said. 'Creepy.' But she took hold of it and rapped it against the door. Three knocks echoed in a muffled way from inside the house and she shrugged. 'Here goes nothing,' she said and fitted the key into the lock. It was stiff and reluctant to turn and Catriona stepped back at the first hint of resistance.

'Maybe this isn't the place,' she said.

'Try turning it the other way,' John suggested and reached out to try his own suggestion.

The key turned smoothly in the lock and it clicked open, the door swinging inwards to reveal a large wood-panelled room ahead.

'It *is* the right place,' John declared, feeling a smile spread across his face.

'Come and help bring the bags in!' Harriet called, as Peter opened up the boot of the car. But John had already stepped past the threshold and Catriona was only a step after him.

'Back in a minute, Mum,' Roley said, catching his own bag from the boot and hurrying up towards the house.

'Go on then.' Peter turned a smile on Katherine, only now getting slowly out of the car. 'You don't want those three to bagsy the best rooms, do you?'

Katherine hesitated. But she could already see lights turning on across the ground floor and shapes moving around inside.

'They can't just have any room, can they?' she asked over her shoulder as she walked up towards the house.

'Looks as if there's plenty to go around,' Peter said cheerfully.

'Tell them that the master bedroom's ours though,' Harriet added. 'I'm not coming on holiday to sleep in a single bed.'

Peter smiled at her, relieved that the journey had reached so positive a conclusion, and reached out to give her a hug. Six steps up, the wind gusted against the door and the knocker clacked down against the brass plate like a bird snapping its beak shut tight around a wriggling worm. Katherine gave it an uneasy glance before sliding round the side of the door and into the house.

2
Slightly Foxed

Katherine could hear the others moving around upstairs as she entered the house. From the noise they were making it sounded as if they weren't just choosing rooms but hauling furniture about, but she didn't think even Catriona would have that much cheek. It was the kind of house she would have loved to explore but since the others were already ahead of her the adventure was spoiled. Like visiting a medieval castle and finding Coke cans and cigarette butts lying about.

The main room was dim, the light barely enough to drive the shadows back into the corners. All around the walls were pieces of heavy furniture: sideboards, bookcases, and a grandfather clock. A long wooden table and chairs for ten people took up the middle of the room, centred on a patterned carpet. But the carpet was threadbare and the books and ornaments dull with dust.

A door on the right opened into what might be a living room, where tapestry-covered chairs and spindly-legged occasional tables clustered around a stone fireplace and a piano lurked in the darkness at the back. Just like the first room, the walls were covered with bookcases, these ones with glass fronts, the books behind identically bound in black leather with gold titles. There was no sign of a TV and Katherine had a twinge of *schadenfreude* at the thought of her stepsister's inevitable complaints.

Turning back, she crossed the main room to the other door—which opened into the largest kitchen she'd seen in a private house. An ancient Aga cooker squatted at one end, between built-in cupboards with wooden counters scarred and pitted from years of use. A kitchen table large enough to seat eight people tried to fill the space on the other side and Kat wondered if they'd eat here or in the main room. If they were only here for a couple of weeks she didn't see how they could make use of all this space.

Peter and Harriet were bringing suitcases in through the front door and she hung back until they'd gone out for the next load. The staircase up was reached through a pair of double doors, both of which hung open at the level of the third step. It turned two corners before reaching the first floor, past a grimy window and flaking plaster walls. Books were piled up in the corners of the stairs and across the deep windowsill, looking as if they'd been there for years.

As she reached the first floor the others were coming down from the second floor, Catriona taking the lead. Roley's footsteps thundered as he followed along the corridor, the floorboards creaking in protest. Katherine had to flatten herself against the wall as they pushed past her but her own brother swung exuberantly around the last banister and came to a halt with a sudden grin.

'This staircase leads up to the attics,' John told her. 'But guess what? At the other end of the corridor there's another staircase which goes all the way up as well!'

'What are the bedrooms like?' Katherine asked, worried that Catriona was already selecting the best one, and John grinned happily at her.

'Which ones?' he asked. 'There's two in each attic and there's more along here. I'll show you.'

The corridor was lined with more books, overflowing from rickety bookcases and stacked up in towers alongside them, not even all facing the same direction. John pointed out the rooms as he led the way down the corridor. The door frames were crooked, or looked it under the slightly sloping ceilings, and the doors themselves had latches instead of handles and each keyhole bristled with a heavy iron key.

The first room, with a mustard-coloured wallpaper, had a high single bed across from an ancient looking computer on an old wooden bureau. The second had blue-flowered wallpaper and contained two single beds with matching blue counterpanes. The third was rose pink and held a brass-knobbed double bed and Katherine thought it must be the main bedroom until John pulled her along the corridor and she saw the next one also had a double bed and was even larger. A pattern of long green leaves dappled the room, like branches of weeping willow, which she thought was the prettiest wallpaper yet.

'This will be Dad and Harriet's room,' she said. 'Unless there are any even bigger.'

'No, this is the largest,' John said, after a pause to think about it. 'The next door's just a bathroom, see?' He opened it to show a loo with a long pull chain hanging from an overhead cistern, a massive bath with little claw-feet, and a china sink.

'Only one bathroom?' Katherine said doubtfully. 'Among six of us?' But John wasn't listening.

'You haven't even seen the attics yet,' he reminded her. 'Come on.'

There were four attic bedrooms, two at the top of each staircase, each with a pointed arch-shaped door. John explained that the two in the middle connected with a door, so you could go round and round the house in a circle, up one set of stairs and down the other. That was what they'd all been doing when she'd arrived.

'Except only the big staircase goes all the way to the bottom,' he added.

As John ran ahead through the attic and across to the other set of stairs, Katherine lingered behind. Catriona had already claimed one of the middle attic bedrooms by leaving her MP3 player down on the bedside table and her coat on the bed. She'd chosen a middle one, so that no one would be able to come through the connecting door without disturbing her. Katherine wondered what had attracted her to it, glancing around the room. There wasn't much furniture, only a bed, a chair, a dressing table, and a built-in cupboard. And of course the bookcases: three of them here with a collection of old school stories and girls' annuals from the 1970s. But, under the sloping roof, the window embrasure was dominated by a three-storey doll's house.

It was a real doll's house, made of wood, not plastic, and with real glass windows. Even the roof was made of miniature pieces of overlapping slate. The front was hinged at one side and Katherine opened the catch gently, feeling the smooth action of the door as it opened. Inside there were three rooms on the ground floor and Katherine had a sense of déjà vu as she saw a kitchen on the left furnished with cupboards and a doll's house Aga, a living room at the right complete with doll-sized piano and spindle-legged tables and a main room full of heavy wooden furniture from which a staircase led up.

On the first floor of the doll's house were bedrooms decorated with miniature versions of the wallpaper Katherine had seen in the rooms downstairs: blue flowers, pink roses, and green willow patterns. The paper couldn't be off-cuts because the prints were the right size for the doll's house instead of being much too big to suit the small rooms, so perhaps someone had painted copies. Katherine was suddenly sure the doll's house had belonged to her mother. The rooms had stone fireplaces and even metal grates. In the single bathroom the furnishings were china and the bath had tiny claw-feet. On either side of the doll's house a staircase led up into the roof. It was almost a perfect replica of the real house, down to the books jostling for space on the bookcases. Katherine almost expected to see doll figures of her family holding little suitcases. But there were no dolls.

Katherine looked again at the roof, feeling along either side for the catch she was sure was there. It clicked in her hands and she lifted it off, holding her breath, wondering what sort of dolls they would be. But to her disappointment the attic was empty. As she'd expected there were four rooms, the middle two linked by a connecting door, but no dolls and no doll's version of the doll's house. There was only the doll-sized attic window, looking out through the real window into the twilight sky.

Katherine replaced the roof gently, treating the carefully crafted toy house with care. As she was closing the door of the doll's house the sound of booted feet on the stairs stirred her from her position and she turned to see Catriona and Roley at the top of the stairs.

'I've already chosen this room,' Catriona said at once and Katherine glared at her.

'I was just looking at the doll's house,' she said, and heard her own voice come out defensively despite the fact this was more her house than Catriona's. After all, it was *her* mother who'd lived here.

'I didn't spot that before.' Roley came over and peered over Katherine's shoulder. 'Hey, this is like the real house.'

'I know.' Katherine closed the door, protectively. 'Where are the dolls?' she asked her stepsister.

'Why would I go looking for *dolls*?' Catriona looked scornful, sitting back on the bed with an air of possession.

'You picked the room,' Kat snapped back, thinking that the way Catriona fussed with her hair and make-up and clothes she was probably the sort of girl who had heaps of Barbies before she started pretending to be too grown-up.

'I picked it because it's the furthest away from *their* room,' Catriona sneered, narrowing her eyes. 'I don't want to be woken up in the middle of night and hear . . . '

'I didn't see any dolls,' Roley said quickly, his nose and cheeks stained by a sudden bright blush. 'But there's a train set in the other attic and a big box of trains.' He hovered at the connecting door and then moved off through it. Catriona deliberately busied herself taking things out of her bag and after a moment Katherine followed Roley, leaving the door open. She'd barely left when Catriona closed it behind her.

The other two attic rooms were as John had described and under other circumstances Kat might have admired the sloping beams and the dormer windows. But with Catriona in the other attic, she didn't want to be up here as well. John had found the train set and was talking to Roley about it as Katherine passed by quickly, walking back down the stairs to the first floor.

She wanted to pick her mother's room and she felt resentful of Catriona's choice. But perhaps the doll's house had simply been put there for safe keeping, and her mother's room was actually another one. With the memory of the doll's house in her mind exploring the rooms felt strange, as if she'd been miniaturized and was walking around the small house instead of the real one.

She only glanced at the double bedroom with the pink roses, feeling uncomfortable as she recalled Catriona's suggestion she might hear noises from there during the night. The room with the computer she mentally assigned to Roley; even if it did look like an antique Roley was geeky enough to find it interesting.

In the blue-flowered room Katherine opened the door of a built-in wardrobe, to find it almost full of clothes. There were long dresses and skirts and shawls, made of silk, lace, and velvet: now faded and smelling of damp. Hippy clothes, Kat thought, and wondered if this had been her mother's room and if these were her clothes. She'd have liked to try on some of them and she shut the wardrobe again carefully, reminding herself to try later when the others weren't watching. Taking off her coat she put it down on the bed before going to take another look at the computer room. It didn't have a wardrobe, just a chest of drawers and the inevitable bookcase crammed full of double rows of paper-backed books. But there was a cupboard door in the corner and Katherine went to open it, expecting a hanging rail or shelves. Instead the door opened into a vast shadowy space.

It took her a moment to recognize it as another room: unplastered and windowless although there were skylights in the roof through which the remains of the day's light filtered faintly.

'A secret door.' Katherine breathed the words softly into the shadows. The room must be an attached barn or something; its shape had been hidden by the bulk of the house when they arrived.

Surprisingly sturdy pine stairs led down from the cupboard door into the barn room, but everything else was old and rotten. Up above her the roof beams were exposed and heavy with cobwebs, a single bare light bulb swinging from the rafters. Down on the exposed and unsanded wooden floor stood a pool table covered by a stained sheet, a rusted swinging chair seat with stained cushions, a couple of old armchairs with torn upholstery and the inevitable piles of books. These were in the worst condition of any she'd seen. Water-damage, cobwebs, and filth had added up so that Katherine didn't even feel like touching anything.

At the top of the pine stairs, she had to turn back before closing the cupboard door just to convince herself she hadn't imagined it. For a minute she had a daydream about claiming the dull computer room as hers and keeping the door in the wall as her secret. But she knew it wouldn't work. The space was some kind of games room, for playing in on wet days. Even if it was filthy, Dad would think it was selfish to keep it a secret and he'd make her share it with the others so that they'd be trooping in and out of her bedroom all day.

Shutting the cupboard door and bolting it again, she knew she'd have to tell. But for now she hugged the secret to herself as she headed downstairs to help with the unpacking.

In the kitchen Harriet was sitting at the table drinking a glass of white wine while Peter rubbed her shoulders.

'It's an incredible house,' Harriet said. 'I must try and find a book of Aga recipes when we buy food.' Turning to smile at Peter she added, 'Mmm, that's lovely . . . did you know it was so large?'

'I had no idea,' he said, shaking his head. 'Anne didn't talk about her childhood much. It wasn't a happy one.' Planting a kiss on the top of his wife's head, he released her and sat down next to her at the table, as Harriet poured a glass of wine for him. 'She didn't get on with her parents and they moved out to the Channel Islands not long after she went up to university—never even came to our wedding. When I wrote to tell him about Anne's death her father sent a very peculiar letter of condolence, implying we were better off. I didn't reply.'

'How terrible.' Harriet looked at him with sympathy but before she could say more Roley came in and she looked up with a smile. 'There you are, Roley Poley. What do you think of the house?'

'It's big,' Roley said. 'There's eight bedrooms and some of them are twins or doubles. No TV though,' he added as an afterthought.

'Thank goodness!' Harriet exclaimed. 'We can do without the idiot box on holiday, surely?'

Roley shrugged, looking at the wine glasses, and asked: 'Can I have some wine then?'

'If you like,' Peter said and Harriet added:

'Just a half glass.' She took the bottle as Roley brought the wine glass and poured it herself to a third of the way up.

John came in while she was pouring it and came to join them at the table. His face was glowing with wonder, obviously enchanted with the house.

'Did you choose a room?' Harriet asked and John hesitated.

'I liked the room with the train set,' he said carefully, looking at Roley for approval.

'You should have that one then,' Roley told him, taking his wine. 'Thanks, Mum.' Turning to Peter he added, 'It's one of the attic rooms, and Cat's taken one with a doll's house.'

'No, I haven't.'

Katherine spoke automatically, unable to let the remark go unchallenged. She saw everyone pause in their movements, Roley with the wine glass at his lips, Harriet replacing the cork in the wine bottle, John and her father looking at each other. Like dolls in a doll's house without people to move them, or puppets with their strings cut. It gave her a feeling of power and guilt at once, reminding them of the injustice she had to bear.

'I meant my sister had,' Roley said, after a moment, even though they all knew what he had meant. 'I'll go and get the bags now, shall I?'

'Peter's already brought them in,' Harriet said, more sharply than she'd intended. 'They're in the hall. Take yours up and for God's sake unpack properly. I hate the way you kids live out of suitcases as if we were in a doss house instead of someone's home.'

Roley didn't say anything but he picked up his glass of wine and took it with him and John hesitated for a second before running after him.

Peter looked at Katherine and smiled as kindly as he could.

'What room did you choose then, sweetheart?'

'A blue one, on the first floor,' she told him. 'Do you want me to show you yours?'

'I suppose we had better unpack ourselves,' Harriet said, making to get up but Peter pressed her gently down again.

'I'll do that,' he said. 'You've done all that driving.'

Putting an arm around Katherine's shoulders he ushered her out and Harriet watched them go. 'You must be pleased to see so many books,' he said. 'Like a treasure trove for you; I hope we'll be able to prise you away.'

'They're just shelved any which way though,' Katherine told him as she led the way up the stairs. 'And a lot of them are stained and torn.'

'Foxed,' Peter said absently and when she looked back at him he smiled. 'It's what booksellers call it,' he said. 'Not stained, just slightly foxed.'

Katherine hadn't said anything about the barn room, during a scratch supper of baked beans on toast, although she'd whispered to John on his way to bed that she had a secret to tell him tomorrow. Harriet had instituted a rota for the bathroom and sent everyone to unpack. Catriona had already headed up into the attics and Roley disappeared into the second double bedroom, which he'd chosen, despite the pink roses, for the sake of the extra space. The dull computer room had been left empty and there was no one to disturb as Katherine crept across to open the secret door.

Rather than turn on the light, she used her torch to find her way down the stairs and across the bare floorboards, wearing her pyjama bottoms tucked into her boots. The floor was littered with paper scraps and bird droppings and crunched softly under her feet.

The bookcases were improvised: long board shelves propped up with logs of wood at each end. Katherine scanned them automatically. She'd already built up a mental catalogue of books in the house. *Swallows and Amazons* books were in the room she'd chosen, neatly jacketed hardbacks, hardly read at all. Downstairs there were factual books of Lakeland walks and bird species, and the living room ones were Shakespeare and histories of England, some so old that the pages were the kind that had to be cut open. The attics had a jumble of fairytales and bible stories mixed in with the old school stories and stacks of yellowed magazines. The computer room had battered and creased modern paperbacks: John Grishams and Joanna Trollopes, perhaps abandoned by the people who'd been renting the house.

The ones in the barn were children's books, the kind you thought of as classics. She prodded them carefully, looking out for spiders or other creepy-crawlies as she studied the spines. When she finally freed one from the shelves and flicked through the pages she realized it had a bookplate, gummed in on the first blank page. It was a black and white engraving of a fox, curled up on a pile of books, and underneath a round childish hand had written: Anne Katherine Stone. Her mother had owned this book.

By the time Katherine crept back up the stairs she'd found two more with the same fox bookplate. There was no central heating and she was shivering when she finally got into bed, pulling up the icy sheets and the rough blanket around her.

Turning on her bedside light she looked at the books she'd chosen: *A Little Princess* by Frances Hodgson Burnett, *Emily of New Moon* by L. M. Montgomery, and *Alice's Adventures in Wonderland* by Lewis Carroll. Picking up the first one she looked again at the bookplate. 'Slightly foxed' was right, she thought, flipping through the pages to see how bad the damage was. The edges of the pages were dog-eared and tattered, the covers stained with the grime of cobwebs.

Suddenly she stopped flipping. She'd read this book before, some years ago, and vaguely remembered the story. It began with Sara Crewe being sent to boarding school in

London while her father went back to India. But as she reached the part about the fat girl the others had laughed at, the one that became Sara's friend, a word had been crossed out. A thick black line, scored so deeply into the page it had almost torn through the paper, went right through her name.

Frowning, Katherine flipped on. There it was again, on every page where the girl's name appeared the same black line was scored straight through it. Ermengarde, that's what she'd been called, Kat remembered. She could still make out the shapes of the letters but all through the book the name was gone.

It wasn't just one name. There had been other characters Sara made friends with, the people who comforted her when she lost her money and the cruel headmistress had punished her by making her a scullery maid. Their names were crossed out as well. Hardly knowing what she was looking for, Katherine turned to the very end of the book. The person who eventually rescued Sara didn't have a real name, she remembered, he was just called the Indian Gentleman. Reaching the part she was looking for she sucked in her breath sharply. A black scribble of jagged lines barred the whole page, ending in sharp spiked points.

Each page after that was crossed and scarred with the same scribble, obsessively crossing and recrossing the words in every direction until not even the shapes of the letters could be seen through it and all that remained was a meaningless jumble of small white marks in the black web, like the scars of the words they had been. The happy ending had been completely obliterated and instead the book ended with darkness and despair.

The other two books with the fox bookplate had the same crossings out. In *Emily of New Moon* the names of the heroine's best friends and protectors had the same black lines scored through them. But it was the Alice book that really frightened her. On every page, names were missing. The White Rabbit, the Caterpillar, the Cheshire Cat, the Mad Hatter, and the March Hare, practically the entire cast of characters, all their names were gone. Alice herself seemed to have escaped the carnage. But there wasn't much of a Wonderland left for her to explore, the pages were so crossed with lines they were falling apart like a paper snowflake cut too many times.

Puzzled and disturbed Kat finally put the books away and turned out the light, but she tossed and turned for hours afterwards, finally falling into a confused dream of running and hiding in corners. Doors opened out of rooms into more rooms and staircases, and she'd wandered further and further through mounds of books, scrabbling through the piles and stacks to try and find her way out. A white rabbit ran past her but when she followed it turned into a fox that grinned at her and vanished away, leaving behind it a crescent of pointed white teeth.

3

A Rag and a Bone and a Hank of Hair

Catriona always woke up early. Back home she had a television in her room and she'd watch MTV before breakfast and while she got dressed for school, letting the beat of her music thump through the house.

The window of the bedroom she'd chosen had pale pink curtains and by seven in the morning the room was as bright as if she'd turned on the light. Getting out of bed Catriona picked her MP3 player up off the bedside table and looked at her suitcase, lying open on the floor. Somewhere in there were her travelling speakers but she didn't really feel like getting them out. Going over to the window she had to reach past the doll's house to open the curtains and she smirked at it, remembering how she'd got the room the day before.

It was weird thinking that this could be Katherine and John's mother's room. She hadn't thought of that when she picked it. Opening the top drawer of the chest of drawers she wondered if there'd be anything there, but it was empty. Putting her make-up bag and her jewellery box away in the top drawer, she unpacked her underwear and some tops into the other drawers and looked about for somewhere to put the rest of her clothes. The only other storage place was the thing like a built-in wardrobe on the other side of the room and she opened it up.

It wasn't a wardrobe but a cupboard, with six shelves inside, all of them covered with junk. She frowned, wondering how she was supposed to hang up her clothes, before actually looking at what all of this stuff was. The top two rows had boxes, too high for her to reach. The next row had a boxy-looking camera and several thick bundles of photographs with rubber bands wound round them. On each the top photograph was bleached and faded so that the images were ghostly white blurs. Curious, Catriona took down one of the bundles and tried to unwind the rubber band. It slithered loose when she picked at it, like the dead skin of a snake, and the bundle sprang apart at one side, the other gummed together by the remains of the rubber band.

Picking off the bits of rubber with her long nails Catriona got the other photos unstuck and began to sift through them. The first group were of three girls sitting in a garden that Catriona recognized as the one at the front of this house. On the back someone had scrawled names: 'Anne', 'Emily', and 'Charlotte' on different photos, depending on who appeared. They were taking it in turns to take pictures of each other because only two of them appeared in each one, right up until the last of that group where they must have found someone else prepared to hold the camera for them. Looking at the three of them Catriona tried to solve the puzzle of the names to guess which one might be John and Katherine's mother.

Emily turned out to be a girl with curling ringlets of blonde hair wearing a blue velvet dress with sleeves that trailed to the ground. She had the figure for it, Catriona thought jealously, looking down at her own almost flat chest. Charlotte was a girl with black hair and dark eyes, dressed in black leggings, pirate style boots, and an almost knee-length white shirt. Anne was easily the dullest one, Catriona decided. Her hair was the same light brown as her children's and she was wearing a patchwork dress and a long white lace shawl.

The next thirty or so photographs in the bundle had been taken in really bad light, making the shadows too dark or the girls look washed out, and in most of them Catriona couldn't make out much more than some trees and sometimes the shape of a building. Flipping on to the end of the stack she didn't see anything interesting and put them back on the shelf next to the other bundles. She might tell John about them later. That way she'd get the credit for doing something nice and she wouldn't have to tell Katherine.

Catriona ignored the next shelf, which was full of little china ornaments of animals, and squatted down to look at the bottom one. This was piled up with shoeboxes. 'CLOTHES' was written on the first one and she opened it up to see doll's clothes, tiny scraps of velvet and silk and even fur, sewn with almost invisible stitches. Catriona took out each item carefully, admiring the work that had gone into it. The next one was labelled 'JEWELLERY' and she opened it expecting something made out of beads or plastic. But instead there was a jumble of bracelets, rings, and necklaces, gleaming silver and gold, or with spots of colour that Catriona thought might actually be small precious stones, or at least semi-precious. She sifted through the box for a while, wondering if it could possibly be real. If so it must be worth hundreds of pounds and she was amazed it hadn't been stolen. She felt a pang as she shut the box but she wasn't a thief.

The third box wasn't labelled and it felt heavy when Catriona dragged it forward on the shelf and she wondered if there might be more jewellery. Inside there was a gleam from metal objects; it wasn't jewellery, but steel blades, poking out of what must have been about thirty pairs of nail scissors all rusted and blunt. Catriona put the lid back quickly, wondering if Anne Stone had been a little crazy. What could anyone need that many pairs of scissors for and what had blunted them like that?

The last cardboard box was the largest and it was the only one that had been tied up with string. Whoever had tied it had used what seemed to be a mile of the stuff, wrapped round and around the box, and tied it up in the most tortuous knot. Catriona had to prise at it for ages, using her nails to tease the knot open; ironically there didn't seem to be a single usable pair of scissors in the room. 'DELILAH and her DRONES' was written on the box and when Catriona finally got it open she caught her breath in shock.

Naked, faceless, hairless dolls lay jumbled up together like bodies in a mass grave. All of those on the top layer had faces rubbed smooth and featureless, except for the gaping holes where their eyes should be, savagely gouged out by something with a small sharp blade.

Catriona dropped the box and it fell on its side, spilling dolls on to the floor. And as the naked, eyeless dolls slid out, something else came with them, something that could only be Delilah.

She was a small girl doll in a white dress. Her blue eyes stared blankly forward and a small smile curved her red lips; her long ankle-length hair was tangled around the arms and legs of the drones and Cat saw that it was more than one colour: blonde, black, and brown.

She could only be home-made, at least Catriona was sure the hair had been, and at first she didn't like to touch any of the dolls. But it was the only way to get them back in the box and when she picked up Delilah she realized the little doll's joints were articulated, so she could move not only her arms and legs but her wrists and each individual finger. Delilah was serious weirdness but she was also a work of art, like a creepy sort of mascot.

It had looked as if her hair was in even worse knots than the string around the box but when Catriona tried to release her the long silken strands came easily, sliding out of its tangles in the same way that Catriona's own hair did. She smoothed out the last few tangled edges of Delilah's hair, and stroked it back into place. It felt soft and sleek under her fingers, and she felt reluctant to put Delilah back in her box after all that work. It was then she remembered Katherine asking about the dolls and, with a feeling of malice, she slipped Delilah and three drones into the pockets of her dressing gown.

It wasn't until they were all sitting around the breakfast table that Catriona revealed her find, standing Delilah up on the table with one small hand resting lightly on the glass of the milk bottle. Across the table Katherine looked at the doll and bit her lips.

'Where did you find her?' she asked.

'In the cupboard in my room,' Catriona said. 'Someone's customized her; I think that's human hair. I bet if I took the head off you could see how they'd done it.'

'Bizarre,' Roley said, through a mouthful of cornflakes, eyeing the doll doubtfully. From her other pocket Catriona took out three of the eyeless, faceless dolls and stood them up next to the girl doll.

'Meet Delilah and her drones,' she said, waiting for their reaction.

'Did you make that up?' Roley asked, picking up one of the drones.

'It was written on the box I found them in,' Catriona told him, adjusting the doll again so that her hand rested lightly on the shoulder of a drone.

'I don't like them much,' John said, looking towards his father.

'Someone made a real house of horrors, didn't they?' Peter said. He picked up the girl doll and looked closely at her hair. 'Delilah, I wonder if you came by that hair honestly?'

'You mean like Samson and Delilah in the Bible?' Katherine asked. 'She cut his hair off, didn't she?'

'How could a doll steal someone's hair?' Catriona said, watching the doll dangling helplessly in Peter's hands.

'Oh, put that horrible thing down,' Harriet said, pouring herself a second cup of coffee. 'I agree with John. Those dolls are extremely unpleasant. It takes a sick mind to make something like that.'

'Why did you bring them down?' John asked, his eyes fixed on Delilah as Peter set her down on the table.

'Your sister was asking about them,' Catriona said, shrugging casually. 'I thought she'd like to see them. You know, someone went to a lot of effort. There are at least thirty drones in the box. All with their eyes cut out like that.' As she spoke she adjusted Delilah's position again, sitting her on the edge of a cereal bowl and stroking her hair back into position.

'Creepy,' Roley commented. 'Sounds like voodoo or something.'

'Voodoo like black magic?' Catriona asked. Her eyes met Katherine's across the table as she added: 'Your mum lived here, didn't she? Do you think she was the one with the sick mind?'

Crockery clattered and glasses jangled as Katherine stood up sharply from the table and Peter had to lunge to stop the milk bottle falling over.

'You're the one who's sick!' Katherine shouted across the table. 'I hate you!' Her voice rose in a scream as she ran out of the room. Replacing the milk bottle, Peter got up and went after her.

'You deliberately provoked that, Cat,' Harriet snapped angrily. 'That was a cruel thing to say.'

'I didn't mean it,' Catriona said defensively. 'You were the one that said it was someone with a sick mind that made them. I just suddenly remembered that her mother lived here. I didn't mean it the way she took it.' She put a

41

plaintive note into her voice and opened her eyes wide, looking innocent.

Roley made a face at her across the table as Harriet started to talk in her 'understanding' voice now, reminding them that Katherine was sensitive about having lost her mother. Catriona ignored her brother and nodded along to Harriet's talk. It was Katherine's fault if she was going to be so sensitive, she thought. Besides, probably it was her mother that had made the dolls, it only made sense.

Suddenly remembering that John was still there, Harriet stopped mid-speech and began to talk brightly about plans for meals. But John hadn't been listening anyway, he was looking at the three drone dolls. They had fallen over when Katherine shook the table and now one lay on its face, the other two on their backs, staring with empty eyes up at the ceiling. Sitting comfortably on the edge of the cereal bowl, Delilah smiled her small hard smile as if the chaos of the breakfast table had pleased her.

Harriet spent the rest of breakfast making a shopping list of things they would need to get from a supermarket. When Peter finally returned, Harriet and Catriona were the only ones left in the kitchen.

'I'm sorry your daughter's feelings were hurt,' Catriona said as soon as he came in. 'I just thought the doll was cool. Shall I go and explain?'

'She's getting dressed now,' Peter said awkwardly. 'Perhaps you'd better leave it a while.'

'I've told Cat she can come shopping with us this

morning,' Harriet said, displaying her list. 'Do you think the boys will want to come too? I don't know if we should leave Katherine on her own.'

'From what I know of Roley I don't think shopping is going to enthuse him,' Peter smiled. 'He and Katherine are old enough to look after themselves, and John too if he wants to stay behind.'

Catriona ran upstairs to get dressed, dumping her dressing gown and nightclothes on the bed and rummaging through her suitcase for something to wear. Her mother had yelled up to her twice to get a move on before she settled on furry desert boots, white jeans, and a fluffy white jumper. Taking her bag from where she'd hung it on the back of the door she looked for her mobile phone and couldn't find it in any of the pockets. Harriet yelled up the stairs again.

'Catriona! Get yourself down here right now!'

Running back across the room Catriona rummaged in her dressing gown pockets, remembering she'd had her phone at breakfast, and felt her fingers touch silky hair. It was Delilah.

She frowned briefly. She couldn't remember having picked the doll up but she must have done it while clearing breakfast away. The mobile phone was in the other pocket but the drones were gone. She wondered if her mother had tried to get rid of them. Looking at Delilah she thought again it would be a pity. She had used the doll to get at Katherine but Katherine was pathetically easy to get at. It seemed a pity for Delilah to suffer the consequences.

'Cat! Catriona Wilde! Get a move on!' Harriet's voice bellowed from downstairs.

Jumping, Catriona put Delilah into her bag and zipped it up carefully before grabbing her MP3 player and running down the stairs. It took her a minute to put on her white coat with the furred hood and let herself out of the house.

Peter had already started the car and Harriet was standing at the open passenger door, looking pointedly at her watch as Catriona came out of the house.

'I don't know what you think this trip is supposed to be,' she said, looking at Catriona's outfit doubtfully. 'We're just going to go to Sainsbury's and maybe Boots. It's not supposed to be fun.'

Catriona shrugged. Shopping, even dull shopping, was bound to be better than sitting in the house with her stepsister or lying around in the garden when there wasn't any proper sunshine. Putting her headphones on and pressing the play button on her MP3 player she watched out of the car window as the car edged carefully through the gate and between the long walls out to the main road.

Catriona often thought that car journeys were meant to happen to music. The things you saw through the window seemed more interesting that way, like the action in a music video. But that was in London. Putting her sunglasses back on, she rolled down her window and looked out as the car turned round some tight corners and came down a winding lane through a small village. There was almost no one about and the place looked dead. But Peter and Harriet pointed out a postbox and a newsagent to each other as if they were fascinating. Catriona turned the volume of her headphones up.

It was a forty minute drive to Windermere and Catriona felt car-sick after only ten. Having the window open helped a bit but the roads went up and down so much and it seemed they were always going around another sharp corner or hairpin bend. Harriet offered her a Polo to suck and a sip of water but Catriona didn't feel any better. Zipping her bag open, she looked at Delilah, lying inside, and stroked her silky hair. Dolls were childish but Delilah was more like a mascot than a doll. Catriona imagined sitting her and a couple of drones on her desk during exam times, the way a lot of girls at school had teddy bears or fluffy pigs. That would be cool.

They parked in the supermarket car park and Catriona wandered around the aisles, picking out KitKats, a six-pack of prawn cocktail flavoured crisps, and two bottles of diet Coke. Peter and Harriet had only reached the end of the groceries aisle by the time she got back. Unzipping her bag again she checked her mobile phone and watched as the signal bar went up to two dots.

'Can I go and look around the town for a bit?' she asked. 'I know where we parked and I won't be long. And my mobile's got a signal if you need to call me.'

Harriet hesitated and then seemed to give in.

'Oh, all right, if you must,' she agreed. 'But don't be longer than half an hour.'

At least in Windermere there were young people. Catriona wandered out of the Sainsbury's and looked in the window of a clothes shop, checking out her own reflection. She thought she looked pretty good. She certainly looked better than a lot of the girls she saw walking past;

not that there seemed to be any boys worth a second glance either.

A narrow alley led in to a row of jeweller's and antique shops and Catriona wandered by, looking in the windows. The fourth shop had a window display that was a mixture of jewellery and bric-a-brac and, laid out on a pine dresser, a collection of doll-sized furniture. Thinking of Delilah, she went in, pushing her sunglasses on to the top of her head so she could see in the dim light. But the furniture was dis-appointing. It was all old stuff, like the things already in the doll's house. Catriona quite liked a set of red velvet chairs that looked just the right size for Delilah but the price tag said they were £14.50 each and she turned away.

The shop owner was sitting in a chair near the counter, reading a newspaper, and he glanced up as she went past and asked:

'Do you need any help, love?'

'I'm just looking,' Catriona said automatically. Feeling as if she couldn't leave right away she stopped in front of a row of jewellery cases, fastened with hook and eye catches. Two were open already, displaying rows of silver rings and pendants and a line of little objects that looked like charms for a charm bracelet.

Catriona did have a charm bracelet back in London, but hers was made of gold and she looked along the row of charms without much interest until she came to one that was larger than the rest.

It was a pair of scissors. The blades were thin and sharp and hinged open as she picked them up. The handles were ornamented with a swirling sort of design and little specks glittered and flashed from the swirls. £28 read the tiny tag attached to them and Cat was about to put them back when there was a sudden ringing noise.

It came from her bag and Cat fumbled to open it. Delilah's hair had got tangled around the phone and it took her a while to get it free. The shopkeeper looked up with a frown by the time she finally stopped the polyphonic ring, dumping Delilah on the counter as she pressed the 'answer' button on her phone.

'Where are you?' Harriet's voice said crossly from the other end of the line. 'We're just packing the car now.'

'In a shop,' Cat said, scooping up Delilah and scrabbling her back into her bag with an apologetic look at the shopkeeper. 'I'll be there in a minute.'

She was already walking out of the shop as Harriet hung up and she hurried back out of the side street and around the corner, reaching the car park in time to see Peter wheeling the trolley back to the front of Sainsbury's.

'There you are,' he said as she came up alongside him. 'I'm sorry we don't have more time to look around this morning, but we can come back later. The woman at the checkout told us that you can hire a boat to take you around the lake.'

'That's cool,' Catriona said absent-mindedly, pulling her sunglasses back down over her eyes. 'I saw a couple of OK looking clothes shops. I might try things on when we have more time.'

She'd thought they would end up going straight back but Harriet looked surprisingly cheerful when they met at the car.

'I know it's almost lunchtime,' she said. 'But I'm gasping for a cup of coffee and there's some bread and cheese back at the house if the others get hungry. What do you say we find a café?'

The café was called a Chocolaterie and Harriet ordered black coffee for herself, a latte for Peter, and a chocolate milkshake for Cat.

'Do you want a cake?' Peter asked, considering the row of cakes and muffins behind the counter, and Catriona shook her head.

'I'm watching my weight,' she said, and Harriet switched from her 'you'll spoil your lunch' expression to 'I don't approve of dieting' instead.

'All right,' Catriona said, remembering that if she had something now she'd be one up on the others back home. 'I'll have a toasted cheese sandwich.'

'Well, I'm going to have a piece of that delicious looking carrot cake,' Peter decided and Catriona said quickly:

'I'll find us a table.'

The one she chose was at the front of the shop, looking out through the plate glass window to the street. Taking off her sunglasses, she unzipped her bag to put them away. Delilah's hair was already starting to tangle around her phone again and when Catriona tried to move it out of the way she jabbed her finger on something sharp.

'Here's your milkshake,' Peter said behind her and Catriona jumped, nearly upsetting it on to the table as she pushed her sunglasses into her bag and zipped it up quickly.

'And here's your sandwich,' Harriet added, 'and you'd better have room for your lunch later.'

'Whatever,' Catriona muttered. Her bag felt heavy and awkward in her lap and she was trying to tell herself she hadn't seen something shining and half-hidden in the strands of Delilah's hair, a gleam like a pair of silver scissors.

She didn't open her bag again during the car ride home; her stomach felt sour and the scratch on her finger stung.

'You shouldn't have had that sandwich,' Harriet said with a sharp look back at her. 'Or that milkshake either. Orange juice would have been healthier.'

'It wasn't the milkshake,' Catriona said crossly. 'You know I get car-sick.'

'Well, then you should have stayed at home,' Harriet snapped back impatiently.

Catriona turned on her MP3 player again and rested her head against the cool glass of the car window. All the time the adults were having their coffee she'd been staring out of the window, expecting to see the antique shop owner following after her. When she got home, Catriona decided, she would put Delilah back in her box and tie the string back up tightly just the way it had been before. She wished now she'd never undone it. Obviously Delilah's wretched hair had tangled round the scissors but in her mind she imagined small hands with tiny articulated fingers reaching out and she shuddered.

4
Rotten Wood

While Harriet and Catriona had been getting ready to leave for Windermere, Peter had gone outside to look for the boys. In the light of day it was possible to see out across the garden lawn, although the fields beyond were still shrouded in mist.

John and Roley had walked around the house to where a line of trees had been bent over into a hedge, bare branches of each tied to the trunk of the next tree. It marked the beginnings of a rough track leading up through banks high with stinging nettles towards the wood.

'Thinking of exploring?' Peter asked, as he joined them.

'If that's OK,' Roley said.

'Of course. You boys have fun,' Peter told him. 'But if you're planning to go that way, I'd take some sting relief.'

'We should have a bottle of water too,' John said seriously. 'Did you mean that I can go too, Daddy?'

'If you want to.' Peter nodded. 'Unless you'd rather come shopping with me and Harriet and Cat. Catriona, that is.'

Roley made a face and Peter laughed.

'If it's all right, I'd like to go with Roley, please,' John said and Peter smiled, ruffling his son's hair. At least the boys had hit it off, he thought.

After the car had driven away John and Roley went back into the house to prepare for their expedition.

'Will you go and look for the first aid box?' Roley asked, filling an empty diet-Coke bottle with water from the kitchen tap. 'Mum probably put it in the bathroom.'

John ran upstairs in time to see Kat coming out of the bathroom.

'Hey,' she said. 'Remember I said I had a secret. Do you want to know what it is?'

'Um,' John hesitated. 'Can you tell me later? Roland's waiting for me downstairs. We're going to explore the woods.' He looked hopefully at his sister. 'Would you like to come with us? Maybe you could tell him the secret too.'

'No.' Katherine shook her head. 'It's not just something you tell, it's something to see as well.' She sighed. 'I'll show you later, when you get back. I'll just read or something.'

'Sorry,' John said awkwardly as she went back to her room. He wished she didn't always want to have secrets with him that Catriona and Roley weren't to know.

Going into the bathroom he found the sting relief and put it in his pocket and then went up the stairs to his room to get the binoculars. He took two of the Tracker bars as well and ran back downstairs to where Roley was waiting.

'Do you want to put your binoculars in my bag?' Roley asked, opening his rucksack.

'Thank you,' John said and he showed Roley the two Tracker bars before putting them in as well. 'I thought we might be hungry,' he said.

'Good thought,' Roley agreed encouragingly, seeing how anxious John looked for approval that he'd done the right thing. He didn't say that if he got hungry he could probably eat six of them.

They took their jackets before going out. The sun was somewhere behind banks of misty clouds, only appearing in starts and flashes.

'I wish your sister hadn't found that doll,' John said seriously as they started up the path towards the woods.

'I'm sorry about what she said about your mother,' Roley said, remembering how uncomfortable he'd been at breakfast.

'That's all right,' John said, looking up at Roley steadily. 'It was true anyway. There was something wrong with Mummy's mind. That's why she had to go to hospital.'

'I didn't know that,' Roley said, feeling awful. 'And I'm sure Cat doesn't or she'd never have said what she did. Does my mother know?'

'I don't know.' John squinted up his eyes as the sun came out again and looked up at the woods ahead. 'I like your mother,' he added.

'She's not so bad.' Roley shrugged. 'When she's not fretting about something.' He was thinking about John's mother and feeling bad that he'd never even asked how she died. He had always assumed it was something like a car crash but what John had said sounded more like a mental illness.

The path came up to an iron gate with a complicated latch. Both Roley and John took turns fiddling with it and it was John who finally made it work so that the gate swung open down the slope towards them.

'We have to shut it behind us,' John said as they went

through. 'Daddy says you always have to shut gates when you're in the country in case something escapes.'

'I don't know what could escape out of a wood,' Roley said, although he pulled the gate shut so that John could latch it again. 'Rabbits and badgers and things like that could just go under it.'

'Maybe there are deer,' John suggested.

'Deer could jump,' Roley replied. 'But let me give you back your binoculars, you can see if you can spot anything.'

John hung the binoculars around his neck and lifted them to look around, adjusting the lenses until it seemed that he was looking through a tunnel. The leaves and branches close by were huge and blurred and beyond them he focused on a fallen tree trunk, the rotten wood seething with grubs.

'Careful,' Roley said, grabbing his arm as John's foot slipped on the path. 'It's muddy here.'

It was cold as well, they were still only a short distance from the house but the trees seemed to have closed in around them. The sunlight only crept in from the edges, in slices between the thickly hemmed trees.

'It feels like being under water,' John said, testing the silence with his voice.

'It does a bit,' Roley agreed, rather breathlessly. The path they were following was getting steeper and he stopped for a breather, sitting down on a log at the side of the path.

John lifted the binoculars to look ahead again, trying to pick out anything in the darkness under the trees. Leaves trembled and shook in the wind, obscuring the path, and as he moved the circle of vision slowly, he saw a white shape slide by. Panning back even more slowly, he couldn't find it again and turned the lenses to try to focus better.

Two eyes stared suddenly into his, dark holes in a blur of a face. With a gasp of surprise John dropped the binoculars and they knocked heavily into his chest as he turned to Roley.

Roley looked up when John gasped and flinched, about to ask what was wrong. But when the younger boy turned towards him his face went suddenly pale. Roley hadn't ever heard John raise his voice and it was a shock to hear him shout so that at first he didn't hear the words properly.

'Up! Get UP!' John's eyes focused just past Roley with a fixed expression of horror.

Roley felt something tickle his arm and turned to see what John had seen: hundreds of crawling bugs with filmy wings, covering the log and across Roley's jeans and shirt. White grubs lay in small curling spots between the crawlers.

Infected by John's panic, Roley jumped up to brush them off and as the log wobbled the bugs twitched their wings and began to buzz. John gave a queer high cry and turned away, slipping and sliding on the muddied grass of the wood as he pelted off. Slapping bugs off his arms and away from his face, Roley chased after him.

'John, wait . . . it's OK!' he tried to yell, but his voice came thin and wheezily through his panting. The younger boy might have been a lot smaller but he was a fast runner and he didn't weigh enough to disturb the piles of leaf mulch that Roley slithered through.

John had run off crossways to the path and the ground was even steeper here. Roley crashed after him, keeping his arms up high to shield his face from the branches that John was able to dodge under. He reached the edge of the wood in a long slipping slide, grabbing at trees to slow himself just in time to avoid falling into a tangle of bramble bushes supporting the remains of a broken fence. Picking a place between two missing fence slats he managed to squeeze through and found himself in a field. John was already halfway across but his speed was beginning to slow and Roley headed after him with a gasp of relief, thanking whoever that his stepbrother hadn't broken his neck.

'John! John, wait for me,' he called. This time John must have heard him, because he turned and waited as Roley finally caught up with him. The binoculars were still around his neck and, seeing them, Roley realized he'd left his rucksack back in the woods. He'd worry about that later, he decided. John's arms were scratched and his jeans muddy, but he seemed to be OK and Roley felt almost cross as he demanded:

'Why'd you run like that? It was only bugs.'

John looked back at him miserably.

'I don't know,' he said. 'They were just so horrible. It made me feel like the wood was . . . I don't know. Something bad.' He shivered and looked up at Roley with a pale pinched expression. 'I'm sorry.'

Roley sighed. 'Never mind,' he said. 'We'd better try to find another way back to the house and get you cleaned up before Mum and Peter get home.'

Lifting his head to try and get his bearings Roley jumped

at the sight of a person standing in the lane on the other side of the field by a five-barred gate. It was a girl, he could tell by her long blonde hair, and she was holding the lead of a large dog. Roley blushed, wondering how long she'd been standing there and if she'd seen him jump like that. John had managed to get him properly spooked, he realized, and he put a hand on the younger boy's shoulder to steer him towards the lane.

'Come on,' he said. 'We'll go that way, OK. And don't run off again. No matter what you see.'

'OK,' John said quietly and Roley felt mean.

It seemed to take forever to tramp across the field and it was almost as muddy as the woods had been. The girl by the gate waited, watching them as they came closer. She was wearing grey jeans and a grey-green anorak and the brightest thing about her was her heavy plait of corn-coloured hair. She was a couple of inches shorter than Roley, about medium-height for a girl. The dog, however, now seemed much larger than it had from across the field.

Roley didn't much like dogs, not since he'd done a paper round and had heard them launching themselves at the doors from the inside as he'd delivered papers through snapping traps of letterboxes. This was exactly the kind of dog he liked least: big and black, reaching up almost to the girl's waist.

'Hello,' she called out as they reached the gate. 'I saw you come out of the woods—are you all right?'

'Yes, we're fine,' Roley said. 'My brother got a bit freaked out in the woods.' Looking around at the field he asked a bit anxiously, 'Is this your field? We didn't mean to trespass.'

'No, it's not ours,' the girl replied and as Roley opened the gate John squeezed through and looked towards the dog.

'May I pat him?' he asked, seeming to have forgotten his fright.

'If you want,' the girl said. 'Baskerville doesn't bite.' Her eyes met Roley's and she smiled at him. Her eyes were grey, with pale lashes.

'Do you live around here then?' Roley asked.

'In the village,' she replied. 'I'm Alice Wheeler.'

'I'm John and that's my brother Roland,' John said and Roley felt a rush of brotherly feeling himself at the description.

'So . . . um . . . Alice,' he said awkwardly. 'Do you know a place called Fell Scar? Can you tell us how to get back there from this road?'

'Of course.' Wrapping the dog's lead around her wrist Alice started to walk up the road while pointing ahead. 'It's just this way,' she explained. 'My mother works there. She's a gardener.'

'Oh. The garden looked very nice,' Roley said, trying to recall it and failing.

'It doesn't really,' Alice said. 'It needs more work than the owners are prepared to pay for. My mother spends most of her time on the vegetable garden. But the place has been empty for years.'

'The man who owns it sent us the key,' John told her, looking up from the dog. 'He's my great-uncle.'

'How long are you staying?' the girl asked John. Her voice was just ordinarily polite and Roley wondered why she was bothering to show them the way when she could have excused herself by now.

'A few weeks, I think,' John said uncertainly.

'Well, I hope you have a good holiday.' Alice came to a halt and pointed out the gate they had seen yesterday and the entrance between two long walls.

'Thanks,' Roley said. He couldn't think of anything else to say and after a moment she raised a hand in a goodbye and paid out the dog's leash and walked off around the corner.

'She seemed nice,' John said after she'd gone and Roley sighed.

'Yes, she did,' he agreed.

He'd never known how to talk to girls and he seemed to be getting worse at it. Still, he thought, since she lived around here he might see her again. As they walked back to the house he silently tried out possible conversations, just in case he did.

Katherine had come downstairs to find breakfast cleared away and everyone else gone. Remembering the door in the cupboard she'd thought of going back through it into the games room but the secret didn't seem as much fun after the fight at breakfast. The thought of finding more books with crossed out words or any dolls like Delilah made her feel sick and instead she'd gone out into the garden.

A terrace of uneven paving stones fronted the house and broad steps led down to the driveway they'd parked on last night. A high hedge separated the drive from a sloping lawn and Katherine walked down another set of steps, this time made of cemented rocks, between which weeds had sprouted. The lawn was more moss than grass and felt alternately springy and spongy beneath her feet. It was bordered by more hedges, twined with brambles, and flower beds choked with overgrown bushes. The only flowers were dead daffodils, clumping at the edge of the lawn, called out of the ground by spring only to be blighted by a late winter frost. At the far end Kat paused to look at a round stone basin, half full of dead leaves, which looked as if it had once been a pond. A central pillar of stone suggested a statue but it was empty now.

Behind the house the track the boys must have followed led up into the woods. Katherine regretted turning down John's offer to go exploring and promised herself she'd go with him next time he wanted to do something with her. She wasn't *really* jealous of him looking up to Roley, she told herself. It was just that she was used to being the oldest, the one who came up with ideas and plans. But ever since her father had married Harriet she felt reclassified as younger, always having to squeeze into the small car seats like left-over luggage and being asked by Harriet what she liked to eat like a baby or an invalid when she was used to actually making their meals.

John getting on with Roley made her feel as if everyone was getting comfortable in their new family except for her. He hadn't said so but she sometimes thought her little brother liked having Harriet around too. Anne had died when he was six and although she'd tried to keep their mother alive for him, telling stories about what she'd been like and showing him photos, she knew John didn't remember Anne the way she did. Katherine wondered if she'd tried too hard, perhaps those stories and photos had actually replaced his memories. Even she now found it hard to remember the little things.

Behind the pond the brambles thickened up to a tumbled stone wall covered in moss and ivy; behind it the branches of trees. Katherine sat on the edge of the pond and looked back at the house, hugging her arms around herself in the chill air of the morning. Everyone had gone off and left her behind as if she was the awkward one, the part that didn't fit in, the stray cat that hung around the doorstep tripping people up. Looking out at the view Anne had grown up with she wondered what her mother had been like at her age. Had she had friends? Or had she played with her doll's house alone, making up stories for Delilah and the eyeless drones?

Katherine stood up abruptly, too cold to sit still. Walking back towards the house, she veered to the right, passing a low stone building at the end of the drive that contained stacks of cut wood. There'd been a leak in the roof and the wood was wet in places and covered with moss. Around the side of the house she saw the outside of the attached barn. There were barn doors at the back, overgrown with ivy and looking as if they hadn't been opened for fifty years.

Anne had lived here until she was seventeen. She and Peter had met at university; her father had said they were drawn to each other because they both came from country villages but unlike him Anne never talked about her family. Peter had never met them, even when he and Anne got married straight after university and set up house together.

Katherine had been born that year, John four years later. And it was when John was still a baby Anne had begun to get ill.

It had taken them a while to notice. The illness that tore their lives apart began quietly and without any fuss. Anne had eye problems. Nothing inheritable, she always said, but she'd overstrained her eyes reading and now she found it hard to read much. Computer screens she found easier but even reading a recipe book she would need thick glasses through which she peered in puzzlement at the simplest instructions. But gradually her reading became more of a problem in her job and there were other things too. She'd forget names, not just people's names but the names of things. She became tongue-tied and uncertain of herself, going out less, worried about making a mistake in public.

Anne hadn't wanted to go into hospital but her doctor had insisted after the incident with the gas. She'd started cooking and had to stop and somehow the gas had been left on for hours and she hadn't noticed. Peter had come home from work and found them all asleep in front of the television and the house reeking with gas. He'd panicked and called an ambulance but they'd all been fine. Even so the doctor had sent Anne for a battery of tests and scans and after too many anxious weeks of inconclusive results she'd scored badly on a test for early-onset dementia.

'So silly,' Katherine could remember her mother saying. 'But I couldn't remember the date and I couldn't draw a shape and now I need more tests and a course of medication.'

The medicine had changed her. The worry had changed them all. By then they were all noticing things. Anne was silent around the family now, except sometimes with John. Peter did most of the cooking and Katherine was responsible for taking herself and John to school—even on the days when her mother was well enough to come with them. Peter had to work long hours to pay for private specialists and the expression of worry became so ingrained into his face that Katherine felt he was becoming a stranger to them as well. Anne forgot conversations and things that had happened just the day before. Katherine told herself that at least she never forgot their names.

But one day she came back from school to find the front door swinging open and the house turned upside down as if it had been ransacked. She sent John to knock on a neighbour's door and shouted for her mother from the front hall. When the neighbour arrived Katherine had gone with him up the stairs and they'd found Anne curled into a ball on the bed. She didn't remember anything then, not even her own name. It was she who'd ransacked the house, the police said later. Nothing had been taken but she'd gone through every drawer of personal papers and ripped apart a book of family photographs and every mirror in the house was broken. This time when Anne was admitted to hospital she hadn't come back home.

By the end she didn't recognize them and Katherine barely recognized *her*. Her mother had faded away from this sick woman who lay pale in the hospital bed, her hair scraped back, her face blank of interest. She'd known her mother was dying before the doctors told them. The person she'd been was already dead. Whatever was left was a shell. All the same Katherine was fiercely resentful when a nurse said it was a mercy. Nothing about Anne's illness had been merciful, it had been a misery almost too great to bear.

Katherine's journey around the house had brought her back to the main gate across a high bank thick with leaf mulch from the wood. A flock of birds were calling from somewhere in the wood, raucous jeers mocking like playground cat-calls. The bird-nosed mask of the knocker watched her with blank eyes as she sidled through the front door. Inside the house she felt the cold stone walls close around her like the vice around her heart. Everywhere she was surrounded by enemies, by traps and pitfalls and secrets that a careless word could spring.

What if her mother had carried the seeds of her illness from childhood? Even her father had called the dolls a house of horrors. And who, if not Anne, could have crossed out those names? When she had lived in Fell Scar perhaps the illness was already lying in wait for her, sharpening its hooks and claws.

5
Who is Alice?

Alice hadn't hurried after meeting Roley and John in the wood, letting Baskerville set the pace, the lead lightly looped around her right wrist as she walked back to the village.

They turned into Mill Road and she let herself and the dog in through the gate of number 27. Alice's house didn't have a name. Lots of those in the village did, especially the ones belonging to newcomers. It seemed that the first thing some people did when they moved in was to put up a little plaque painted with wildflowers with names like Shangri-La or Rose Cottage or Danandemma.

But number 27 wasn't a particularly attractive house and perhaps Alice's mother thought it wasn't worth naming. It had belonged to her parents and she'd inherited it when they died.

As Alice came in the front door of the house, an insistent Baskerville preceding her into the kitchen and looking mournfully at his empty bowl, she called out to let her mother and Charlotte know she was back.

From the sound of clanking and running water she could hear that Emily was in the scullery, an area off the kitchen comprising a small extension and the length of a ramshackle lean-to against the side wall of the house which she used as a combination greenhouse and potting shed.

Alice filled Baskerville's bowl and, as he inhaled its contents noisily, began getting out bread, cheese, and tomatoes for lunch. Sound carried through the thin walls and down the crooked stairs and while she gave a lettuce a cursory splash under the sink she could hear the sound of typing coming from Charlotte's room at the back of the house. Charlotte always typed as if she was trying to hammer the keyboard into submission even though her computer was reasonably modern. She tended to wear out keyboards every six months. Either that or upset cups of coffee over them, which caused more dramatic burn-out of the components and necessitated emergency trips to Windermere for replacements.

As Alice was laying out plates her mother came in from the scullery and squeezed past Baskerville who was as always fascinated by the smell of newly turned earth from the plants. Pushing the dog out of the way Emily shut the door behind her and came to join Alice at the table.

'Thank you, Alice,' she said, pushing Baskerville off towards the front room. 'I rather lost track of time. Shall we call Charlotte?'

'I heard her typing,' Alice said and Emily nodded her understanding.

'I expect she'll eat when she's done,' she agreed. 'She's been just staring at the screen most of the morning so probably better not to disturb her.'

Charlotte wrote for the local paper as well as occasionally having articles in the nationals, but a writer's life seemed to involve long periods of not being able to write anything followed by frenetic banging of the keys until finally Charlotte would appear with a bulging envelope and run off to catch the last post, still sticking down the stamps.

Dumping the lettuce into a bowl, Alice brought it to the table and began making herself a sandwich while Emily assembled bread, a slice of cheese, and two tomatoes on her plate to eat separately.

'I took Baskerville for a walk,' Alice said, slowly buttering her slices of bread. 'There's a family staying up at Fell Scar.'

There was a pause. Emily hadn't moved, a piece of cheese still held in one hand as she looked back at Alice. After a couple of seconds she blinked and put it down carefully on her plate.

'A family staying at Fell Scar,' she repeated. 'On holiday, I suppose.'

Suddenly Alice felt the need to be very careful. She mentally edited out the part where the little boy had seemed so frightened of something. In a light tone of voice she said:

'Two boys asked me for directions. They said they were staying there.'

'I'll remember that for tomorrow,' Emily said slowly. 'There's a lot of vegetables in the garden there at the moment that they should feel free to use. A lot of the produce from the empty houses is just going to waste.'

'Is that why the salad drawer is full of leeks?' Alice said and Emily gave her a quick grateful smile before replying.

'Guilty as charged, but I only take a fraction of what goes to waste—honest. Perhaps we can have them in tomato sauce this time instead of cheese.'

Alice nodded but through the rest of lunch the sense of being precariously balanced didn't leave her and although she finished her sandwich, Emily barely ate any of hers, putting most of it back when she cleared the table. As she went into the scullery with a smile and another thank you, Alice watched after her, struggling to decide if she felt more curious or guilty.

Emily Wheeler had grown up in Stirkley in the same house she lived in now. Her father had been the local doctor. That much Alice knew because everyone knew it. Everyone also knew that Emily had moved away when she was sixteen and not come back until her parents died and left her the house.

She'd come back with Charlotte, another village girl. Charlotte Dean had gone to university and the rest of her family had long since moved away. Village rumour vaguely spoke of her having failed her degree and she'd been generally believed to be living in London. But she'd arrived with Emily, driving a car full of boxes, and Alice.

Alice had always called her mother by name. In a cardboard box somewhere lay blobby nursery school paintings with a stick figure person holding a plant and labelled ƎMILY in five-year-old hand-writing. Alice had a vague memory that might have been her imagination of seeing a wall of similar paintings pinned up, with all the rest labelled MUMMY and thinking that the others had all spelt *Emily* wrong.

But she couldn't remember much from that age so perhaps it wasn't a real memory. She had only dim recollections of her school in London and the flat they had lived in. It had been Charlotte's flat and Emily had always called it that, as if keeping up the pretence that they were only visitors there. But they had lived in that flat for seven years until Emily's parents died and left her Number 27.

Alice had vague memories of arriving at the house. It was still full of hard and uncompromising furniture and fussy chintz covers and cushions jostling uncomfortably for space in the irregular sized rooms. Emily and Charlotte had covered most of these with prints and throws which Alice felt added to the confusion. Her own room was plain and white, the only ornaments her wall of photographs. It was the only room Emily and Charlotte had decorated, making a fresh start. Emily herself now occupied the master bedroom and Charlotte had filled the L-shaped spare room with a single bed and the chaos of her desk and papers.

Back in London Alice hadn't thought her mother being different was very important. With Charlotte around she hadn't felt left out when Emily went to her botany night classes. Charlotte was better at helping with homework anyway and at playing games, even if she never read stories and was much stricter about when bedtime was. It wasn't until they had moved to the country with their boxes loaded up in a pile in Charlotte's rusty car and came to this house that Alice had begun to wonder what kind of a person her mother was.

It had started at school when Alice had got into a fight and come home with a muddy dress, bruised feelings, a note from her class teacher, and a lot of questions. It was

Charlotte who'd been in; Emily was still out trying to establish the beginnings of her gardening business.

'Julie Manferd said I'm a bastard and that Emily's a lezzy,' Alice had admitted while Charlotte was finding her clean clothes. She hadn't properly known what either word meant, only that she hadn't liked being called them. 'So I punched her in the nose.'

'Julie Manferd should take her foul mouth to the library and try bringing her language into the twenty-first century,' Charlotte had said calmly. 'It's been a good while since either of those was much of an insult. And you shouldn't punch people, it makes them much angrier if you just turn your back and walk away.'

By the time Emily had got home Alice had forgotten about it in the excitement of a new board game where pirates sank each other's ships, but although she didn't get into any more fights, somehow the feeling grew that Charlotte's answer hadn't been entirely satisfactory.

In fact Julie Manferd had proved the exception by saying straight out what everyone else thought in private. Those words were the reason that people hadn't wanted to hire Emily as a gardener and that Charlotte had done the local shopping in a whirl of speed like someone running a gauntlet, and that the old ladies would come out of their houses and look at Alice as she passed without saying anything.

Gradually the village had got used to them. Emily's little green van made trips to all the bigger houses and Charlotte had made a friend of the newsagent who ordered in extra copies of the paper she wrote for. Old ladies would look at Alice approvingly after she'd stopped to say good afternoon and tell each other in overloud voices after she'd left 'that Alice Wheeler has really good manners for a girl of her age and she's growing up to be quite a beauty as well'. When it came down to it the people from the village thought of Emily and Charlotte, and now Alice, as local girls. Their personal quirks were public property but, like Mrs Farraday's affair with the butcher or Mr Belter's Saturday morning stagger home from the pub, not all that interesting once people knew what was going on—or thought they did.

But Alice didn't find other people's acceptance so easy to accept. She couldn't help noticing that Emily and Charlotte, who were so matter of fact on almost every other subject, had managed to brush three subjects under the rug. Their own relationship was one. Two and three were why Charlotte had dropped out of her university degree and who had made Emily pregnant when she was just sixteen. Alice never had asked those questions outright and each time they dodged around one she felt less able to tackle it head on.

Going upstairs, Alice walked quietly past the shut doors of the other rooms. Her own bedroom was at the front of the house; her bed fitted into the only possible space under the sloping walls, the other furniture a small white chair, a chest of drawers, and a hanging rail for skirts and dresses.

It was the one room in the house with none of the original furniture in it. It had been Emily's room when she had lived here as a girl but, although Charlotte had toys and games and more blobby childish artwork in a trunk labelled 'Charlotte' which had come with them from the flat, there was nothing that had belonged to Emily, not even a photograph of her as a child.

Sitting down on her chair, Alice looked across the room at the pine-framed mirror hung over the chest of drawers. Her own freckled moon-face with vague grey eyes and almost invisible eyebrows and lashes. Her blonde hair was plaited back and out of the way, but Emily's pale face and light blue eyes were framed by a corona of curls the colour of new minted gold. Alice couldn't see Emily in herself any more than she could see Charlotte's dark snapping eyes or sleek black cap of hair.

Tilting her head Alice looked up the sloping walls at the room's only decoration: the layers of photographs glued to the walls and across the ceiling. Herself aged ten dressed as a milkmaid for the county fair, Emily and Charlotte on either side of the garden door, Emily sitting on a red rug in a wheat field, Charlotte sitting on a wall with a book forgotten in her lap, Alice and her friends at school holding up a netball trophy. She had started taking and collecting photographs when she'd found a camera in the attic with a half used film. Her own photos of Baskerville asleep in a ruined flower bed and the view from her bedroom window had come out but the rest of the film had been spoiled by light. There had been no photos of Emily's parents, the grandparents Alice had never and would never meet.

Alice had no way of knowing what those people were like or what they would have thought of the grand-daughter living in their house, their village, without ever having so much as put flowers on their grave.

At fifteen Alice would have thought she'd have given up wondering about the things her mother kept from her. If anything her curiosity had increased—but with it her fear. Rationally she was sure Emily was stronger now, more confident than she'd been in London, but Alice was more aware of her need to protect her mother. Perhaps it was something she'd picked up from Charlotte, or an instinct that Emily needed defending, because she would never defend herself.

Now more than ever it was her own curiosity Alice thought her mother needed protecting from. She thought of the secrets as cobwebs layered with dust hiding spider thoughts that might scuttle out at any moment. If you didn't look into the shadowy corners you wouldn't see the cobwebs, but you couldn't forget they were there.

6
The Make-Believe Game

By the time the bags of shopping had been unloaded and put away, and everyone had had lunch, accompanied by an extra argument when Catriona revealed she had had a sandwich and milkshake already, Harriet said it was too late to go and do anything that day. Instead she produced a pile of books about attractions, walks, and local wildlife and suggested they each go through them and pick a thing they wanted to do. Roley despaired of this method working. Catriona would never pick until everyone else had, just in case she accidentally chose something the others wanted to do. John was too shy to suggest anything and Katherine always chose something that Catriona hated.

Roley thought that anything like watching a film or finding a computer games shop would probably be criticized roundly by his mother for being insufficiently holiday-like and he wasn't about to admit that what he really wanted to do was get some exercise. After a cursory glance at the books he said he was going to walk around outside for a bit.

'I think it's coming on to rain,' Harriet pointed out, just as John asked:

'Can I come with you, Roland?' John was the only person who ever did call him Roland, and although he'd felt

73

fed up with him earlier, Roley was about to say yes when his sister said abruptly:

'No, you can't, I'm going with him and I've got something I want to discuss *privately*.'

John's face fell and Katherine snapped back instantly:

'Well, I've got something to tell John anyway, so that works out fine.'

'Catriona, it would be polite to ask Roley first,' Peter said awkwardly.

'She didn't ask John,' Cat replied instantly, levelling a stare at her stepsister.

'Would it be too much to ask for this family to do something without an argument?' Harriet asked irritably and Peter got up to make her a cup of tea.

'I'll make dinner for seven o'clock,' he said. 'You lot can be left to your own devices until then. But if you go out, take coats. There are extra waterproofs in the cupboard in the hall if you need them.'

'And for heaven's sake no more rows,' Harriet added.

Roley noticed that no one had actually asked if he wanted Catriona along with him but as he put on a heavy grey leather coat with thick sheepskin cuffs she joined him, ready in time for once in case he went without her.

'You look like a bear in that coat,' she said, as they went out of the door. 'Or a troll, maybe.'

'And you look like a Barbie doll,' he said looking askance at her bright pink jacket, out of place in the muted grey-green colours of the garden. That reminded him of the row over the doll and he added: 'You're not still carrying that horrible thing around, are you?'

'I left Delilah in my room,' Cat said, shooting him a quick resentful look as she walked alongside him. 'Where are we going anyway? I'm not going into the woods. I'll get my boots all muddy.'

'*I'm* walking down to the village,' Roley said. '*You* can go where you like.'

'If you're hoping you'll find a sweetshop or something you'll be disappointed,' Cat smirked. 'It looked completely dead when we drove through earlier.'

Roley said nothing. He wasn't about to admit that he thought he might run into Alice again. He'd been imagining conversations with her all through lunch.

The road was a winding country lane, the views of fields and trees and distant hills.

'Wait a bit,' Cat said, fumbling in the pocket of her jacket, and Roley paused and then sighed when he saw what she was doing. She'd taken a packet of cigarettes from an inside pocket and she took one defiantly as Roley watched. It was a packet of twenty, already a third empty. She lit one with a pink plastic lighter that Roley found almost as annoying as the cigarettes and inhaled deeply, before coughing suddenly.

'So when did you pick up this charming little habit?' Roley asked sarcastically and his sister shrugged.

'Everyone does it,' she said. 'And it's relaxing. Anyone would smoke if they had to go through what I've been through.'

'You mean what you put us through,' Roley said, feeling irritated. 'Why can't you just let it rest once in a while? Even if you can't think of the rest of us, you should think about John. He's only a little kid, for God's sake.'

75

'Oh, he's all right.' Cat shrugged it off. 'Little kids adjust. And he's got Mum running around trying to make everything wonderful for him. You know she's going to try and get him into your school.'

'So what?' Roley shrugged. 'It's a big school.' He actually thought it would be almost fun to have a little brother at the same school as him.

'Whatever,' Cat said. 'I couldn't stand having *her* at mine. What if people thought we were related?'

Roley tried to tune her out as she continued in this vein over the next few minutes. He was trying to make out the shape of a distant figure some way down the road, and it was a while before something his sister said grabbed his attention.

' . . . and I think their mother was actually mad . . . '

'What?' He looked across at her as she took another casual drag on her cigarette.

'That's why *she* got so freaked out this morning,' Cat said, widening her eyes at him. 'A sick mind, like Mum said. I think Anne went crazy.' Dropping her voice unnecessarily she added: 'She might even have killed herself.'

'Where do you pick this stuff up? Mum would have said,' Roley objected, feeling uncomfortable.

'Maybe she doesn't know,' Cat pointed out. 'You think Peter would want her to know his wife was insane? It doesn't say much for him as a husband.' Tossing the butt of her cigarette into the bushes at the side of the road, she added: 'Besides, what if it's inherited? You realize we could be living with a couple of potential psychotics?'

'You're over-reacting,' Roley said, remembering uncomfortably his conversation with John that morning. 'And even if she was insane, it doesn't mean it's something inheritable.'

Cat shrugged, and Roley realized she wasn't actually worried, but that didn't mean she wouldn't pretend to be, just to have something else over Katherine. He wondered if there was any way he could persuade her to drop it, when she suddenly stopped herself, in mid sentence.

'Looks as if the local talent isn't too bad . . .' she breathed softly, looking away from him and towards the village ahead. For a second he thought she might be talking about Alice, but when he looked he realized it was a boy she had seen.

'He's too old for you,' Roley said, knowing she wouldn't listen.

It was true though. The boy Cat had seen looked at least eighteen. He was standing on the top of a stone wall, looking down across the back gardens of a row of village houses. He was standing there quite unashamedly staring, and Roley looked at him doubtfully. He seemed a very unlikely type to be hanging around a remote country village; his red hair was shoulder-length and he was dressed showily in a sleeveless T-shirt, leather trousers, and big black biker boots. Roley wondered if he was on holiday here as well and had the sudden irrational thought that the boy was looking for Alice as he stared down the row of gardens.

As Roley and Cat came down the road, the stranger turned away from whatever it was that had absorbed him, with a calm air that suggested he'd known they were there all along. He was tall anyway, and standing on the wall he looked alarming, especially when he jumped down without looking and landed lightly on the road next to them. But Cat was already looking impressed and she smiled at the stranger, before saying with a confidence Roley envied:

'Hi, are you on holiday here too?'

'No.' The boy looked them up and down, coolly. 'I live here,' he added.

'We're on holiday,' Cat went on, now embarrassing Roley, who had the conviction the stranger thought them both interlopers here. 'I'm Cat and the bear's my brother Roley.'

The boy raised his eyebrows. He had a thin sharp face, although Roley had already noticed the muscles in his bare upper arms. He met Roley's eyes for a moment, looking amused.

'I'm Fox,' he said and Cat crowed with delight.

'We've both got animal names,' she said. But Roley couldn't shake the impression the boy had been talking to him. He felt more lumbering and bear-like than ever.

'Is there anything to do around here?' Cat was asking, obviously angling for an opportunity to see Fox again.

'We manage to amuse ourselves,' Fox replied, his eyes flicking back for a moment towards the gardens in a way that Roland distrusted.

'Do you know Alice?' he blurted out, causing Cat to look up at him in surprise and Fox to smile slowly at him, showing a gleam of white teeth.

'Oh yes, I know Alice,' he said. 'I know Alice very well.'

Roley blushed. Fox was leaning against the wall now, very much lord of the manor. He was obviously Alice's boyfriend or he wanted to be and next to all that glamour Roley didn't have a hope. He looked at his sister, planning to suggest they leave, and inwardly groaned when he saw she had taken out her packet of cigarettes again.

She stuck one in her mouth and began to fumble for her lighter and Fox suddenly reached out a hand.

'I'll take one of those,' he said.

Cat looked delighted, not fazed at all by the cool way he assumed she'd give him a cigarette, and gave him the whole packet. He took one and held it between finger and thumb, waiting as Cat continued to look for her lighter. He and Roley were both watching as suddenly a worried look crossed her face and she pulled out Delilah.

The doll hung limply in her hand, the lighter entangled in the strands of her hair. Cat looked frightened for a moment and then her eyes quickly went to Fox.

'Sorry,' she said. 'That keeps happening.'

'You said you'd left that creepy thing at home,' Roley said, annoyed enough to glare at her despite Fox's presence.

'I thought I had,' Cat said, sounding a bit subdued. She disentangled the lighter and shoved the doll back into her pocket.

'Delilah's not easily left behind,' Fox said casually, taking the pink plastic lighter from Cat and lighting the cigarette before inhaling. It took Roley and Cat a moment to process what he'd said and when they did, Cat dropped her own cigarette.

'You know Delilah too?' Roley said, trying to put a bit of a challenge into the question and Fox raised his eyebrows.

'Oh yes,' he said. 'I told you, I live here. I know everyone that matters.'

He took another drag from his cigarette and then dropped it, crushing it beneath a boot. He pocketed the packet and turned to the wall and picked up a long coat that had been folded and left on it. Roley hadn't registered it before but now Fox swirled it around his shoulders in another stagey gesture and thrust his arms down the sleeves. It was a fur coat, a reddish brown that matched his hair and his name. Roley wondered if he could perhaps be a member of a local hunt, and if Alice was too. He wondered why someone would wear a fur coat and call himself Fox but perhaps it was a joke he didn't get.

Cat hadn't said anything about Fox taking her cigarettes and Roley wondered whether he dared. He thought the other boy might be on the lookout for a fight and even as he thought it Fox gave him another of those long assessing looks. Then he leapt up on to the wall and down again into the first of the back gardens.

'Catch you later,' he said with a glance at Cat before adding, with a smile: 'I'll give your love to Alice.'

Roley and Cat watched as he strode off down the line of gardens, vaulting the next wall with an athletic ease that left Roley sick with envy. Cat was looking with a kind of dazed amazement that worried him all the more. When Fox was finally out of sight she seemed to come out of her daydream and turned to him.

'Who's Alice?' she asked.

Cat and Roley walked all the way around the village, not going inside the small church although they stopped for a while at the village green to have an argument about whether or not Roley would buy Cat some more cigarettes.

'I don't have any ID on me,' he said finally. 'So stop asking, because even if I was willing to fund your horrible habit they probably wouldn't sell them to me anyway. If you want to smoke ask Fox for your fags back.'

By the time they got back to the house it was almost dinner time. Harriet and Peter both enjoyed cooking although in Harriet's case it was always a whirlwind of chopping and slicing and dicing while Peter's puddings involved a slower process of tasting and mixing and the eating of raw ingredients.

The smell of roasting potatoes and lamb casserole filled the house, wafting out of the kitchen and up the stairs. All four children tended to make themselves scarce while the cooking was going on, to avoid being given jobs. But Roley and Cat arrived in time to be told to set the table and Katherine and John clattered downstairs shortly afterwards.

Cat had almost forgotten her stepsister mentioning a secret until she noticed John's face was flushed and excited and Katherine looked smug. As their parents brought in the dishes, even they noticed something was up.

'You look pretty excited, old chap,' Peter said, putting a hand on John's shoulder. 'What've you been up to all afternoon?'

'Kat's been showing me something,' John replied. He looked hopefully at his older sister and said, 'It's a secret but she said we could tell at dinner.'

As they took their seats people turned to look at Katherine and she waited until they were all watching before she spoke, spinning out the moment for as long as she could.

'I've found a secret room,' she said.

'Like a priest's hole?' Peter asked. 'Where?'

'In the back of the computer room,' she replied. 'There's a door that looks like a cupboard and it leads to . . .'

'The magical land of Narnia,' Cat said, cutting her off. 'Are we playing Let's Pretend?'

'No!' Katherine flushed. 'It leads into the barn. There's a games room down there with a pool table.'

'Whoo hoo,' Cat murmured. 'A pool table.'

'Catriona.' Her mother frowned at her and Cat fidgeted.

'Well, it's not exactly an exciting secret is it?' she said defensively. 'You can see the barn from outside.'

'If you're not interested you don't have to look,' Katherine snapped back. 'You can stick to playing with dolls.'

Cat was caught without a comeback, her eyes flicking to her coat, slung over the back of an armchair on the other side of the room. She hadn't had time to put Delilah back in her box before going for the walk with Roley, so she'd just put her in the doll's house for safe-keeping. She could remember opening and shutting the door. But Delilah hadn't stayed behind. Giving Katherine a filthy look over the table, she wondered if her step-sister had put the doll in her jacket, trying to get her in trouble.

Roley was trying to make peace, asking questions about the barn room and John was swallowing quickly in order to answer.

'It's got all these really old books,' he said. 'Piles and piles of them, and some games too. Like Cluedo and Mousetrap.'

'Maybe we can play one after dinner,' Roley said and John beamed at him.

Cat rolled her eyes but didn't say anything more. As the conversation became general she dragged her mind away from Delilah. Instead she replayed her first sight of Fox standing on the wall. Roley had answered her question about Alice awkwardly, muttering something about meeting a girl in the lane earlier. It was weird thinking of Roley meeting girls. He'd never seemed interested before, preferring his computer games and TV programmes to going out clubbing or to the pub. Cat was a year younger than him but everyone at school said girls were naturally about four years more mature than boys, so she'd got used to thinking of herself ahead of him.

Fox was exactly the right age and exactly fitted Cat's daydreams of the ideal bloke. He was tall and gorgeous and coolly confident. Her friends had talked about holiday romances with boys called Romeo and Jacques and she had a vision of herself coming back to school with photos of her and Fox like the ones other girls had pinned up in their lockers. She smiled to herself, wondering how she could get to meet him again and if he really was seeing this Alice girl. Glancing across at her mother she felt her good mood sink. This stupid holiday was supposed to be a *family* thing and she bet her mother wouldn't let her run around with the local boys when she was supposed to be bonding with her stepsister.

But replaying her meeting with Fox led to the moment her fingers had felt for her lighter and touched silky hair. Cat remembered Fox saying 'Delilah's not easily left behind' and felt her stomach turn over. Feeling sick, she asked to be excused from pudding. Harriet hesitated but the family rule was you could leave when you were finished if you asked politely and Cat was already carrying her plate back into the kitchen.

As Roley practically drooled over the dessert, she ran up the main staircase, across the landing and up the second staircase to her room on the attic floor. Her clothes were still all over everything and she wished she'd chosen a room with a real wardrobe. Or any room but the one with the doll's house. She looked over the miniature house with its real glass windows and froze, as if she had seen a snake. At one of the gabled windows on the attic floor of the doll's house was a face: a pale face framed in long silky hair.

Cat stared at Delilah across the room. She could see that the doll's house door was slightly open, the catch not properly engaged. One of Delilah's small hands was against the window, as if she was pushing it open. In the silence of the attic, Cat thought she could hear the catch creak. Whirling around, she fled through the door into the other attic and slammed it behind her. There was no way any of the others could have set that up. They hadn't had time to get Delilah from her jacket pocket and put her in the doll's house.

Sitting down on John's bed, neatly made with a stuffed bear on the pillow, Cat stared at the door to her own room. Perhaps there was more than one copy of the Delilah doll, she thought. But the idea just made her shudder and she lay down on the bed, rumpling the covers, wishing she was at home in her own room with its band posters and stereo system.

She heard the others' feet thundering on the stairs and sat up, hoping they wouldn't come up here. But instead they stopped on the floor below and she guessed they were going into the barn. Getting up from the bed she glanced back at the door to her own room again and then left through John's door. She walked slowly down the main stairs, one hand on the smooth banister, trying to steady herself. Perhaps Harriet had put the drones in the doll's house, she thought suddenly. The face she had seen might have been one of them, not Delilah at all. She'd only glimpsed it for a second before she'd freaked out.

All the same, she didn't feel like going back up there right now, or like going back down to check her coat pocket either. Instead she went to find the others.

Katherine, Roley, and John had been making themselves at home in the barn. Katherine was on her knees looking through the tottering piles of books stacked higgledy-piggledy against a wall. Roley had pulled the dust sheet back from the pool table and located the balls and a frame.

He was showing John how to line up shots as Catriona came down the stairs to join them.

'How's the magical world of Barnia?' Catriona asked as she came in and John laughed and then looked guiltily at Katherine.

'Just fine,' Katherine said, sitting back on her heels. 'How're Delilah and her drones?'

That morning Catriona had been crowing over Delilah but Kat had noticed how she'd fallen silent at dinner at the mention of the doll's house and she saw that for once she'd managed to find a raw spot in her stepsister's cool attitude.

'I've dumped them somewhere,' Catriona said, throwing herself on to a chair. 'You can have them, I'm not into voodoo dolls. That's more your family's kind of thing, right?' Kat flinched and bent her head, feeling stupid to be hurt by Catriona's casual cruelty. Over at the pool table John looked shocked and Roley glared over his head at his sister.

'Shut up, Catriona,' he said and she gave him a betrayed look.

Even Katherine was surprised to hear Roley take her side and it changed the mood in the barn from hostile to wary. Everyone was tense and as Catriona began to pick stuffing out of the chair with her long fingernails, John and Roley began a game of pool. Over in her corner Katherine continued sorting through the books. With the light on, it was easier to see what she was doing but even so the books had been so crammed together that mildew and damp had stuck some of them in solid blocks.

Many of the books were unsalvageable and she wondered why her mother had just left them here in the barn. None of the others were watching her as Katherine looked through the heap, hooking her hair behind her ears as she scanned through book after book. But gradually she was forming a pile of books with the fox nameplate and her mother's name in the front. Each one had the same savage crossings out of names. It was always the nice characters who were excised, the kind and the good. Villains survived and petty thugs and people who sneered and jeered at the heroes and heroines. When you thought about it, most stories involved the main characters overcoming problems to reach a happy ending. But her mother's books were evidence someone had hated happy endings, hated them enough to damage every one of her books. Had that person been Anne herself?

There were still piles and piles of books to look at and Kat was finding the hunt depressing. Her eyes travelled the piles to a heap she'd disregarded. Old school exercise books, the thin notebooks with ruled lines that came in different coloured covers, now faded and bent. Kat's school used A4 paper and ring binders but she had a brown notebook just like the ones in the pile for rough work—although actually most people used theirs for writing notes in class or doodles of boxes and smiley faces.

Suddenly interested again she crossed to the pile of exercise books and began to pick through them. They weren't all Anne's. Some said *Charlotte Dean* in black uncompromising capitals, or *Emily Wheeler* in swirling looping curlicues. Something about the names was familiar. It took Katherine a while to track down a memory from her own school lessons. Emily, Charlotte, and Anne were the names of the Brontë sisters. They were common enough names but it was an odd coincidence that the names of these three girls matched. *Or perhaps that's how they got to be friends,* she thought, *if they all liked to read.*

Charlotte had left a stack of English notes defining words like 'synecdoche' and 'metonymy'. Emily had painstakingly inked-in maps of countries and geographical features, all faded now. Anne seemed to have abandoned years and years worth of Religious Studies homework, notes on gods and angels and folklore all in the same round regular handwriting as her bookplates. It was nice to have them and Kat put them aside to show to John but they weren't what she was looking for.

People never used rough work books for homework, only for writing notes to friends or drawing caricatures of the teachers. One girl in Kat's class had written a story in hers, not a very imaginative one, about a pop-group she liked. A group of boys used theirs for fantasy football league tables. Rough work books were like diaries, full of people's secrets.

Near the bottom of the heap she found a scuffed brown notebook which didn't have a girl's name or a subject title on the front. Instead it read in block capitals: **THE MAKE-BELIEVE GAME**.

Kat carefully brushed the cobwebs off with part of a ragged curtain someone had thrown over the bookcase in an unsuccessful effort to protect it. The book hadn't escaped the damp and some of the later pages were gummed together but when she lifted the cover it opened easily to the first page. *Rules for Sacrifices* headed the page in Anne's writing, but beneath it the next few lines were written in alternating styles.

Names crossed out cannot be spoken—
A character dead is a story broken.
Every sacrifice must cost:
You can't recover what's been lost.
Stolen words must be spent,
Borrowed power can't be lent.
The name-eater must be fed
By the living or the dead.

Beneath the words three names were written. *Anne Katherine Stone* was the first, followed by *Charlotte Miranda Dean* and *Emily Jane Wheeler.*

This was the reason for the names being crossed out of Anne's books. It was part of the 'Make-Believe Game', something she and her friends had invented together when they'd written these rules. Rules for sacrifices. Kat swallowed, the dust from the books had got all over her and she suddenly felt grimy and depressed. She didn't much like the idea of a game where you crossed names out of books and she remembered how savage some of those crossings out had been.

She closed the book, but she didn't like to leave it where anyone could find it and she hid it in the pile of novels, carrying them back to her room. John barely looked up from the pool game when Kat said she was going to her room. Catriona was commenting contemptuously on Roley's lack of skill and Katherine wondered why she hadn't shut herself up in her room with her music the way she usually did.

Katherine slinked up the stairs and into her own room. The words of the poem were still running through her head, puzzling and disturbing at once. She eyed the book uneasily as she changed into her pyjamas. She didn't want to know what else was written in it. But, in the bathroom, as she washed her hands clean of grime she knew she'd read the rest of the book. She felt as if she'd found her mother's diary—that the book might be the key to understanding her.

7
Whispers in the Walls

John's bedtime was normally nine o'clock but on holiday the rules were different and when he finally got to bed it was past ten.

Lying in his bed with his brown bear tucked up next to him, John tried to fall asleep. Downstairs he could hear the others moving about, floorboards creaking and murmurs of voices. There were other sounds too, gusts of wind outside and other noises he couldn't identify but he supposed were sounds of the countryside. But as well as those there were noises from inside the house, scraping scrabbling scratching sounds that seemed to come from the skirting boards and the walls and ceiling. He wondered if there were mice living in the walls. A boy at school had tame white mice he kept in a cage in his bedroom and he said that they were always trying to escape. Once he'd lost one for a month and finally found it bringing up a nest of baby mice in the under-stairs cupboard.

John would have liked a pet mouse, or something larger like a cat or a dog. If he had a pet he'd have something to play with when Roley was busy on his computer and Katherine was reading and Catriona was listening to her music. But the scratching sounds kept him awake and, hugging his bear closer, he pulled the covers over his head.

He must have fallen asleep because in his dream he was back in the wood. John always knew whether he was asleep or awake, but with a strange sort of knowledge that made dreaming seem just as important as the real world. The wood ahead was dark and there was a buzzing noise coming from somewhere close by. He was running, before he remembered starting to run, and he knew there were other people in the wood, people who couldn't get out. He could feel them around him, a crowd of invisible people pushing and shoving, shadowy figures with arms shaped like wings or the branches of trees, all pushing to get past.

A girl in a golden dress ran by, a long plait of blonde hair hanging down her back and John reached out to grab it. The plait turned into a rope and he clung to it, finding himself halfway up a tower, with Alice looking down at him from a high window. The rope of her hair was slippery and the golden strands had other shades of brown and black wound through it, like Delilah's. He opened his mouth to ask her to help him up and felt his hands slip. Then he was falling, falling past stone walls and tall trees as a flock of black birds swooped and dived around him.

He opened his mouth to scream and his eyes snapped open, staring at the dark room. As his heart hammered in his chest he heard his own scream as if it came from somewhere else: a raw terrified noise that made his heart race faster.

It had come from somewhere else. After another moment John realized it wasn't his voice screaming. It came from the other side of the wall, from Catriona's room. Throwing off the covers he sat up and heard footsteps running up the other staircase. On the other side of the wall he heard a door open and people come in. His father murmured something and Harriet's higher sharper voice say through another choked off scream:

'Cat! Wake up, darling, you're having a nightmare.'

Sitting in his bed John heard Catriona gasping for air as if she'd been drowning. The sound was mixed up with sobs and soothing murmurs and another rumble from his father before his heavier footsteps went back downstairs. The gasps and sobs continued, overlapping with Harriet's soothing voice.

'No, no . . . I don't want to. Don't let her . . . '

'It was just a nightmare, darling.' Harriet was easy to hear, it sounded as if she was sitting on Catriona's bed, looking after her. John felt tears prickle behind his eyes. He wondered if his mother had ever come and sat with him when he was little and he wished he could remember.

'Oh,' Cat was still sobbing. 'Mum, please, I can't bear it here. Let's go home, please. Please.'

'Don't be silly.' Harriet's voice was suddenly sharp. 'We've only just got here. We haven't seen the lakes or anything. We're going to Windermere tomorrow, you'll feel better then.'

'No, I won't,' Catriona cried. 'Mum, please. Please just let's go. I'll be good, I promise . . . '

'It's not about being good,' Harriet said. 'I just want us all to have a nice holiday as a family.' There was a pause and she added, 'Do you want me to get you a glass of water?'

'No.' A mutter of something else from Catriona and then Harriet said:

'We are NOT going home. Lie down and count sheep. It'll be morning before you know it.'

'You're horrible.' Cat's voice rose to a wail. 'Mum! Don't go!'

But John could hear Harriet's footsteps crossing the room in quick sharp steps that showed she was annoyed. It wasn't fair though; Catriona was still sobbing and she sounded really frightened. Harriet shouldn't leave like that. He remembered his own dream and thought Cat's sounded worse. She was still breathing in gasps, and he doubted that she would be able to sleep when she was that upset.

John looked at the wall which separated them. He normally found Catriona overwhelming. He thought older sisters were quiet and nice, helping you with homework or explaining how to play rounders. Catriona with her loud music and her strange clothes and her hysterics was older than Katherine but she didn't seem like a grown-up. She was more like an alien. But she was still crying and John raised a hand and made a fist, knocking on the wall.

'Oh no, no please.' Catriona's voice shook and John felt himself go hot and cold as he realized he had scared her.

'Don't cry,' he said. 'It's me. John.'

'John?' Catriona's voice levelled out and he heard her ask: 'Did I wake you up?'

'It doesn't matter,' John said. He picked up his bear and looked at the wall. 'I had a bad dream too.'

'About her?' Catriona's voice started shaking again. 'D-Delilah?'

John hesitated. He didn't think his dream had been about that. But there had been something about hair, something that even now he was forgetting. As he tried to think of the right answer he heard Catriona get up from

94

her bed and walk to the door between their rooms and knock quietly.

'Come in,' he said, and the door opened.

'Sorry,' Catriona said as she came in and John realized it was the first time he'd ever heard her say the word. She closed the door to her own room behind her and came to sit on the end of her bed. 'I don't want to stay in there,' she said, her voice still shaking.

'Because of your dream?' John asked and she shuddered and wrapped her arms around herself. She was wearing shorts and a top that left her arms and legs bare and her hair was tousled. 'Do you want some of my blanket?' he asked and Catriona mumbled something and pulled the bottom end of it around herself.

'I wish I'd never found that stupid doll,' Catriona said and then glanced sharply around as if she thought Delilah might have heard her.

'I thought you said she was cool?' John said carefully.

'Well, she isn't,' Cat said, huddling into the blanket. 'She's horrible and creepy and she was *in my dreams*.' Her voice dropped to a whisper as she continued: 'She was cutting . . . ' Her hands reached up to touch her own hair. 'Cutting my hair with her scissors . . . '

John felt chilled and he looked at Catriona's hair. Over by her right ear there was a part that looked a bit shorter than the rest and as he looked he saw her turn even paler and twist her head, pulling at her own hair to look at it.

'Oh shit, oh shit,' she said. 'No, she couldn't, it's not possible.' She'd pulled the shorter strand forward so she could see it and she was staring at the clipped ends with a fixed look that made her face seem dead.

'Perhaps you tore it,' John said quickly. 'Maybe there was a loose nail or you got it wound round your hand and you pulled some out and that gave you the bad dream?'

Catriona was quiet for a moment and then she said slowly: 'I suppose.'

John realized that there was something else, something she hadn't told him. Catriona was normally so cool and stand-offish. The nightmare must have frightened her a lot or she wouldn't have come into his room. But she wouldn't have been scared if there hadn't been something more. He remembered her holding the Delilah doll at breakfast, adjusting the position of the doll's arms and legs. Something must have happened since then to scare her so much.

'What scissors?' he asked and felt Catriona jump.

'Nothing,' she said quickly. 'It doesn't matter.' She moved as if she was about to throw the covers off and leave and then she stopped.

'Do you want to stay here?' he asked. 'It's a big bed. There's lots of room.'

'If you want,' Catriona said after a moment.

John had almost forgotten his own nightmare but now that he'd heard Catriona's he was a bit worried he'd have it too. But when she had bundled herself up beside him in the blanket he actually felt better. It wasn't the same as having his sister here. Katherine would have put her arm around him or said 'sweet dreams'. Catriona had taken most of the blanket and her feet were cold but once she was lying down she relaxed and he could hear her breathing become slower and more regular. Relaxed by it, John felt his own eyes get heavy and soon he was deep in a dreamless sleep.

On the floor below Katherine heard Harriet come back downstairs and cross the corridor to enter her own room. There was a distant buzz of voices for a while, too far away for Kat to make out what was being said. Only once she was sure no one was going to get up again did she turn the bedside light back on. She'd barely slept at all, imagining what the book might contain.

Now she picked up the book once more, feeling the roughness of the mould-speckled cover as she looked at the black inked title. Make-Believe was a game for children younger than John but the handwriting was too neat for children that young. She guessed her mother and her friends had been teenagers when they'd written the poem. She recalled more than one of the notebooks had been marked 'Upper V' which would be Year Eleven now.

Opening the musty pages Katherine looked again at the words of the poem. It read like something a teenager might write. Carefully she turned the page, feeling its stiffness in her hands as if it had got damp and then dried out in cardboard-like corrugations. *Order of Service*, read the next heading and beneath it was a series of what looked like stage directions beginning, '*The sacrifice is placed upon the altar, the celebrant takes the paperknife and the*

97

congregation kneels.' It was like a black mass, she realized, a sort of parody of a church service. The lines of the poem were interspersed with directions about using the paper-knife to cut the spines of books or a fountain pen to blot out words.

Katherine told herself it was only books being damaged, inanimate objects. Anne and her friends hadn't been sacrificing animals, or anything truly horrible. But the thought wasn't very consoling. The descriptions of the books made them seem like animals, roped and bound for slaughter on the stone altar. She skipped ahead to the end of the service and came to a double-page spread.

It was a map. Perhaps it had been drawn by Emily, the careful geography student. The ink was faded now but Katherine could still make out the different colours. Black for houses, green for trees, brown for fields, blue for water, and grey for the lines of roads. Following a wandering loop of road past a cluster of buildings that must be the village and around a sharp right bend she followed the route they had taken to a black-inked house. Behind the house the green trees were so thick the ink had merged and blobbed together. Waving gradient lines showed that the wood rose up the hill and surrounded a puddle of blue marking a tarn at the top. Here and there were place names: '*Blyght Wood*', '*Blyght Tor*', and '*Shystone Tarn*'. All over the landscape were marks and symbols that you wouldn't find on any ordnance survey map.

Katherine sometimes read the kind of fantasy novel that began with a map at the front, showing the landscape of another world. Now, looking at this map she began to have an idea of what the Make-Believe Game was supposed to be about. The three girls had used the real world as the landscape of their game. The house, the wood, the hills, and the tarn were all places they went and the symbols marked the places they had their rituals. She could all too easily imagine the three of them slipping off into the woods together with their books and paperknives or whispering together about the places they planned to meet.

The next twelve pages were a calendar, dates marked with symbols for full or crescent moons, signs of the zodiac, festivals from more than one religion. Katherine didn't pay much attention. She thought she understood what the girls were doing—what she wanted to know now was why. After the calendar the pages were stuck together and she had to peel the first back carefully, fraction by fraction. A piece of art paper had been glued into the book, and on it was drawn Delilah, standing as she had stood on the breakfast table this morning, surrounded by hairless, faceless, and eyeless drones. The drone faces covered all the available white space, repetition after repetition of the same blank expression, the pits of the eyes scoured into the art paper deeply enough to shred it.

The drawing was in black ink except for Delilah's hair. That alone was coloured in with Lakeland pencils, in whorls and loops of wheat gold, mud brown, and raven black. The coloured loops reached out to hold the drones at neck, wrist, or ankle, like ropes binding them to Delilah.

Katherine had to put the book down; she was finding it hard to breathe. She was already sure she'd have nightmares enough of gravestones surrounding the house, books trussed for sacrifice, and an army of drones tied together with hair.

8
The Hanging Tree

It was just after dawn when Alice let herself out of number 27. She'd not been sleeping anyway. Baskerville had barked several times in the night and each time Alice had sat up and listened for a while before lapsing into an uneasy sleep.

Both Emily's and Charlotte's doors were shut when she walked quietly down the stairs, carrying a heavy bag and her walking boots. She stopped to leave a brief note on the kitchen table before lacing her boots up. Outside in the garden Baskerville came to meet her eagerly, putting his paws up on her shoulders when she bent down to him. His muzzle had black feathers caught on it and she took them from him thoughtfully.

'Where did you get these, then?' she asked and walked him around the garden to see if there was any sign of a bird. It would have to be quite a large bird, a raven perhaps. The feathers were long and slightly glossy. She found more of them caught in the back hedge, near the gap where an apple tree had toppled down in last year's gales. All around the fallen trunk were signs of battle, broken feathers lying about on the ground.

Letting herself out of the side gate, she called Baskerville to her, clipping the lead on to his collar as she walked through the village. It was a misty morning and Baskerville seemed calm as he walked at her side. Alice passed the milkman and the butcher's van and the usual early morning travellers.

No one was paying her any attention. But even when the village was lost behind the bend of the road, Alice felt as if eyes were watching her as she headed towards the fell. Letting Baskerville off the leash she wrapped it around her hand loosely, adjusted her sports bag, and then quickly scrambled up a high bank and into the shadow of the trees. She whistled to the dog and he came exuberantly up the bank, excited by the change to their walk.

Technically she was trespassing but that wasn't why she was cautious. Her mother was mostly reasonable about letting Alice out alone but she wasn't rational on the subject of the wood. Alice thought she knew why but she hoped she was wrong and so she hadn't asked for an explanation. She'd not had much reason to visit the wood anyway, not many people went there. It wasn't even a useful shortcut, straggling across the hill behind Fell Scar and then down again on the other side. But today she had a reason to go there.

With the dog running ahead she began to walk through the trees, looking at the patterns of green light and black shadow that crossed the path ahead. In term time Alice worked after school in the drama department, sewing and mending the costumes they used for the school plays. She didn't want to act herself, always feeling unconvincing when they read plays in class. But she enjoyed working on the scenery, watching the sets take shape for each production. The drama department kept almost exclusively to Shakespeare, not seeking to surprise the audience. Until Alice had joined they'd relied almost exclusively on an old stock flat of a formal garden and some painted cardboard imitations of Greek statuary.

Alice was now in charge of the scenery. She might not be one of the bright beautiful girls who went up for leads in the plays, flirting on stage with the good-looking guys who wanted any role that let them wear a sword, but she'd made friends with the team of geekier guys who worked on lights and made props and with their encouragement she'd starting working on set backdrops. Her night-sky curtain with hundreds of individually sewn sequins showing the constellations and one brightly glowing star had been used in the juniors' nativity play. Last year she'd painted a huge flat for *Macbeth* with a lowering sky coloured with a flaming sunset over a craggy Scottish hillside.

This year they were planning to do *A Midsummer Night's Dream* and Alice had plans to use green branches to create a bower around Titania's throne. But for the backdrop she wanted to work from photographs, to make the wood seem real behind the bower.

'The woods are lovely, dark and deep,' she said to herself, quoting something she'd read in English. Her voice seemed to fall silently into the wood so that she wondered if she had spoken out loud. But Baskerville had pricked his ears up.

Alice's feet crunched on layers of old dead leaves. Really *Midsummer Night's Dream* should have a slightly brighter forest than this, she realized. Just a few minutes into it and already the path ahead seemed shrouded in gloom.

She stopped, calling Baskerville back and wondering if this was such a good idea. She was thinking of her mother. The mystery had something to do with these woods. Emily wasn't rational about them and without knowing the truth, Alice feared she had guessed it. Emily wasn't easy with anyone, although among people she worked with she managed to hide it, and among large groups of men like the crowd at the kennel club she seemed almost afraid. Whatever lay at the heart of her relationship with Charlotte it was true she had no boyfriends, no men friends of any kind. And yet there was Alice.

Alice stood between the shadows of the trees and tried out again in her mind the unpleasant knowledge that Emily had become pregnant at sixteen. With no one in the village ever having mentioned a boyfriend, there remained the appalling possibility that Emily had walked alone in this wood and something had happened here that frightened her even now.

It had been a mistake to come here and a double mistake to come and think these thoughts. The shadows of the trees seemed imbued with menace. In the patterns of light and shade Alice's artist's eye could draw blurred faces and watching eyes. Baskerville whined at her feet, picking up on her growing unease, and Alice crouched down to ruffle his ears, reassuring herself as much as him.

'We'll just take a couple of pictures and then we'll go,' she told him.

* * *

With a dog you didn't need to feel frightened, Alice told herself, as she set up her camera and tripod. It had taken longer than she'd expected to find a suitable clearing but Baskerville's wholehearted approval of the adventure had banished some of her dark thoughts.

He was a gun dog, trained to respond to voice commands. Alice had worked at the kennels at weekends for a while and Baskerville had been a birthday present from the owner. He was a Labrador cross, black like the 'Hound of the Baskervilles', and he'd grown quickly to become much larger than his litter-mates. Alice considered him company rather than protection but it couldn't be denied that sometimes out late it was reassuring to know Baskerville had been trained, among other things, to 'hold' a burglar or attacker. She worried more that he might get hurt than that she would.

When she finally settled on a stretch of moss within a rough clearing, Baskerville ran around the boundaries snuffling at the tree roots and then bounded back past Alice to explore the centre of the clearing. There was an old stump there, the trunk of the tree sliced off about a metre up. Moss had grown over the flat place now and other branches had grown up from the sides of it, splayed out and twisted around each other, groping their way back up to the sky. At the base, tentacular roots wrestled with the ground as if the tree was trying to drag itself free.

It made a fantastic focal point and Alice adjusted her camera to frame it. She was already rethinking her idea of Titania's bower. A seat made out of a tree like this, with withered branches like an old man's arms, would make the elf queen seem more other-worldly, less like a tinselly Christmas fairy. Shooing Baskerville away from the stump she draped a green blanket across it. Moss might sound poetic but if Alice was going to stand in for Titania in the test shoots she'd rather not sit on anything slimy and the stump had more than moss growing on it: fungus and lichen were all over the roots and the lower branches.

Looking around the clearing again, Alice felt a more normal nervousness about what she was going to do next. Fearing a hypothetical attacker from sixteen years ago was obviously paranoid but walkers might still come by, like the boys she'd met yesterday. Slowly, Alice removed Titania's golden silk gown from the bag. This was the reason she'd gone far enough into the woods to be sure no one was watching her. She didn't want to act Titania, but she wanted the costume to look right on stage.

Taking off her baggy jumper, she shivered in her thin T-shirt as she worked the gown over her head. It was rough inside with the knots of embroidery and it scratched her arms as she smoothed it down. She had to take her boots off before undoing her jeans and kicking them on to the pile. The wood bark and dead leaves felt spongy under her feet as she changed and she stepped back into her boots. It was too cold under the trees to take authenticity too far.

She set up the camera for a series of time-delayed shots and crossed the ground to compose herself on the stump. Titania's hair would be loose and she dragged the band from the end of her plait and raked her fingers through her hair, shaking it out. She wasn't used to being the focus of attention, even of her own camera, and felt more than a bit stupid in the gold gown with her hair loose. *Think Titania,* she told herself, trying to relax. *Think Ophelia and the Lady of Shalott.*

The camera flashed, blurring her vision with the sudden light, and she blinked and then winced at herself. She hadn't imagined it would be so difficult just to sit for a photograph— she was too used to being behind the protective lens of the camera. Everything seemed to distract her: the rough bark of the tree against her back, the spongy texture of the moss underneath the blanket, and the rustle of the branches above her, shaking dead leaves into her lap. The camera flashed again, catching her unprepared. In the distance she heard Baskerville barking and wondered when he'd got so far away.

Alice glanced uneasily around the clearing. The only faces were the ones she'd invented in the knots of bark and clusters of leaves and still she felt as if she was being watched. The branches shook again, this time more noticeably, and there was an ominous creak from the roots of the tree. She hoped it wasn't going to topple over; some of the branches seemed more than half rotten. Another flash went off just as she'd shifted to look at the twisted trunk behind her and she flinched and tried to turn back.

Pain flared in her scalp as her hair tangled on a branch, and she reached up to free it and felt her wrist caught suddenly in a vicelike grip. Her instinctive cry of alarm was muffled as her hair wrapped more tightly around her head and her free arm scraped agonizingly against twigs. The grip on her wrist was rough and when she struggled to pull her arm free it was wrenched behind her back, pulling her up against the trunk of the tree. Somehow the blanket seemed to have got tangled around her legs and when she tried to kick free it drew tighter around her and she felt herself lifted from the ground.

Through her own hair Alice could see nothing but the branches shaking wildly above her and she heard only her own breath coming in shocked gasps in turn with the creaks and groans of the tree. Her arms were caught above her, twigs scraping her shoulders hard enough to draw blood, and as her legs flailed to find a purchase against the shaking branches her dress rode up to her waist.

'Poor little partridge tangled in a tree, flutters up her feathers but she can't get free . . .' The voice was old and cracked, the words seeming to come from somewhere behind her head, and at the sound of it Alice froze. Up until now she'd been thinking she'd had a weird sort of accident. Only now did she realize it was a deliberate attack. Despite her own stillness the tree was moving and creaking as if shaken in a high wind. Branches were wrenching her body as twigs snared the fabric of her dress and she kicked out suddenly and heard wood snap.

'Wicked little bird, made a bad mistake. Forgot that bone, like branch, can break.' The croaked words came with a savage yank of her twisted arm and the pain brought tears to her eyes.

'Stop it!' Alice had to force the words out past her suddenly dry throat and heard them sound as cracked and broken as the voice that taunted her. 'Please don't . . .'

The voice laughed creakily and the branches wrenched at her legs and arms, scraping roughly against her skin.

Finally giving way to panic, Alice screamed and heard the woods echo with the sound an instant before a flock of birds repeated her scream with their own harsh calls. A dog barked and Alice fought the invasive branches of the tree to shout again.

'BASKERVILLE!'

The barked reply sounded closer but still too far away to help her and Alice was running out of strength. Her body was forced up against the trunk of the tree, rotten bark breaking away against her skin as branches squeezed her breathless so that she couldn't scream again.

The birds screamed for her. Suddenly the tree was shaking this way and that as bird calls rang out all around her. There was a flurry of black feathers and Alice was shaken backwards and forwards as the voice of menace roared a wordless curse. Wings beat about her body and this time it felt like hands that pulled at her as she was grabbed and lifted, torn free of the branches and thrown from the tree.

The birds were still screaming as she hit the ground, jarring the last of her breath from her body. A moment later a volley of barks added to the din as Baskerville charged past her. Alice slipped on damp earth and sobbed a breath into her lungs to call the dog back.

She grabbed his collar and hauled him away, bent over and leaning on him as she broke into a limping run. They pushed through a stand of bushes and skidded down a muddy bank into a ditch full of weeds. Somewhere back behind her in the clearing was her camera and her clothes but Alice couldn't think of anything but getting away. She'd twisted an ankle coming down the bank and, with one arm limp and useless at her side and the other clutching the dog's collar, she couldn't get her balance again. Baskerville was bristling all over and his lips rolled back into a snarl. He continued to growl as Alice pushed herself to her knees and then to her feet. Her next steps were stumbled but fear forced her on. All around were trees and she shied away from every branch and flinched whenever she tripped over a root, lurching like a cripple on legs that protested at every step.

In the end she told Baskerville to find the way out and had to trust to his instincts to lead her wisely. When she finally saw a glimpse of the fields through the thinning branches of the wood, relief gave her a last burst of energy, enough to climb over a tumbledown wall into a sheep pasture and sag back against the stone.

It was covered with moss and the sensation pushed her upright at once with an unpleasant flashback to the mossed trunk of the rotting tree. Baskerville had heaved himself over the wall and was calming down, pushing his nose against her hand and then licking it. She patted him, looking him over for scratches and finding one nasty gash on one of his legs. He whined when she touched it and Alice winced, reminded of her own scrapes and bruises. Finally, she called him to heel and set off across the pasture. She recognized where she was now and it ought to be possible to cut across it to reach a footpath that would take her most of the way home. As she walked, her wrenched arm ached and she had to hold it against her chest to stop it protesting with every movement she made. Even then she could feel the torn muscles screaming at her. Luckily she met no one along the footpath and she took a short cut behind the back of a row of gardens to reach number 27 through the gap in the fence.

Her gaze fell on the scattering of black feathers for the second time that day and she left Baskerville to sniff at them as she limped up the garden to the back door. Emily seemed to be out and upstairs Charlotte's fingers rattled the keys of her computer behind her shut door. Alice walked quietly past it and into the bathroom to take stock of the damage.

It was bad. Her hair was a mess with leaves and twigs—dragged through a hedge backwards was almost literally true in her case. The golden dress was a wreck, the embroidery torn and snarled, and covered with smears of mud and sap. Underneath it her arms were scored with scratches, her legs bruised and scraped bloody.

Dropping the dress on the floor, Alice sat down on the closed lid of the toilet and turned on both the bath taps to full. She was biting her lips, to keep from making any noise, but now that she was home and the danger was past she couldn't seem to stop shaking. Her legs were weak as she kicked off her boots and got into the bath, still wearing her T-shirt and underwear. The water was as hot as she could bear, but she still felt cold. It was shock making her shake like this, she knew, but she couldn't seem to stop it. Crouched in the bathtub with the water rushing, she wondered if Emily had also lain here crippled by fear and pain.

9

Fractured Light

Roley had gone to sleep with his stereo headphones on and woken early in the morning with an uncomfortable crick in his neck to hear birds squabbling somewhere outside on the lawn. He'd muzzily thought something about the early bird getting the worm and fallen into an uneasy dream of being a pale grubby worm hiding in the grass from huge cruel beaks.

He was woken for the second time by his mother knocking on the door and then walking straight into his room.

'Time to get up,' she said brightly, as he blinked blearily at her through the motes of dust floating in a spar of sunlight from between the curtains. As she swam into focus he saw she was wearing her 'positive face', a sure sign that family bonding was ahead.

'What time is it?' he asked and she laughed trillingly. She was whisking the curtains open as she spoke and light came dazzling in.

'Already eight o'clock, sleepy-head. Get yourself washed and dressed quickly, we're going to go into Windermere after breakfast and take a boat trip across the lake.'

As she whisked out of the room Roley reflected that adults were always like this on holiday. His father was the same way. It was as if they took being on holiday as seriously as going to work, you always had to get up and go and do things instead of simply relaxing and having a lie-in.

Harriet had left the door open behind her and Roley went to shut it so he could get dressed. He could hear the sound of crockery clinking in the kitchen downstairs as Peter laid out breakfast and Harriet rousing the others. Outside the house the garden was wet with dew and bright with sunshine in a way that made his eyes ache. He still felt sodden with sleep and, after he'd pulled on jeans and a T-shirt, went to splash his face with water to try to wake up. The bathroom mirror was spotted with brown dots and his face floated blurrily behind smears and smudges. He met his own eyes warily, trying to tell himself it would be OK. But Harriet's forced brightness had depressed him, and he didn't feel ready for a whole day of 'doing things as a family'.

When he got downstairs Peter greeted him cheerfully with a 'hello, old man' and a plate of bacon and eggs, which went some way towards making him feel more human. John and Katherine were already sitting at the table eating their own breakfasts. Unsurprisingly Cat wasn't down yet. She always took forever getting up and Roley knew they'd end up waiting for her ages after everyone else was ready. Harriet was usually irritable about the delay but when she joined them in the kitchen her first remark was:

'Catriona had a bad night last night, so I think she's feeling a bit fragile.' She smiled at Peter as she added: 'No eggs for me, darling, I've got my cereal,' pouring out a bowl of the wholegrain fruit and nut mix she'd brought with her from London. 'Can you all be especially gentle with her today?' she continued, not looking at any of them.

Katherine said nothing but John nodded seriously. Roley swallowed a mouthful of bacon and asked:

'What's up?'

'She had a bad dream,' Harriet said quellingly and John said softly:

'So did I.'

'Me too,' Katherine finally spoke. 'Last night and the night before.'

'Horrid for you,' Peter said sympathetically. 'Probably sleeping in a strange bed. Let's all have a great day today and try and wipe away the bad dreams, shall we?'

John nodded again but Katherine's eyes were haunted and Roley felt uncomfortable remembering what he'd learnt about their mother yesterday and thinking their nightmares weren't likely to be dispelled by a boat trip or an ice-cream.

Catriona was the last to be ready, just as Roley had expected. She was dressed to impress in a leather mini-skirt and a low-cut top and he thought Harriet was taking the gentleness a bit far not to point out it would probably be cold on the lake. But Catriona did look as if she'd had a bad night. Her hair was pulled back into a tight ponytail and the skin of her face looked stretched and false, behind a mask of make-up.

It had obviously rained in the night since the Lakeland countryside they passed had the same bright wetness that made Roley scrunch up his eyes. Roley sometimes had problems with his vision, which Harriet blamed on

114

watching too much TV and playing computer games. Today he wished he'd thought to bring sunglasses because something about the quality of the light was giving him a headache.

When they reached Windermere town, Roley realized they were still a long way from the lake itself. He could see it far down below a steep hill, a wide stretch of water mirroring the blue sky. He had plenty of opportunities to admire it, because it seemed to recede like a mirage as they walked down the hill. A helpful passer-by told them Windermere and Bowness were two towns next to each other and Bowness was the one actually on Lake Windermere. Both Harriet and Peter were brightly humorous about this as they walked past what seemed like a hundred bed-and-breakfasts and another five car park signs and pointed out what a nice day it was for a walk until Roley wished it would rain just to make them shut up.

At the bottom of the hill the bed-and-breakfasts were replaced by shops. Catriona made a beeline for the nearest and their progress slowed to a dawdle as Harriet followed her in and Peter paused to admire a display of wicker baskets. John looked at the baskets with his usual quiet politeness but Katherine didn't even pretend to be interested. She'd taken a book out of her bag and stood outside the first shop reading it, only stirring to park herself outside the next as the others moved on.

Roley wished he'd brought his Game Boy but he knew his mother wouldn't have stood for it. Instead he shuffled onwards from shop to shop, trying to step around the hordes of tourists who thronged both sides of the pavement. The lake was more like a mirage than ever, dazzling unexpectedly from around corners and at the end of side streets. Roley felt as if it was ambushing him; each new glimpse of it made his headache worse and he had to raise a hand in front of his face to block out some of the sunlight. The sudden flashes of light glinting across the water and shining from the plate glass of the shop windows were enough to set up a dull beat of pain in his head.

He began to wish seriously for rain, for grey clouds to cover the sun and damp down all the shininess that glimmered and glistened from different directions, distorting his vision like a hall of mirrors. The headache was a dull throb in the back of his mind, drumming a warning that it was going to be a bad one.

Harriet and Catriona had gone into another shop and Roley stopped outside, looking at the display of handbags in the window with a sort of blurred incomprehension. He needed painkillers, he realized, but he couldn't quite make his mind work enough to think through the steps of finding a chemist's and buying something. If his head would just stop pounding perhaps he could think. He closed his eyes for a moment, leaning against the window, and feeling the cool glass against his forehead.

When he opened his eyes again, he saw the reflection was dimmer and darker than the street itself. The passing crowds were shadows in which individual faces and clothes were blurred into a shifting moving mass. Two white blurs moved across the reflected street and resolved into people. Mimes, Roley realized, as they began the traditional trapped-in-an-invisible-box routine. Their exaggerated movements had called his attention to them. That and the white suits they wore. But in the reflection the darker crowds seemed to move through them rather than past them.

He could see their pale pointed faces as they moved up behind him, whispering to each other behind their hands and pointing at him, before laughing and whispering some more. Roley hated mimes at the best of times. There was something mocking and unfriendly about the way they mimicked people. He turned away from the window, intending to tell them to cut it out, and was assailed by a wave of light from a jeweller's window across the street.

His eyes watered and the others came out of the shop behind him, collecting him up in their wake. As Catriona suddenly announced she was tired of shopping, Roley realized the mimes were nowhere to be seen. But he hardly cared. They'd finally reached the lake and as the view ahead opened up into one vast mirror of shining silver the drumbeat in his head erupted into a timpani of warning bells and crashing cymbals of pain.

From a great distance he seemed to hear someone speaking and he brought his head around slowly to see John's small worried face looking up at him. Reading his lips more than hearing him, Roley mumbled:

'I'm fine, just a headache.'

'Oh, Roley.' He heard his mother's voice behind him, ringing with disappointment. 'You won't let it spoil our day, will you? Drink some water.' Light scattered from the water bottle she held out to him, turning it into a rainbow prism. Roley looked at her dazedly until she pushed it into his hands.

'Why don't you sit down for a minute while we buy the boat tickets?' Peter suggested and Roley let John tug him towards a bench at the side of the lake.

He slumped into the seat and shut his eyes. But the headache seemed to swell behind his closed eyes, shutting him up inside his skull, and he opened them again to see the sun flash upside down from the sheet of water ahead.

'Do your eyes hurt?' John's voice pattered into his ears. 'They look as if they do.'

Roley mumbled something uncertain. The ache in his skull felt bone-deep now; as if moving might shake something loose. John was a blur, reaching up towards him, and Roley felt a small gentle hand on his forehead checking his temperature. The cold touch soothed the ache in his skull for a moment and he turned his head blindly towards it and felt John's hand cover his eyes as he closed them.

'Roland . . . ' It didn't sound like John's voice at all; it was quiet and commanding and behind a shield of welcome darkness the sunspots faded from Roley's shut eyes and he opened them again to see through watering eyes the shape of John's hand retreating.

It took a moment to recognize that he could see. A cloud had at long last passed over the sun. Fumbling for the bottle of water again, Roley opened it without looking at it. Over John's shoulder Katherine was approaching and she held out a packet of painkillers.

'Harriet said to give you these,' she said, before adding sympathetically: 'You look really sick. Shall I tell my dad you're not up to it?'

'It's OK.' Roley took two painkillers and washed them down with a glug of water. 'It's not so bad as it was, I think John fixed me.' He smiled at the younger boy. 'I should have brought sunglasses.'

'Dad's got some.' John got up from the bench. 'I'll go and ask if you can borrow them.' He was already darting off through the crowds, throwing the last words back after him.

Katherine and Roley looked at each other awkwardly. Roley thought that Katherine probably knew it would be more trouble than it was worth to cry off the trip. She looked as if she was about as excited by 'doing things as a family' as he was. But it didn't make any difference. There was an inevitability about the boat trip and about the family fight that Roley was sure lay ahead. After all, why would this occasion be any different?

It was a small boat with an outboard engine and seats for ten people. The skipper had counted them all on to the boat and then frowned saying:

'Only six of you then? I've seven ticket stubs. Where's the other lad?'

'We've just the two,' Peter said, helping John on to the boat and turning to offer a hand to Roley.

'I can manage.' Roley felt embarrassed to be treated like an invalid and climbed down into the boat to take a seat on a padded bench. Peter helped Cat and Harriet on board as the skipper said:

'Well, I leave in five minutes. He'll have to take the next boat, whoever he is.'

'Four's enough for us,' Harriet said in her jolly voice as Catriona and Katherine took seats as far away from each other as possible. Peter and Harriet sat together in the middle of the boat and John slipped in next to Roley.

'It's the fox-man,' he whispered. 'I saw him on the quay.'

Roley wondered if John was making something up. The words 'fox-man' and 'key' didn't mean anything to him. By the time he'd remembered the boy who'd called himself Fox, John had moved back to join his father and had taken out his nature book.

The skipper had climbed down into a small cabin and started the engine. Roley craned his neck to look behind him and saw Catriona in the back of the boat sticking her hands in the pockets of her bomber jacket and hunching down on the bench. There was no sign of anyone else waiting for the boat and Roley looked back to the front where Katherine was only just putting her book away.

His head still hurt but the painkillers were beginning to kick in and he had to confess Peter's sunglasses were impressive. His stepfather had handed them over willingly, explaining them as he did so, and Roley realized Peter was a bit of a geek for high-tech gizmos. According to him the sunglasses were achromatizing, blocking out certain wavelengths of light and making sense of scenes that would otherwise be a blur of dazzle.

Light sparkled from the water again as the boat pulled off into the lake. Roley tried to imagine the sunglasses as a wall, a transparent one like the mimes had acted but a wall all the same. He paid no attention to the skipper's commentary, telling them about the islands they were going to pass. Instead he shuffled to the end of the bench and looked down at the lake. The boat's shadow lay on the water and he could see the reflections of the passengers riding in it.

A blurred face turned and waved to him and Roley blinked. Looking back across the benches no one was waving. And from that angle he couldn't have seen it anyway. Scooting closer to the edge of the bench he looked more intently over the side. Just then the boat turned and a dazzle of light sparkled across the water, making his eyes water. Through the sun-sparkle and blur he saw a ripple of movement before his eyes closed to blink.

This time he fixed his gaze on the lake intently, determined to identify whatever light effect or mirage he was seeing. From a clear grey sheet of water the mimes stared back at him from either side of his own reflection. Roley saw his mouth fall open, making him look as dopey as his mother always said it did. What he was seeing seemed impossible. But whether or not it was a trick of the light, the faces were there, floating in the water or swimming in the blur of his vision.

They were pale, very similar looking, both with short hair. It was hard to tell if they were male or female, but both faces were smaller and sharper than his own. Their hair looked bluey-green but that might have been the water colouring it. Their eyes were similarly water-coloured and as he looked from one to the other they waved again, both white-clad arms moving in unison in the same mocking salute.

Roley gaped at them. This surely wasn't possible. What kind of photophobia could give you visions of mimes? But before he could come up with an answer the faces dissolved into ripples and were gone.

'Roley!' Harriet's voice cut across the air. 'Why don't you leave the fish for a moment and admire this beautiful scenery?' As Roley looked over at her she added: 'Have you finished with Peter's sunglasses?'

'Not yet.' Roley suddenly felt very annoyed with his mother. Her hectoring everyone to enjoy themselves all the time grated on him and he was on the verge of telling her so as she swung around in her seat to start in on Catriona.

'I told you you'd be cold,' she began. Then, remembering her own injunction to be gentle, 'Do you want to borrow my jumper, darling?' Then, abruptly descending into anger, 'That'd better not be what I think it is!'

Roley looked with the others, expecting to see Catriona smoking. But instead she was staring at her own cupped hands where a small doll reclined. Delilah observed them dispassionately with wide glass eyes as the argument began.

'How many times do you have to be told to put that thing away!' Harriet's voice crested to a pitch of fury.

'I did, I didn't . . . ' Catriona's voice tumbled into confusion and she hunched her shoulders against a barrage of recriminations even as she placed Delilah carefully on an empty bench.

'You said you didn't want her,' Katherine's voice was sharp. 'And taking from the house is *stealing*!'

'Let's calm down for a moment.' Peter's voice was more-in-sorrow-than-in-anger. 'Catriona, please put the doll away.'

'It's not her fault.' John's whisper was for once heard by someone else besides Roley and Katherine turned a betrayed look at him as he insisted, 'Delilah brought herself.'

Then Catriona dissolved into hysterical tears and in the end Peter picked up the doll in his handkerchief as if it were something he didn't want to touch and hid it away in his rucksack. Harriet was a wall of frozen fury at his side and John pale as a ghost next to them. Catriona was left to sob herself into silence and Katherine pointedly picked up her book. The skipper was studiously ignoring the lot of them and Roley could hardly blame him. When they reached the other shore that was the boat's destination he could see the man wasn't best pleased about having to take them back across the water in a few hours.

As the others got themselves off the boat Roley was thinking hard and when his own feet touched the jetty he turned to Peter and said:

'How about we explore separately? You and Mum could look at the church while we go around the shops and things.'

'Let's do that.' Peter took up the suggestion with relief. 'Why don't I give you some money for lunch and we'll meet up at a quarter to three here for the boat.' He glanced at Harriet for approval and she nodded tightly, silently opening her bag and removing three ten pound notes.

'Thanks,' Roley said, taking them from her.

As the adults moved off up the shore he winced as he saw the two girls looking daggers at each other and John trapped between them and realized he was in charge.

123

The trouble was that no one but John seemed to see Roley as in charge.

'I'm not walking with *her*,' Katherine began.

'Who wants to walk with you anyway?' Catriona rejoined.

'Can't the two of you give it a rest for once?' Roley asked and it was his turn to receive a betrayed look from his sister.

'Give me my share of the cash and I'll spare you my company,' Catriona snapped, sticking her hand out.

'I don't need your mum's money anyway,' Katherine added.

'For Christ's sake.' Roley shoved a tenner at Catriona and held out another to Katherine. 'Just take it,' he said. 'John and I'll get fish and chips or something, won't we?'

'I'm not very hungry anyway,' John whispered and Roley put a hand on the boy's shoulders.

'Fish and chips,' he said. 'And we'll leave these two to their cat fight.'

He steered John ahead of him up the road. He could feel the younger boy's shoulders trembling and felt angrier than before. It wasn't until he'd got them into a cheerful-looking chip shop with wooden booths and a reassuring smell of salt and vinegar that he felt able to calm down.

'I've got some cash of my own anyway,' he said. 'We won't starve. How about a milkshake to start with?' He winced, realizing that he sounded like Harriet, but it was hard to look at John's tense face without trying to cheer him up.

Roley's headache had died away but as he sat back in the booth and glanced idly at the mirror glass of the window, it spiked again with shock as he saw four people sitting in the reflection of the booth. On the other side of him and John were the mime-artists again, barely distorted at all by the plate glass. As he watched they went into a charade of exaggerated silent laughter.

He couldn't help looking over his shoulder and was startled to realize there was someone there. But it was only a waitress and Roley ordered milkshakes and fish and chips, feeling the blue-green eyes of the mimes boring into his back from the glass mirror. When she'd gone he leaned over the table and muttered to John.

'Don't laugh, all right? But can you see anything reflected there?' John looked at the window and then back to Roley.

'You mean the clown people,' he said calmly. 'They've been following us all morning. I saw them in the shop windows before.' He dropped his voice though when he added, 'They don't like it if you ignore them.'

'Then you can see it? Them?' Roley stared back at the window where the two white-suited figures were applauding John with slow silent handclaps. 'It's got to be some trick of the light. Or holographics . . . something.'

In the window the two watchers fell about with laughter, shaking their heads and wiping their eyes at Roley's folly and he glared at them, squinting to do it as the sun came out again outside.

'I think the one with green hair's a boy,' John said. 'The one with blue hair and green eyes is a girl.'

'I think you see them better than I do,' Roley said faintly.

John scrunched up his face and then shrugged, as if it was just a question of eyesight. He seemed to have cheered up anyway. Roley was now the one feeling tense and he found it hard to finish his food, pushing the milkshake aside after only one sip. John drank it for him although the mound of chips defeated them both. It didn't help having the two reflections watching them and miming hunger like starving orphans outside a Victorian workhouse. John seemed to manage it better than Roley did, observing them dispassionately in the glass.

'I think they come from the house,' he said.

'You mean our house?' Roley asked and John shook his head and nodded, contradicting himself.

'Not our London house,' he said. 'From Fell Scar. They followed us, like Delilah and the fox-man.'

'Fox-man? Do you mean Fox? A boy about my age in a fur coat?'

John nodded.

'A fox-man,' he repeated. 'I think he was the one I saw in the wood that time.' He shivered suddenly. 'Before the bugs . . . '

'Don't worry about that now,' Roley said quickly. 'Why do you think they come from the house?'

'Maybe near the house,' John said, suddenly uncertain. 'But they're there, all the time, watching us. More than just the ones you can see. Can't you feel them?'

'With all the screaming and fighting I've not noticed any-thing much,' Roley said wryly but John shook his head.

'They *like* that,' he said. 'They pay more attention then.' Roley didn't like the sound of that at all but again John surprised him. 'I think they're lonely,' he said.

* * *

Someone else who seemed lonely was Katherine. She was sitting by the jetty when Roley and John got back there, still immersed in her book, her long hair hiding her face. Roley wondered if she'd eaten anything and reminded himself she'd started the fight. But he felt guilty remembering how she and John had come to check on him earlier.

'Are you all right?' he asked, sitting down beside her. She took a long time to turn away from the book, finally registering him so vaguely that her gaze seemed to come from a million miles away. Roley wondered if she'd also been seeing visions, although how she could when her nose was always in a book he didn't know.

'OK,' she said finally. Then, 'How's your headache?'

'Still lurking about,' Roley replied. John had moved off to the water's edge and Roley and Katherine watched him in silence for a while. After a moment her head bent again to her book but this time Roley spoke before she could vanish into the pages again.

'Have you seen a boy in a fur coat?' he asked. Katherine raised her head to consider the jetty and Roley added: 'Not here, around the village.'

'The only person I've seen was the gardener,' Katherine said. 'This morning.'

'The gardener? Was there a girl with her?' Roley was embarrassed by the eagerness in his own voice. 'Um . . . a blonde?' That sounded worse. 'Alice.'

'I don't know,' Katherine said. 'I only saw a woman weeding vegetables. She wasn't there long.' She sounded bored now and Roley drew back, leaving her to read.

Standing up he rubbed his eyes and realized he was nervous, expecting bogeymen around every corner. His mind was still casting about for a rational explanation for what he'd seen. Ghosts seemed to be the best explanation. Ghosts were almost scientific, he thought. There were experiments people did to find cold spots in haunted houses. He was suddenly impatient to get back to the house. With all the books around there must be something on parapsychology or supernatural happenings.

Peter and Harriet arrived back at half past two, both looking refreshed and positive. Roley felt a mixture of relief and despair at the sight. He didn't want his mother to be miserable and furious but at least he found that more honest than her bright trilling tones as she called to John:

'Have you been having a good explore?'

To Roley's amazement John seemed to have found time to tick more animals and plants off in his nature book and as he showed it to the adults Roley looked around for Catriona, praying that she wouldn't be late.

It was five to three when she finally came sauntering down on to the jetty and the skipper had been muttering darkly about the time while everyone else waited tensely beside the boat. Cat's face was flushed and her smile brilliant as she approached, the long fur coat she wore flapping loose like a banner. Beside her, a narrow smile on his face as he joined them, was Fox.

10
Fox Brush

Fox was the sort of person who made people pay attention. Kat watched him as he handed Catriona into the boat with a bow and then twitched his fingers in a conjurer's gesture to make a ticket appear in them for the boatman.

'Come along in another boat, did you?' the man grumbled. 'You didn't ought to do it.'

'Most humble apologies.' Fox's teeth gleamed whitely when he smiled. His incisors were very sharp. Katherine wrinkled her nose as he passed her, taking a seat beside Catriona on the boat. She didn't approve of him or his fur coat. Even Harriet was frowning at her daughter as Fox slung an arm across the bench behind her shoulders.

Katherine hoped Catriona would get in trouble for being late but instead, disgustingly, her mother seemed to be trying to make a friend of Fox. She was the one who asked him his name. Catriona actually said nothing at all, glorying in her conquest, one hand occasionally stroking the fur coat. It was Roley who asked Fox where he lived and then, when he'd replied 'Not far from you,' Peter who invited him to tea.

'There's not room in the car,' Katherine pointed out and Catriona shot her a triumphant look.

'Fox has a motorbike,' she said.

He would have a motorbike, thought Katherine. Any moment now he'll be telling us he's a film star. Something about Fox just didn't seem real. Real sixteen-year-old boys didn't lounge around in fur coats and make lazily confident conversation. They staggered about in old jeans and smelly T-shirts and grunted at you on their way to the bathroom. Like Roley. Fox was like a character in a book, or an actor in a play. He's playing a part, Katherine thought, and it's working.

Harriet at least put her foot down about Catriona accepting a lift on the motorbike. But Katherine could have done without listening to her whinge the way back up the hill about the walk and then insist on having the window open the whole way back home. Everyone else seemed to accept Catriona was car-sick even when she was craning her head for glimpses of Fox's bike. When it finally zoomed past them Katherine actually shook her head. Who rides a motorbike in a fur coat? Feeling Catriona's eyes on her she took the book out of her bag and opened it.

She was almost halfway through now. Most of it was more of the same sort of poem she'd found on the first page. Again and again there were three different handwritings, taking it in turns to write lines. Whatever else Kat felt about the Make-Believe Game she realized her mother had at least had close friends. Later on there were maps of the Lakes, with black lines crossing and recrossing them. But all those crossings reminded her of the missing names and she'd riffled quickly onwards.

After the Delilah drawing, the next section was still gummed together with the sticky remains of spider

webbing and Katherine had to peel back the page carefully, making sure not to tear it. But when she had it open
she stared down at the page in confusion. Another piece
of art paper had been glued into the book, and on it was
drawn a face: a handsome male face framed by darkish
hair and wearing a narrow smile. Underneath the face
handwriting she recognized as one of the other two girls
had written: *Fox*.

It certainly looked like Fox. The drawing was in black ink
so you couldn't tell hair colour, and it wasn't a perfect like-
ness simply because the artist wasn't that good. But it was
much better than anything Katherine could have done.
Someone had spent a long time on this. Katherine closed
the book up and put it back in her bag, thinking furiously.
Fox had known where they lived and he was plainly the
boy Roley had mentioned earlier. Perhaps the picture was
of his father or an uncle or cousin—someone her mother
had known with the same name. Suddenly Katherine was
as impatient as Catriona to get back to the house so she
could ask him.

Roley had barely noticed the motorbike pass them. His
eyes had been glued to the rolled-up window on his side of
the car. Whenever the scenery outside darkened, as they
passed under the shadow of trees or a high wall, he could
see his own face reflected in the window and behind it the
faces of the two ghostly watchers.

They didn't act like ghosts but they were definitely haunting him. They'd chased the boat back across the lake, their

faces watching him from underneath the water. During the walk back up the hill in Windermere he'd caught glimpses of them from the glossy finish of car bonnets. When the car pulled up at Fell Scar they were waiting for him in the windows on either side of the front door.

Fox was waiting too. He'd left the motorcycle on the drive and was looking at the front of the house. He could see the ghosts too, Roley was certain. He'd been looking at the windows as they arrived. Katherine didn't seem to and Catriona only had eyes for Fox. The adults plainly saw nothing, since they paid no attention when John went up to the glass and touched it.

'Tea on the lawn in half an hour,' said Harriet, adding, 'Don't anyone wander off before then.'

'Can't I show Fox the house?' Cat said and to their surprise Fox remarked:

'I've seen it before.'

Peter had unlocked the door and they were standing in the front hallway, taking off coats. Fox alone kept his on. He had wandered across to the big mirror and was studying his reflection in it. Behind it the two watchers lifted fingers to their lips as if choreographed.

'You've been here before?' To Roley's surprise it was Katherine who spoke. 'When?' Her tone was challenging and Fox's casual as he replied:

'Many years ago.'

'Did your family know the Stones when they lived here?' Peter asked, hovering undecidedly.

'No one knew them,' Fox replied. 'They kept themselves apart.'

'Oh.' Peter obviously didn't know how to take this. 'I didn't know them myself,' he said. 'Anne didn't stay in touch with them.'

'It's always sad when families don't get on,' Fox said. He seemed to have an answer for everything and it was clear Peter found him disconcerting. After a moment he vanished to help make the tea.

Harriet's words about tea being in half an hour seemed to pin them all in the hall. For all that Fox claimed to have seen the house before he seemed interested in it, strolling around the room inspecting things. He opened the case of the grandfather clock, lifted a dusty goblet off a mantelpiece and looked inside it, and ran his fingers across a row of books.

'Looking for something?' Roley asked.

'Just noticing how old everything is,' Fox said in the most natural tone he'd used so far. 'It's the same but . . . older.' There was a look of distaste in his eyes.

'Did you know my mother?' John's voice piped up suddenly. This time even Roley had forgotten him. John seemed to be keeping his distance but he met Fox's eyes directly.

'He's not old enough,' Cat said.

'Even if I were, not many people knew Anne,' Fox said coolly. 'She had the friends she wanted, she didn't look for more.'

'Who were her friends then?' Katherine asked, just as Roley was thinking that Fox was playing word games with them, hinting at things he pretended not to know.

'Books, of course,' Fox smiled. 'They were her friends.'

'Seems to run in the family,' Catriona said. '*She's* the same way.' She jerked her chin at Katherine. 'No real friends at all. Sad, really, isn't it?'

'I have friends,' Katherine snapped, distracted from Fox.

'Make-believe friends, maybe,' Catriona replied. She was showing off, Roley realized, and he wished she didn't have to do it by putting other people down. In the old days it'd have been him she called sad while a legion of rail-thin glossy-haired girls regarded him with identical pitying expressions.

'Why shouldn't she? Imaginary friends are very loyal,' Fox said smoothly. 'They don't forget you, even if you turn your back on them.'

Roley frowned, wondering what that was supposed to mean. Fox made it sound like a threat. What did Fox want here anyway? Certainly he seemed to have lost interest in Catriona. He'd barely looked at her since arriving. Make-believe people, imaginary friends, mirages, ghosts, and mental illness jostled for space in Roley's head as he tried to fit the pieces of the puzzle together.

'Has anyone ever said the house is haunted?' he asked abruptly.

'Not to me,' Fox told him, again with that sly look that suggested he knew more than he was telling.

'Aren't you a bit old for ghost stories, Roley?' Catriona moved closer to Fox, trying to retrieve the ground she'd lost with the make-believe friends gibe. 'What'd haunt this place, anyway? The ghosts of dead books out to get vengeance on the people who trashed them?'

'Um . . .' Roley wished he hadn't brought the subject up. He didn't like the conclusions he was coming to. 'I don't know.' He ducked his head.

'He means Anne,' Fox said, leaning against the mantelpiece in a casual pose. 'She lived here and she died . . .'

Behind him in the mirror the two white-faced figures moved up towards the glass. For once they weren't cavorting. Instead they pressed their faces up against the other side of the glass, hands flat as if the mirror was a window or a wall.

'She died,' said Fox again. 'And a ghost always comes back to the place it lived the longest.'

Katherine made a noise, something between a gasp and a whisper and Roley saw that she was staring at Fox. Roley had heard of people looking as if they'd seen a ghost; Katherine looked as if she was seeing one right now. Horror and fear were written across her face. Abruptly Roley realized that she might have seen the people pressed up against the mirror. But perhaps it was just what Fox had said, what Roley had thought, that made her so afraid.

To his surprise, that made Roley feel angry rather than guilty. Admittedly he'd thought it but he didn't plan to say it just straight out like that. What gave Fox the right to come wandering in here and bait them with his sly hints and verbal traps?

It wasn't just Katherine who looked frightened. John had moved closer to his sister, his hand creeping into hers. Even Catriona was regarding Fox doubtfully, as if she was realizing she'd brought something dangerous into the house.

They were still frozen there, like chess pieces waiting for someone to make a move, when the door opened and Peter held it wide for Harriet to bring in a tray loaded with tea cups and saucers and a mound of scones.

'Here we are!' Harriet said merrily and Roley cringed inside as she added: 'What've you lot been chatting about then?'

There was an awkward silence. A silence filled with Fox's gently mocking voice.

'We've been telling ghost stories,' he said.

No meal in the family ever passed without an argument. Tea was no exception. John thought probably the wasps enjoyed it the most. They descended in droves as soon as they got a whiff of the jam and clotted cream that came with the scones. Peter swatted them and Harriet fanned at them with her hat but the wasps regarded these feeble efforts with contempt. They seemed to feel that anyone foolish enough to eat jam near a wasp's nest didn't deserve their respect.

John sat still while the wasps dive-bombed the jam pots. Being fanned and flapped at only seemed to enrage them and he wanted to prove to Roland that he was brave, after having been so scared of the flies in the wood. But Roland himself looked queasy and left his scone to the wasps after one of them drowned in a puddle of jam next to it. His eyes were squinted up again against the light.

Katherine and Catriona sat on opposite sides of the table, separated by their parents. Catriona flinched and squeaked when the wasps buzzed past, the rest of the time her eyes were fixed on Fox. Katherine had refused food and tea. She'd withdrawn into herself, not speaking at all, but she too was watching Fox warily.

Fox didn't eat either, he left his plate and his cup of tea untouched and smoked a cigarette instead. He lounged in his chair, unconcerned by the wasps. One of them alighted on his neck and began to crawl slowly up the side of his head. John couldn't take his eyes from it, feeling his own skin prickle as if it were his ear the insect was walking past on six tiny legs. When it finally buzzed off John slumped back in his seat with relief. He'd had a nasty image of it crawling all over the man's face like that while he sat there smiling.

Harriet was getting upset that people weren't eating and although she told them to ignore the wasps John could tell she thought they had spoilt her nice idea. John wished he could tell her Fox had already spoiled things. But he knew the grown-ups wouldn't listen. Even Roley who was nice and did ask him things hadn't listened when John tried to tell him Fox wasn't a real man.

John only wished he knew what Fox was. Sometimes he felt he almost did know, like with the reflection people and Delilah. He knew things about them without realizing it. He knew the reflections were lonely and he knew Delilah didn't need Catriona's help to appear on the boat. He concentrated on Fox, trying to encourage that sense of his to wake up and tell him something. But it was like not thinking about pink elephants. It didn't work if you were trying to. All he knew about Fox was that he was sly like a fox and that hardly helped.

Yet more wasps were arriving all the time as if the first had sounded a jam alarm. Everyone was twitching and jumping like puppets on strings.

'Roley, can't you put something over your plate?' Harriet asked irritably. 'Why you had to take such a great lake of jam, I don't know.'

Roley obligingly reached for the lid of the crockery dish the scones had been served in. As he picked it up both Kat and Cat on either side of the table made noises. Katherine's was a choking sound and Catriona's a sharp gasp but for once they were united in shock.

The crockery pot had been almost empty. Now it was full. Naked, hairless, faceless dolls with holes for eyes lay jumbled together, arms and legs twisted at ugly angles. In the middle of the bodies sat Delilah, like an evil queen on a throne.

Suddenly everyone was moving at once. Roley dropped the lid and it crashed on to his plate with a shattering noise. Harriet pushed herself back from the table and upright in one motion. Peter stood as well, perhaps intending to separate the two girls, who had both jumped up and now faced each other across the table.

'Do you think that's funny?' Katherine demanded, her face white with rage. 'Why do you have to be so horrible? I hate you!' Her words were choked off with a sob and her eyes had reddened even before she started crying.

'I didn't do it!' Catriona shouted back, her voice raw and desperate. 'I told you before, it's not me moving her around.' She looked at Harriet for support. 'It's not, honest. It's one of them doing it to wind me up.'

'That's ENOUGH!' Harriet's eyes blazed. 'I don't care who it is. I'm sick to death of both of you.'

'Someone took Delilah from my bag,' Peter said. His voice was serious. 'I want whoever that was to admit it now.'

There was silence. John's head turned to Delilah, afraid that she might raise a small porcelain hand. But it was Fox who moved, crushing his cigarette out on his plate. He was the only one except John who was still sitting down. He alone didn't seem to be shocked by the appearance of the dolls.

Peter looked around the table. He considered Roley, then Katherine, barely spending more than a moment on John before finally settling on Catriona.

'It wasn't me!' she said. Her tears were more glamorous than Katherine's, sliding smoothly out of her eyes and over her cheeks. Perhaps that made them look unreal because Peter didn't seem convinced.

'I'm sorry, Catriona,' he said. 'But you're the one who's been playing with Delilah.' He paused and then looked at Catriona's mother.

'Peter's right,' Harriet said. 'And I'm disgusted that any child of mine would steal and then lie about it. I want you to take that horrible thing back to your room and leave it there. Do you hear me?'

'But I . . . ' Catriona looked as if she'd been asked to pick up a wasp's nest. 'Mum . . . '

'DO YOU HEAR ME?' Harriet banged her hand down on the table, clumsily furious, and then cried out, pulling her hand back and turning it over so that they all saw the

139

wasp. It was half-crushed, its sting embedded in Harriet's hand and its wings trembling as it attempted to tear free.

'Oh lord,' said Peter.

'Don't move, Mum,' Roley said.

'I'll get the first aid kit.' Katherine looked as if she was about to be sick as she pushed off from the table and raced towards the house.

'Mum . . . ' Catriona took a step forward and Harriet's face contorted as she spat back.

'To your room. Now!' Her face was as hard as granite as Catriona picked up the crockery pot with shaking hands, fumbled the lid back on top, and set off across the lawn with her burden held out as far away from her body as she could manage.

Another meal had ended in disaster, even for the wasps, John thought. But one person looked untroubled.

'Thank you for tea,' Fox said, standing at last. 'And for the entertainment. I can't remember when I last had such an amusing time.'

Even Peter and Harriet were speechless as he sketched a bow and then turned on his heel and left.

11
What's in a Name?

The motorcycle droned like an angry wasp as Fox rode away from Fell Scar. The road curved around the edge of the hill, the woods rising up on one side, the fields falling away on the other. Fox rose up in his seat, urging the heavy bike onwards, and saw a figure ahead on the road.

She was heavily dressed for the spring day. Honeyed sunshine lapped the fields and the horizon was a pale clear blue, but she seemed not to have noticed. Her jeans were blue and her hooded sweatshirt was dark green but silhouetted on the road ahead she seemed clothed in shadows as she stared into the wood. The only colour about her was the wheatsheaf gold of her hair.

Alice looked up as the motorcycle's drone stuttered and stilled and the rider dismounted, leaving the bike at the side of the road as he walked towards her.

'There's danger in the wood,' he said.

'I know that.' Alice met his green almond-shaped eyes. 'But do I know you?'

'Once, perhaps.' His voice was low. 'And perhaps in the future.'

'I'm in no mood for mysteries,' she said sharply, looking away from him again.

'No?' he asked. 'Then why did you come here? This is where the mysteries begin.'

Alice gave him another longer look. Whoever he was he'd posed the question that she'd been asking herself ever since she'd begun the walk up the hill. Even before that, she'd wondered if she really dared to do this. She certainly had no desire to return to the wood. She'd left her bag and the rest of her clothes there and her camera. Even so, *things* could be replaced, even though they weren't rich. But the thought of the camera had nagged at her like a hangnail all through the long afternoon of pretending that everything was fine.

There was no way she could have spoken to Emily, she feared too much what she might hear. And even with Charlotte the words wouldn't come. But the thought of the camera couldn't be dismissed. Words were chancy but it was hard for pictures to lie. All through the attack by the tree the camera had been flashing, and the truth of what had happened to her might have been preserved on a thin roll of film. It was for that she'd returned to the wood and this time she wasn't coming unarmed.

The haft of the wood-axe fitted her hand comfortably. She'd used it often enough splitting logs for the fire. She'd never thought of using it in anger, but it wasn't truly anger she felt right now—or fear. *I'm still in shock*, she'd thought more than once. But what she felt was a colossal calm, blanketing other feelings with the strength of her resolve.

'Alice.' The boy in the fur coat had become very still and in the wood the twitters of birdcalls had fallen quiet as well so that the silence seemed immense.

'Who are you?' she asked. 'What do you want?' She was delaying, she knew, wasting time with this tourist instead of setting about the task she'd steeled herself for. But he acted as if he knew something about why she was there, so perhaps it wasn't wasting time after all.

'I'm Fox,' he said, with a gleam of white teeth that was not quite a smile. 'And I want to help you—if you'll let me.'

'I don't have time for this.' She was suddenly impatient. 'I don't need your help, Fox, or whoever you are.' The name was too appropriate for her to believe in it and she thought it was more likely he'd named himself. Remembering the boys she'd met yesterday and the direction he'd come in she asked: 'Are you one of the family? The people staying at Fell Scar?'

'Yes and no.' Another flicker of a smile and his voice was gently teasing, trying to draw her into his game and she wondered if he was making a pass at her. If so he'd chosen a really bad time for it.

'Whatever,' she said brusquely. 'I'm not looking for company.'

'Then you'd be wise to avoid the wood,' he told her. 'And even the boldest knight would fear to go a-questing without his horse, hawk, or hound and you have none of those.'

It was true. She'd wanted to bring Baskerville but Charlotte had seen the gash on his leg and decided to take him to the vet to have it looked at. She could hardly be blamed for that but Alice wished she hadn't had to go back alone—even if she did have a weapon.

'I'm not a knight,' Alice said flatly.

'Nor a simple woodcutter's daughter either,' Fox said. 'Although you carry an axe.'

'What if I do?' She wondered if he was playing some sort of game, if he'd mistaken her for someone else. But he'd known her name and said that he knew her.

'An axe might not be enough,' he said. 'To slay the dragon.'

'A dragon?' That gave her pause for thought. On any other day she'd have laughed at him. But today was a day for believing in dragons.

'A dragon or a demon,' Fox said. 'Or perhaps a dark god. There are no names for what dwells in the wood. You've seen only the palest of its shadows and there are darker dangers ahead.'

'You know what . . . ' Again Alice lost the words and had to stop and start again. 'You know what happened before . . . in the wood. How?'

'A little bird told me.'

Alice froze, chilled by the reminder of what the twisted tree had said. It had called her a little bird and for an instant she felt like one again; the fear cresting up inside the calm ocean she'd made of her mind.

'I don't want your warnings,' she said fiercely, gripping the axe tighter as she stepped away from him. 'Or your riddles or your games.'

'But . . . ' He looked as if she'd slapped him, hurt written across his face, as she took another step away.

'Leave me alone,' she said. 'I don't need your help either.' She was at the edge of the wood now and she turned her back on the boy to face the tangle of trees.

'Alice!' she heard him call after her as she stepped beneath the trees. But this time she didn't reply.

It was cold in the wood. The sunshine struggled to break through the canopy of leaves. The air felt damp and smelt of mould and mildew. Alice walked softly between the trees but even so dead leaves and broken twigs crunched beneath her feet. No other sound broke the stillness. Last time she'd walked here she'd tried to damp down her own unease, this time she listened to her instincts and as she went deeper into the wood her calm slipped further away.

She had planned the route she would take on an ordnance survey map. This time she'd come to the tree from uphill. Perhaps that would give her an edge. She would grab the camera and run, not stopping to ask questions. The only answers she wanted were the ones on the film. But despite her brushing him off, Fox's warnings had stayed with her and this time it was impossible to ignore her own feelings of being watched.

She picked her way between tangles of bracken. She could have hewn out a path with the axe but, despite everything, she was reluctant. It felt too much like starting a fight. Instead she stepped around the bushes and ducked beneath the low branches. Even tree roots she stepped over carefully, alert for the slightest twitch of movement. But when the moment finally came it took her by surprise.

A touch on the back of her arm had her whirling, axe raised defensively, her free hand tightening into a claw. Her heart seemed to skip a beat and then slam back hard in her chest as a dark shape leapt backwards. Her right arm, already swinging the axe-haft, fell and the blade sliced across empty air before she tensed her arm to pull the blow. Across the space that had opened up between them, she saw fear flicker in a pair of grass-green eyes.

It was Fox. How he'd managed to creep up behind her without Alice hearing him, she'd no idea. But he'd almost lost an arm for his pains. He looked as if he knew it too, breathing quickly and shallowly in short rasps she could hear.

'What do you think you're doing?' she demanded. Anger and fear were now so mixed in her, she wasn't sure which was stronger. The last vestiges of her calm had shredded when she'd felt that soft touch on her arm. 'Is this your idea of helping? Stalking me? Or are you one of those dangers you warned me about?'

'Yes.' This time Fox did smile and she read menace in those bared teeth. 'To all three. But never a danger to you, Alice.'

'Stop saying my name,' she said; the way it sounded on his lips was more sinister than anything else he'd said.

'Names are powerful,' he said. 'And here you need that power more than most.' He'd recovered from his own shock and now seemed more relaxed than out on the road; it was easy to believe he was at home in this wood. 'Don't tell me to leave again,' he said, anticipating her reply. 'You need me, even if you won't admit it. You would not have escaped the Knarl before without my help.'

'Your help?' Alice remembered the whirl of black wings and the force that had ripped her from the tree. 'I didn't see you.'

'I wasn't there,' Fox said. 'But your rescuers came from me all the same.'

Alice was beginning to believe him. It wasn't so much his words, which seemed to threaten and plead her to trust him both at once. But he'd crept up behind her and done no more than touch her arm; and when she'd swung the axe he'd jumped back not forwards. Whoever he was, he seemed to know more about what had happened than she did herself. Perhaps he really did want to help her.

Ultimately, it looked as if he'd follow her whether she liked it or not and she was tired of telling him to go home.

'What was the name you said just now?' she asked instead.

'The Knarl,' he said, seeming to know what she meant. 'It is the name of the being that attacked you. Named for its knotted and cross-grained nature. It lost some stature in the winter storms but its roots go deep.'

'What is it?' Alice asked. Putting a name to the thing did seem to make the fear more manageable. 'A tree spirit?'

'Of a kind. A tree with a name, that was part of a game.' He fell into the same rhyming cadence as the Knarl as he spoke of it. 'Shunning the light. Rotten with blight.'

'Stop that,' Alice shivered. 'This isn't a game.'

'It is,' Fox told her. 'But games aren't always innocent pastimes. Take it from one who knows something of blood sports.'

She had nothing to say to that. But as they walked onwards together, him taking the lead as if he knew the way through the woods, she was remembering what he had said about names. A boy named Fox who wore a fur coat and watched her with sly green eyes as he walked silently through the forest—if names had power, what power had he gained from his? He'd been right when he'd told her she stood on the brink of mysteries. Now she was within the woods the mystery had deepened, along with the shadows that surrounded her.

As they penetrated further into the wood, Fox took the lead. There were no true paths here, although sometimes the haphazard arrangement of the trees made it look as if there were. Fox moved quietly, neatly side-stepping drifts of leaves and broken twigs. Mimicking his caution, Alice followed in his footsteps from tree to tree; stopping when he raised a hand and moving quickly to join him when he beckoned her on.

They followed a zigzagging path, skirting the slope of the fell. Alice could hear the sound of water from further up, a ragged murmur that thinned to a trickle of sound as they began to move downhill again. The ground was damp underfoot and, even through her boots, Alice could feel the sponginess of it. She was looking down with distaste at the half pound of mulch her boots had picked up when Fox stilled with a new tension, more alert than before. He raised a hand and pointed ahead to where the trees thinned out for a short distance ahead, around a stunted tree with wizened limbs.

All around the clearing black feathers lay scattered. The Knarl clutched handfuls of them in clusters of twigs. It was scored with claw marks and long curls of bark hung down in strips, gouged out of the trunk.

'It has been weakened by the fight with the Rookery,' Fox said softly. 'Wait here.'

Alice might have protested if she could have spoken. But the sight of the thing had brought back memories of its attack and she could only swallow dryly in an effort to ease the tightened muscles of her throat. Hanging back she watched as Fox stepped out between the trees and began to move around the Knarl, green eyes watching it warily.

He was halfway across the rough clearing when the branches began to creak and sway. This time there could be no denying it. The tree twisted around in its place, roots churning at the earth as it turned a scarred and knotted patch of trunk towards Fox. The cracked whispery voice snapped across the space between them:

'*Foolish Fox should stay away, or a hunter will be prey.*' A branch reached out towards Fox who evaded it easily, taking a quick step back.

'Not today.' Fox pulled back his lips, showing white teeth. Before the Knarl could speak again he continued quickly: 'How long have you stood here, hollow and rotten? All your past is long forgotten. When you fall to storm or frost, even your name will be finally lost.'

'*A wish or a lie. My roots go deep. You will die and I will sleep.*' Branches creaked and groaned as they lunged for Fox, who again stepped back. The Knarl was at an angle now, canted over almost at a diagonal as once again Fox stepped back. However much movement it had, enough to tear the ground, was not enough to catch Fox. Even this much was shaking loose more bark and Alice grimaced as she saw wingless insects crawling and squirming in the hole left by the writhing roots.

Looking past the cursing Knarl she saw that her tripod was still standing on the other side of the clearing. Her bag lay near it, her sweater lying on the ground just where she'd left it. The Knarl had obviously had no interest in her possessions. Carefully, moving as Fox had shown her, Alice began to skirt the clearing on the opposite side to Fox. He didn't look at her, still taunting the Knarl, but she was certain he knew what she was doing. Her right hand was sweaty on the axe-haft and she moved the weapon to her other hand as she wiped her palm on her leg and then switched back.

Snatches of words floated across the clearing. The Knarl's words all sounded like threats. Fox's rhymed replies sounded more like a game, lightly amused whenever the Knarl wrenched itself around for another strike and openly mocking when the strike missed. As Alice came level with her camera she clenched her fist around the axe and prepared to run. As she broke free of the tree cover her boots crunched heavily on the leaves and there was a wild rustle of branches.

'The Fox doesn't hunt alone today . . . Wicked little vixens should have stayed away!'

It was coming for her. Alice could feel the ground trembling beneath her, earth opening as roots wrenched themselves up through layers of soil. She had eyes for nothing except the strap of the camera, hanging loosely as it sat on top of the tripod. As she drew level with it she grabbed for it and the tripod toppled as she caught the camera up.

Dead leaves crackled furiously and she heard the branch above her whip through the air before it landed across her back with bruising force.

There was an angry growl and for a moment Alice thought Baskerville was with her after all before she pulled free and swung around to see that her rescuer was Fox. He had hurled himself into the branches of the twisted tree, wrenching and tearing at them with a fury, holding the Knarl back as she made her escape. Already the Knarl was returning battle, slashing wildly at its attacker, Alice forgotten for a moment. She didn't waste the opportunity. Stringing the camera around her neck she placed both hands firmly on the axe-shaft. She took a deep breath and then hurled herself forward, swinging the axe high and bringing it down hard to bury it deep in the Knarl's trunk.

The Knarl made a noise like furniture splintering as its trunk split apart where the knots of its face had been. The wood had broken open easily and as Alice twisted the axe to get it free, the bark crumbled, falling away from the side of the split. A shower of bugs and maggots began to pour out of the split and Alice hesitated, still trying to pull the axe free. Fox dropped out of the branches on the other side, and caught her arm.

'Leave it,' he urged her, pulling her back from the spreading tide of insects falling from the hole that had been a mouth. 'There are greater dangers than this old stump.'

'What?' Alice let Fox pull her away from the axe but her eyes were still fixed on the creaking form of the Knarl, trying to hold its trunk together with its branches even as the split widened, exposing the hollow trunk, black with mould. Not all the insects were wingless. Inside the broken stump filmy wings twitched and a low buzz began to sound from within the wood.

Reaching for the camera around her neck she focused it on the remains of the Knarl, hoping there was still enough power left in the flash, and snapped the shutter, taking three photographs in quick succession.

'Come on.' Fox pulled her away with him and broke into a run as the buzz grew angrier behind them.

'What is that?' Alice risked a glance behind and saw a mass of filmy wings rising out of the tree, enough for her to put on a turn of speed.

'Vampiries . . .' Fox replied breathlessly. 'Like wasps, but without the charm.'

'What charm?' Alice asked, imagining a swarm of angry hornets after them as they pelted through the trees.

'Exactly.'

Fox slammed suddenly to a halt, pulling Alice in close against him as he sheltered in the shadow of a tall tree. The buzzing had dropped away and the woods were quiet again. Alice felt his coat soft underneath her hands as she steadied herself against him, feeling his muscles gradually relax underneath the fur.

'Alice,' he said and she looked up to see him regarding her with a questioning look as he studied her face. 'You shouldn't come here again,' he told her, pressing her back against the tree. 'The Knarl almost caught you.'

'But why me? And why did you help me?' She found his expression incomprehensible. Her hood had fallen down and she watched as his hand reached to pull a dead leaf from her hair and the gentle stroking touch made her shiver suddenly.

'Because I love you,' he told her and she felt her own expression become incredulous even as his shifted into a wicked smile.

'You can't possibly!' she said, suddenly angry and feeling that he was making a game of her. 'You don't even know me. Let me go.'

He released her, frowning as if she'd puzzled him and she raised the camera suddenly like a weapon. Through the lense she saw him look startled.

'What are you doing?'

'Stealing your soul,' Alice told him defiantly as she clicked the shutter. For a moment he looked frightened. Then he laughed.

'I don't have one,' he told her and suddenly from the trees all around them the sound of mocking laughter echoed through the woods. Jeering bird calls taunted her from high above and looking up she saw a flash of black feathers.

Clutching the camera tightly Alice backed away, leaving Fox standing alone, still smiling as all around the unseen birds screamed with laughter.

12
Ghost Hunt

Roley stood in the main room of the house and tried to think. His mother's hand had been bandaged and she'd gone to her room to lie down. Peter and John were washing the tea things in the kitchen and Katherine had disappeared off somewhere to read and he guessed that Catriona was sulking in her room.

It felt as if the family had fragmented. A ridiculous thought, he realized, since they'd never been united. His gaze turned towards the mirror over the mantelpiece and was actually surprised to see it empty, except for his own reflection. His own pale face looked back at him with a frown, not appearing to think much of his chances of sorting out this mess.

'But someone has to,' Roley said out loud, coming to a decision even as he spoke.

He recalled his own thoughts on the boat about ghosts and his plan to search the house. Now seemed like the best opportunity he'd have to make the house give up its mysteries and with new resolve he set out to explore.

He began with the room he was in and its collection of books. Scanning quickly across the shelves he ignored the books of walks and Lakeland tourist guides, looking instead for anything historical. If the house was haunted, he hoped there might be a reference to it; but none of the indexes mentioned Fell Scar. Then again, if it was Anne's ghost who was responsible for the apparitions it hadn't been long enough ago to be mentioned in a book. He'd have better luck questioning the local villagers. His thoughts went inevitably to Alice and he bit his lips, thinking that of all the ways he'd hoped to get to know her, enlisting her in their family problems would be the last one he'd pick.

Returning the books to the shelves he tried to recall what he'd heard about haunted houses. All he could remember was something about cold spots: places where the temperature changed because of the presence of ghosts. It wasn't much to be going on with but unless he found a book about ghost hunting, it was all he had to go on.

Methodically he began to search the house, avoiding the kitchen since it seemed an unlikely place anyway, paying attention in a way he hadn't when they first arrived. Floorboards creaked as he moved from room to room; looking at bookcases, opening cupboards, and even peering behind paintings. It didn't help that he had no idea what he was looking for: something out of the ordinary, he supposed.

Midway through his search the ghosts joined him. A glimmer of white from the polished surface of a wardrobe alerted him to their presence. This time he didn't turn to look at them full on. Instead, as he searched, he glanced at reflective surfaces from the corner of his eyes. Unlike John he still couldn't tell the difference between them and only glimpsed in flashes he couldn't see much more than their strange water-coloured eyes watching him first idly, then with mounting curiosity. They practically pushed each other out of the way to stare at him from every reflective surface, craning to see where he was going when he left a room and waiting expectantly when he arrived in another.

He left out the adults' room, peering through the narrow crack of the hinges to see his mother lying on the bed. But the door to Katherine's room was open and he went inside cautiously. Her suitcase was open on the floor and he stepped past it carefully, not wanting to invade her privacy. Instead he turned to the wardrobes and found them crammed with old clothes, vintage seventies, he thought, considering the velvet and lace with which they were trimmed. That was the right sort of period, but he didn't see how it helped. He glanced quickly across the bookcases and turned to leave, before noticing the pile of books Katherine had put on her bedside table. She'd been collecting them, he remembered, from all over the house.

As he picked up the first book on the pile he saw a movement from a looking glass on the dressing table: the ghosts were vying for space to watch and that alone made him pay closer attention to the book. It was something girly, a school story, and he'd never normally have bothered with it. But on the front page was a bookplate with Katherine's mother's name on it under a stylized fox. A coincidence? Roley somehow doubted that. He hovered indecisively, holding the book. Katherine had collected them for a reason and he was beginning to suspect she had been on her own version of the ghost hunt when she did so. Taking a couple of the books from the bottom of the pile, he told himself he wasn't stealing, he was collecting evidence. But he still felt uncomfortable about invading his stepsister's room. Turning away he met the twinned gaze of the people in the looking glass.

'Where next?' he said, as if they were real people accompanying him on his quest. Realizing what he'd done he laughed at himself, shaking his head, and it took a moment to notice they had responded. For once their faces were grave as they raised their hands and pointed upwards.

'The attics?' Roley said and they nodded before whisking themselves out of the looking glass, leaving only his own reflection looking warily back from the mirror.

He caught up with them on the way up, as they flitted from frame to frame of the paintings on either side of the stairs. The one on his left beckoned almost flirtatiously as he followed them. He was finally seeing the difference between the two and this one did seem a bit more feminine and its eyes were slightly more green, its hair tinged with more blue than the other. There was something about the face as well, he thought, although he couldn't define exactly what. On the landing the other one, the boy, raised a finger to his lips and cupped an ear with the other hand. Roley obediently stopped moving and listened.

If he hadn't been listening for it he wouldn't have heard the noise, a sort of irregular whooping noise ending in a mewing sound. He looked back at his ghostly companions for an explanation and the boy lifted his eyebrows in a patronizing look before raising both hands to his face and wriggling his fingers as he brought them past his cheeks. Roley had never been any good at charades. The girl joined the boy in the picture frame and gestured for Roley's attention. Abruptly she dropped her head in her hands and her shoulders started to heave. Roley moved closer to the painting instinctively, wondering what was wrong, and then froze as she raised her head again to look at him with contempt and stabbed a finger at Catriona's shut door.

Roley felt himself blush and looked away from them both, feeling very guilty. Catriona was crying. That was the sound he could hear, she was gasping for air in between sobs and he hadn't realized. He hadn't even cared, if he was honest with himself. Like the others he'd blamed her for the latest appearance of Delilah and hadn't believed one word of her excuses. No. He shook his head. That wasn't right either. John had believed her and Roley heard again in his head his stepbrother say: *'Delilah brought herself.'*

Gently, almost afraid, Roley raised a hand to knock on the door. The sobbing sound was abruptly silenced and after a moment a voice said harshly:

'Go away!'

'Catriona? Cat . . . It's me, Roley. Can I come in?'

Another silence and then he heard the key turn in the lock and the door opened. His sister stared at him silently from the room. Her hair was tangled, as if she'd been lying on the bed, and her eyes were red-rimmed and bloodshot. She'd changed out of the clothes she'd worn on the lake, into jeans and an old favourite jumper she'd had for years; she looked younger than she usually did and Roley felt protective. Behind her in the centre of the room he saw the crockery pot the scones had been in, its lid on so it was impossible to see what it held. Somehow that convinced him of her innocence in a way that nothing else would.

He'd seen her do something similar with flies and spiders, putting cups or glasses over them and leaving them like tombs until the insect or whatever it was died, too phobic to try and move them.

'Do you want me to get rid of that for you?' he asked, looking at the lidded pot.

'You can't.' Catriona sounded snuffly; she'd cried enough to have trouble breathing and he could hear it in her voice. She threw a quick nervous glance at the pot, reassuring herself the lid was still shut tight. 'It won't help,' she told him, and he heard the edge of panic behind the brusque words. 'No matter what I do . . . she keeps coming *back*!' Her voice was already rising to hysteria and Roley realized he had to tread very carefully here.

'Don't worry, Cat,' he told her, trying to sound calm and confident. 'I'll take care of it.'

'You?'

The tone of contempt actually hurt. He was used to Catriona thinking he was useless but the fact that even when half-hysterical she still thought it made him feel angry and ashamed at once.

'Yes, me,' he said, annoyed. 'And while I'm at it, what else do you have in here that's not yours?' He saw a flash of fear in her face then before he added: 'Anything that belonged to Katherine and John's mother.'

'Oh, that junk.' Catriona stepped back into the room and sat on the bed, shrugging a shoulder at a built-in cupboard. 'There's a pile of old photos and stuff in there.'

The too-casual tone didn't fool him. He'd missed something. She'd looked guilty for an instant. As Roley gathered

159

up a stack of shoeboxes and bundles of old photographs he looked carefully along the shelves for anything else that might be important. A row of china animals didn't seem likely and he left them where they were.

'Do you have a bag?' he asked and when Catriona didn't move he added: 'I need to carry this downstairs, I can't manage it and the scone dish unless . . . '

'Here.' She'd started moving the second his eyes had gone to the pot, getting a plastic bag from her suitcase and shoving it at him. Roley put his hoard inside it and went to pick up the pot. She tensed as he touched it and he was certain that whatever else his sister might be concealing, she really wasn't responsible for the appearances of Delilah. She acted as if the pot was full of creepy-crawlies and, to be honest, he didn't much like the thought of carrying it downstairs.

He paused in the doorway and looked back at his sister, sitting on the bed again and waiting for him to leave.

'You're sure there's nothing else?' he asked. 'In the doll's house, perhaps?'

'Just the furniture,' Catriona said. 'What do you want all this junk for anyway?' She seemed genuinely curious, behind the casual act. But Roley didn't feel like telling her. Behind her head his eyes travelled to the shiny surface of her make-up mirror on her bedside table and in it he saw a white-gloved hand move in a shadow-puppet gesture. The forefinger and index finger opened in a sideways V and shut again, opened and shut.

'Scissors!' For once he'd actually guessed what was being mimed and he felt proud of himself for a second before he heard Catriona's sharp intake of breath.

'I don't have them!' Guilt and fear warred across her face as she stared at him. No, at the crockery pot, he realized. 'She took them! Not me!'

'What do you mean?' For a moment he thought she might be going to tell him but instead she flung herself on the bed, turning her back and burying her head in her pillow.

'Nothing!' Her voice was muffled. 'Just leave me alone!'

At least he'd tried, he told himself, as he carried his cargo of items downstairs. But under the ironic gaze of the two mirror mimes he felt he hadn't tried hard enough.

As he reached the landing he heard a door open along the corridor and quickly whisked himself into the computer room. He didn't fancy being caught with the crockery pot, suspecting that the sight of it would send his mother into another screaming fit. He wasn't exactly keen on the idea of keeping Delilah imprisoned in his room either.

Awkwardly, balancing the pot in one hand and holding the bag in the other, he sprang open the latch of the barn room and pushed the door open with his foot. Inside the light was dim but he could see a figure curled up on the old swing seat, reading. She looked up as he entered, frowning up at the door and Roley hesitated, his foot still on the top step.

'Oh, am I disturbing you?' he asked.

'That's OK,' Katherine said. 'I was just reading.'

Roley wished he'd realized she would be in here but it would feel odd to turn back now. Shutting the door behind him, he came slowly down the stairs and went to put the pot on top of the pool table.

'What have you got that for?' Katherine asked quietly and Roley wondered if she would object. If she thought of the barn room as her own private den she might not be too keen on him bringing Delilah into it.

'It's a sort of . . . um . . . experiment,' Roley told her, putting the bag on the table and turning to face her. 'I thought perhaps if I locked it up . . . ' He was thinking aloud but the idea actually didn't seem like a bad one.

'Are you sure she's even still in there?' Katherine asked, coming slowly towards the table. They both looked at the pot and then met each other's eyes and laughed nervously at the same time.

'I'll do it,' Roley said, not wanting to look like a coward and Katherine looked nervous.

'Hang on,' she said. 'I'll get a stick.'

Roley didn't object as she looked around and then picked up a broken spar of wood, handing it to him. Carefully he levered the lid up and pushed it back, letting it slide down on to the pool table. Inside the tangled limbs of the drones formed a grisly image but there was no sign of Delilah.

'Oh, arse,' Roley said out loud and then turned to Katherine. 'Look, don't tell Cat . . . Catriona. Don't tell her Delilah's gone.'

'Since when do I ever say anything to your sister?' Katherine snapped back angrily, glaring at him.

Roley winced. He could have said that she'd said plenty in their fights but it wouldn't have helped. Instead, he reached out for the lid of the pot and put it back on again.

'Sorry,' he said. 'But I'm still trying to decide what we should do. You were right though, about Delilah not being inside.'

Katherine shrugged awkwardly.

'I just thought she might not be. She's never where people think, is she?'

'No.' Roley leant back against the pool table and tried to decide what to say to Katherine. In the two years they'd lived together he'd never really had a conversation with her about anything important. He'd got used to thinking that he didn't know either of his step siblings but actually he knew John much better. He realized he didn't even know if Katherine could see the ghosts the way her brother could or if she really thought Catriona was responsible for the appearances of Delilah.

'What's in the bag?' Katherine asked and Roley only hesitated for a moment.

'Have a look if you like,' he said. 'I was looking for things that might have belonged to your mother.'

'Really?' Katherine looked suddenly frightened rather than pleased. She reached for the bag and pulled out the bundles of photographs, seeming to relax a bit as she did so. 'That's . . . that's really great, Roley. Our photos were damaged and I don't have any of Mum when she was younger.' Picking up a bundle she began to look through them, carefully, holding them as if they were precious.

'Katherine,' Roley wasn't sure how to begin. 'You know what Fox said before? About the house being haunted.'

'It's not true,' Katherine said instantly. 'I don't believe it.' She put the photographs down and he could see that her hands were trembling.

'No, but seriously, I've seen some weird things . . .'

'It was just a game,' Katherine said, not letting him finish. 'That's all. It doesn't *mean* anything. It wasn't me who started playing with Delilah anyway—your sister did that. And she brought Fox here too. It's nothing to do with Mum.' Her face looked blotchy as it always did before she was about to cry and Roley felt his spirits sink. He hadn't meant to upset her but, like Catriona, she seemed to turn everything into a drama.

'Look,' he said, trying to keep his voice reasonable. 'I'm just trying to find out . . . '

'It's none of your business!' she said furiously, backing away. 'Just leave me alone. I don't want to talk about it!'

Before he could try to speak again she'd turned and scrambled back up the stairs, opening the cupboard door and pulling it shut behind her, leaving him on his own in the barn.

'Well, that went badly,' Roley said and turned instinctively towards a mildew-dappled mirror propped up against the wall. Inside the frame the figures in white met his gaze. The girl rolled her eyes at him but the boy was looking at something behind Roley. Turning, Roley saw that Katherine had left her book behind on the swing seat.

For the second time that day Alice came out of the wood as if the fires of hell were after her. Breathing hard she came down a sloping track and found her path barred by a wooden gate. Flopping over it she tried to catch her breath as she turned and looked behind her. There was no sign of Fox and she didn't know if she was disappointed or relieved or some strange mixture of the two.

It took her a while to work out where she was. The rambling shape of the house she could see ahead of her wasn't familiar. But as she carefully opened the gate and closed it behind her she came to the sudden realization that this was Fell Scar. She'd only ever been here once or twice to help her mother with the gardening but nowhere else had the same aura of decay surrounding it. Coming out of the wood, Alice saw how even with Emily's work to keep the vegetable garden clear, the trees needed thinning and bracken had built up in the hedges and borders.

Fox's touch had frightened her. His air of mystery had taken on an abrupt sexual slant that stirred up unpleasant memories of the Knarl's attack. Alice was still processing all that he'd shown her but her normally orderly thought processes were jumbled up with her reaction to Fox. *Who the hell did he think he was?* As she tried to quell her rising anger and consider the question properly she realized she was hearing voices from the garden beyond the hedge.

' . . . she didn't do it.'

'I can't believe you're defending *her.*' The indignant tone raised the voice loud enough for Alice to identify it as a girl, a bit younger than she was.

'But she didn't, Kat. I know she didn't. She's frightened of Delilah.' The other voice was softer: a child's voice and gently hesitant. Alice had heard that voice before, asking if it was allowed to pat Baskerville. It was the younger of the two boys she'd met in the wood. He had one of those names that was easily forgettable, Alice thought, as she listened.

'Is she frightened of Fox too? *She* brought him here. Now he's got Roley looking for ghosts. He said he was doing an experiment . . . '

'Shh, listen . . . '

'What?'

'Did you hear something?'

The mention of Fox had made Alice start and as she stilled herself she heard the boy—John, that was it—shush the girl again. Abruptly she realized that it was her he'd heard and blushed. Deliberately she took a step across crunching bracken and walked around the edge of the hedge into the garden.

'I'm sorry if I startled you,' she said. 'I got lost in the wood.'

'You came from the wood,' John repeated. His small pinched face turned to look towards the mass of trees smeared across the hillside above them and Alice remembered that he too had seen something in the wood that had frightened him.

The girl was frowning at her. She looked much more like John than Roley did. She had the same light brown hair and the same nervous look, although in her it was a more active tension—as if she might suddenly snap.

'Who are you?' she asked and it was John who replied.

'Her name's Alice,' he said. 'She has a dog.'

'My mother's the gardener here,' Alice added, placatingly. 'Emily Wheeler? She keeps up the vegetable garden and . . . Is something wrong?' She couldn't help but ask. As soon as she'd mentioned her mother's name the girl had turned as pale as if she'd seen one of the ghosts she'd been talking about.

166

'Nothing's wrong,' the girl glared at her angrily and Alice blushed again, feeling that she'd been rude to intrude on them.

'Kat, it's not Alice's fault,' John said unexpectedly. 'Even if she did come from the wood.'

This time both girls looked at him and his golden brown eyes looked back earnestly. Alice had no idea what the girl called Kat was thinking but she herself was beginning to realize that there was something very odd about this little boy.

'I'm not planning to go back there,' she said carefully. 'And if you don't mind me mentioning it, I don't think you should either. It can be dangerous.'

'It's not just the wood that's dangerous,' John began. 'There are . . . '

But then the doors of the house opened and a man came down the steps into the garden. It was obviously the children's father but he looked nothing like Roley. He gave Alice an enquiring look as he came across the lawn and again John seemed determined to explain her presence.

'Dad, this is Alice,' he said. 'Her mum's the gardener.'

'Pleased to meet you. I'm Peter.' He seemed distracted as he shook Alice's hand. 'Look, guys, Harriet's not feeling too great. I'm going to take her out for dinner. What do you say to getting yourself some pizza or something?'

'I can make dinner,' the girl said and her father smiled.

'I'm sure you can, but why not order in. If somewhere here will deliver, that is.' He glanced at Alice and looked enquiringly.

'There's a fish and chip shop in the village,' she said. 'But they don't deliver. It's only a short walk though.'

'Does the pub serve food?' Peter asked and she nodded.

'It's got three stars,' she said. 'My . . . my parents eat there on special occasions.'

'Sounds great. I'll ask Roley to sort you kids out.' Peter seemed to have forgotten his daughter's willingness to cook and she looked sulky as he continued. 'You staying, Alice? Let Roley know if you are.'

'Um . . . ' Luckily Alice didn't have to think of a more eloquent answer because he was already heading back across the lawn.

As he reached the house, a woman who had to be his wife came out of the door and he opened the passenger door of the car for her. Alice wondered if his wife was ill; he had the same air of careful concern that Charlotte displayed when Emily was sick. As the car started up both adults looked out of the window and waved and the children waved back mechanically.

Alice wondered if she might have asked them for a lift. She had an idea that Fox might be waiting for her in the lane and she didn't feel ready to face him again. Glancing awkwardly at the two children she said:

'I didn't mean to intrude . . . '

'Why don't you stay?' John asked. 'You could help Roley hunt ghosts.'

'Um . . . ' said Alice again but Katherine's reaction was explosive.

'Help Roley do what?' she demanded. 'I thought it was an experiment.'

'I think he's ghost hunting,' John said. 'Because of what Fox said.'

Katherine's face was red and blotched with anger as she almost screamed at her brother.

'Why does everyone listen to Fox? He's not even a real person! He's not!' Suddenly she looked around her wildly, her hands searching the empty seat next to her. 'The book,' she said. 'Where is it?'

Before either of them could say anything she'd taken off, running for the house and slamming the front door behind her so the knocker clattered noisily after she'd gone. Alice and John watched her go and as the last echoes of the knocker died away, John said earnestly, 'She's not cross with you, honestly, Alice. It's because of the ghost people. She's frightened of them.'

'Is she?' Alice said. 'What about you? Are you frightened of ghosts?'

'I wasn't.' The little boy looked serious. 'But I think they're getting stronger. I can feel it.' He looked towards the wood. 'It got worse again just before you came out of the wood,' he said.

'But that doesn't make sense.' Alice gave up any idea of pretending not to know what he was talking about. 'I think I killed one of them. They should have got weaker, shouldn't they?'

John looked up at her, his expression shifting from impressed to doubtful.

'Are you sure?' he asked. 'Aren't ghosts already dead?'

1 3
Sticks and Stones

Catriona wasn't exactly overwhelmed by the fish and chips idea. But when she'd suggested she go out with the adults, Peter had frowned at her and said her mother needed a break from her in particular. Catriona had glared at him as he let himself out of her room but when he was gone she slumped back on her bed, feeling helpless.

She was beginning to hate this little room with its sloping ceilings and crumbling plaster walls. Every little sound in the house seemed amplified up in the attics: the creaking of floorboards, the wind in the chimneys, the hundreds of almost inaudible noises at the edge of her hearing that made her strain to identify them. The doll's house squatted in front of the window like a rat cage. She'd tried covering it with a blanket but the shrouded shape seemed more menacing and she'd taken it off again.

She'd counted her holiday spending money three times, trying to decide if it was enough to pay for a train ticket home, but she didn't even know if trains ran from the local station. She wondered about calling her father in France and telling him how unfair everyone was being. But she didn't know how she could explain about Delilah. It was ridiculous to be afraid of a doll. Catriona knew that if someone at school had told a story about being followed around by a creepy voodoo doll she'd have laughed at them. It just sounded like a practical joke, one you'd play on someone gullible.

Cat knew she wasn't gullible. But, faced with the choice of believing that Delilah was stalking her or one of the others was playing a trick, her mind kept shying away from the idea that a doll could move on its own. Automatically she suspected Katherine, who could have inherited some sort of loony mindset from her mother who'd made Delilah in the first place. She actually didn't like to think it was John, not after he'd talked to her after her nightmare, but every time he talked about Delilah moving by herself it made Catriona wonder if he might be playing a weird game with the dolls. Little kids could be odd like that and John was a strange little boy. Roley was a possibility; even though he ought to be on her side he'd been spending more and more time with the Brown children. And then there was Fox. He'd hardly paid any attention at all to her when he'd come to visit, watching everyone else as if he'd been waiting for something to happen. Fox could have put Delilah in the dish but Cat couldn't work out how he might have been involved all the other times.

Outside the house, tyres crunched on gravel and Catriona realized the adults were leaving. With a sudden feeling of abandonment she went to the window, twisting her body to avoid touching the doll's house, and looking through just in time to see the back of the car disappearing into the lane. Suddenly every horror film she'd ever seen came flooding into her mind. Doors locking themselves, hands tapping at windows, stairways extending endlessly as you stumbled down them until you lost your balance and fell. Despite the presence of the doll's house next to her, Catriona couldn't shake the idea that she was inside the miniature house and somewhere downstairs a life-size Delilah was assembling an army of drones.

Every moment the sensation got worse, the feeling that there was something out there coiling to strike. Suddenly Catriona felt a fierce craving for a cigarette. She'd bought another packet in Windermere and she fumbled for it inside her rucksack. Her fingers slipped against something silky that moved beneath her fingers and she snatched her hand back as if it had been bitten.

'It's not Delilah, it can't be Delilah,' she said out loud, staring at her own pink rucksack and rubbing her fingers as if to soothe away a sting. The rucksack had been lying on the floor at the end of her bed for hours since before the wasp tea, and Roley had taken Delilah away. But in her own mind Catriona conjured an image of Delilah lifting the lid of the crockery dish and climbing out, her miniature form climbing slowly but inexorably up the human sized staircase, one stair at a time, before reaching the attics and creeping through a crack in the wall . . .

'It's impossible,' Cat said. Then, more defiantly: 'I don't believe it.'

Reaching for her bag she upended it on her bed. A jumble of pens, sweets, make-up and disposable lighters came cascading out together and there, reclining amongst the debris, limbs akimbo at an inhuman angle, was Delilah.

Catriona tried to scream and heard it come out as a thready whistle. Delilah smiled up at her, her hair fanning around her like a cloak: blonde, black, and mid-brown. But a streak of another colour striped through the blonde section: a stripe of dark chestnut brown. Catriona's hands went to her head, feeling for the raggedy section John had spotted. The chopped-off ends felt as rough to her questing fingertips as Delilah's had been smooth but there was no mistaking the colour. It was a strand of her own hair.

Blundering from the room, she banged into the door as she pulled it open violently and lost some skin off her hand slamming it shut behind her. Her feet slipped on the worn stair runners and she fell down three stairs of the first flight before picking herself up and hurling herself down the next set. She was gasping for air, the scream she hadn't managed to get out sticking in her throat, and dizzy from the fall. The walls seemed to go in and out of perspective and she was gripped by the fear that she'd reach the door only to find the whole front of the house swing open like the doll's house to dump her back into the attic.

As she skidded down the last set of stairs into the main room the front door flew open and a female figure was silhouetted black against the early evening light. Catriona threw up her hands to protect her face as it rushed towards her and felt the collision with bone-jarring force. Feeling herself falling, her fingers tangled in long hair and she pulled hard, and felt the other fall with her as they landed on the hard wooden floor. The wind had been finally knocked out of her and she scrabbled to get upright again, only realizing as she pulled herself to her knees that her antagonist was not Delilah but Katherine, eyes blazing as she suddenly launched herself forward.

Katherine slapped her face before she could duck and then took hold of her hair with both hands and pulled hard. Catriona had to claw at her wrists to make her let go and then, faced with an enemy she could at least fight, tried to box the younger girl's ears.

'You bitch,' Katherine was crying as she tried to fend her off. 'You complete *bitch*.'

'Psycho,' Catriona spat back. 'I know it was you who cut my hair. You should be in a mental asylum.'

'Cut your hair? Why don't I rip it all off and save everyone from your stupid prinking and posing?' Katherine snapped, lunging for her again.

As they scrabbled and fought Catriona registered other people surrounding them.

'What the hell's going on?' Roley's voice boomed out above them from the stairs.

'We just found them like this,' a girl's voice replied from the door. 'Can I help?'

Then suddenly there was a blast of icy water over her body and Catriona felt Katherine letting go as she did, sitting up to blink water out of her eyes. John was standing next to them holding a large flower vase. Its contents, a bunch of bedraggled flowers, now lay all over the floor along with the rapidly spreading puddle.

'Nice work,' said the girl. She was dressed in dark clothes and carrying a camera, holding it protectively to her chest.

'Yeah, well done, John,' Roley added, smiling briefly in his direction before putting on a parenting face of disapproval. 'Who started the fight?'

'She just came running into me and pulled my hair,' Katherine said, brushing daffodils off her clothes as she stood up.

'She ran into *me*,' Catriona snapped back, getting up herself and facing the other girl down. 'And slapped my face and called me a bitch.'

'She said I was a psycho,' Katherine insisted and Roley's face clouded over.

'ENOUGH!' he shouted. 'I'm sick to death with both of you. Do you want the rest of us to be miserable? Do you want our parents to get divorced? Have you any idea how sick and tired everyone is of the two of you fighting like—like alley cats—every single bloody day?'

Surprised by the force of the criticism and feeling the injustice of it, Catriona felt first one tear and then another slide out of her eyes and down her face.

'Don't even bother,' Roley said coldly. 'Either of you. Katherine dissolves like a wet tissue and Catriona's a past master in crocodile tears. Why don't the two of you just go to your rooms, put on something dry and try and pretend to be human beings just for a change?'

Catriona felt her stomach churn at the idea of going back to her room but before she could speak Katherine replied hotly:

'I don't have to do what you say. You're not in charge of me. Our family was just fine until your lot turned up and tried to take over everything. I can look after myself.' Turning on her heel she broke for the front door dodging past the hand the blonde girl put out to stop her.

'You can't send me to my room either,' Catriona said

quickly. Suddenly she had the thought that Roley might actually try to carry her up there and lock her in. He was certainly big enough to try it and, before he could take another step forward, Catriona pushed John out of the way and ran out of the door into the grey twilight.

Katherine was a flying figure in the distance heading along the road to the village and Catriona instantly turned the other way, running for the shelter of the wood. From the house someone called a name, a short syllable drawn out into a shout. But Catriona couldn't know which name they had called and she didn't stop running.

Roley saw his attempt at controlling the situation dissolve into chaos and rubbed his temples, feeling a headache threatening. For a moment he had thought it might actually work, that the girls might actually listen to him for a change. Fat chance of that. All he'd achieved was to convince himself there was no way the two of them would ever make peace.

John was standing at the open door looking into the garden where twilight had descended. Still cradling her camera Alice looked over his head at Roley. He had no idea why she was there and he wondered if the scene with the girls had shocked her enough for her to walk straight out again.

'Can I help you?' he asked uncertainly.

'I'm actually wondering if I can help you,' she said, a faint blush on her cheeks as she added: 'Um . . . Roley, isn't it? Your sisters both seemed pretty upset.'

'Understatement of the century,' Roley said, awkwardly. 'I suppose I should go after them.'

'They went different ways,' John pointed out, turning back from the door and Roley sighed.

'They would,' he said, grimly. 'Look, don't you go haring off, John. Shut the door for a minute and let me think about what to do.'

'We should bring them back,' John said although he at least did what Roley had asked and closed the heavy front door. 'It's dangerous outside.'

Roley didn't like to say he wasn't sure it was so safe inside either. With the front door closed the room was dark and he ran his hand over the three light switches, the yellow electric light making the room jump into sudden bright relief. Putting her camera on the table Alice bent and started picking up the flowers. Unasked, John ran into the kitchen and came back with a cloth, mopping up the water. The sudden return to normality made Roley feel a bit more normal too. Cudgelling his brain into thought he realized that whatever happened his mother would almost certainly hold him responsible for losing the girls. But that wasn't as important as making sure they were safe.

'Alice,' he said and was surprised when she started so abruptly she nearly dropped the vase of flowers.

'Sorry.' She was blushing as she put the vase quickly on the table. 'I'm a bit jumpy.'

'That's all right. Look, can I ask you a favour?' Standing up he moved towards the living room. 'John, we'll just be in here for a moment, OK?'

John looked up with a sudden brilliant smile and he nodded before busying himself with the water. Roley smiled back automatically, wondering if his little stepbrother was deliberately trying to keep out of the way. Alice followed him into the living room and Roley shut the door. He actually felt like an adult for the first time in this house, something to do with the two of them being the only authority around.

'I think I am going to have to ask you for help,' he said. 'Would you mind watching John while I go after the cats?' She looked puzzled and he laughed when he realized what he'd said. 'Cat-riona and Kat-herine,' he explained, stressing the similarity of the names. 'It's a long story. Like an opera but with more screaming. Katherine's John's sister, Catriona's mine.'

'Families can be complicated,' Alice said. 'You really don't have to explain. I'm happy to help. I did meet your father— your stepfather, I suppose—earlier so if they come back . . . '

'It'll be awkward for you, though, won't it?' Roley worried. 'I'd probably better leave a note.'

'It's OK,' Alice said. 'John will help me explain. And with any luck you'll be back before they are. I should warn you though . . . ' She hesitated and the hesitation became a longer pause as Roley realized she was looking over his shoulder.

She was looking at the reflective surface of the bookcase cabinets. Roley realized what she might be seeing and turned in time to see the two reflections acting out a scene. The girl leaned back against the bookshelves while the boy drew a tress of her watery hair through his fingers. Alice looked alarmed and Roley said quickly:

'Don't worry, they're harmless. All they seem to do is watch.'

'What are they?' Alice's eyes narrowed as they watched

the embrace become more intimate and Roley blushed, wondering if he was being sent up.

'I've no idea,' he admitted. 'But according to a book Katherine found, they're called Mirror and Glass.'

'Which is which?' Alice asked, more calmly than he'd expected.

'Your guess is as good as mine,' Roley said. 'Ignore them. John isn't bothered by them and he seems to have a sense for this stuff.'

'John thinks the wood is dangerous,' Alice said, forgetting the reflections as she picked up her train of thought. 'That's what I was going to tell you. I think he's right. There are things, people, I don't know . . . '

She was frowning and Roley could have happily kicked his sister and stepsister for ruining the first chance he'd had to talk to someone about what was happening. For that person to be Alice was a stroke of luck he'd not expected and now he had to charge off into the night after hysterical teenage girls who would doubtless refuse to come home without a lot more screaming.

'Look, don't go anywhere,' he said. 'I'll get the girls and then maybe we can talk about this stuff. There's something very weird going on.'

'Take care out there,' Alice said, looking as if she really meant it and Roley nodded.

'I'll just get a torch,' he said. 'I've got a mobile phone too so call if anything happens, OK? John knows the number.'

'No problem,' Alice said. She looked a lot calmer than Roley felt and he added:

'Look, I am sorry to dump all this on you.'

'Don't worry about it,' Alice said. 'Really, I'm happy to help.'

They stood there looking at each other and then Roley opened the door.

John had finished mopping up the water and was sitting in a window seat looking outside. Roley explained to him what he'd decided, as he gathered up a torch and his jacket.

'Be careful,' John said anxiously as he went to the door and Alice echoed him from across the room. Roley actually felt kind of tough and brave as he let himself out of the house. Outside in the garden the mood abruptly faded, replaced by the conviction that he was letting himself in for more than he bargained for. But what other option did he have?

He turned the torch on and directed the circle of light across the hedges. He'd infinitely prefer to take the road to the village where by now at least one sobbing girl might be halfway to the pub. But instead he turned towards the wood, facing the inevitable.

Alice watched Roley's torch light bob out of sight and then deliberately closed the curtains. She hoped he'd be all right out there. He was heftily built but after his initial show of authority he'd turned out to be rather diffident and uncertain. She hoped she'd done the right thing by agreeing to stay behind.

'I'm afraid you'll have to wait for your supper,' she said, trying to strike a note of normality. 'Would you like a hot drink or anything?'

'No, thank you,' John said politely. He wriggled off the window seat and looked around the room before asking abruptly: 'Would you like to see the house?'

'If you like,' Alice agreed, thinking some kind of distraction was probably a good idea. But as the little boy grabbed her hand determinedly she wondered if he had an ulterior motive as well.

As he led her up the stairs, he started explaining it to her. Alice's experiences with young children were fairly limited and John's careful way of speaking interested her. It was as if he investigated each word for hidden traps before using it which gave him an adult air of astuteness. Before they'd finished exploring the first floor he'd explained the family to her more completely than Roley had managed.

'So this Kat and Cat thing's been going on for two years?' she asked, trying to imagine it.

'Two and a half years,' John corrected her. 'They get cross when we use their full names but if you say the short one they both pretend to think it's them you meant. And my sister gets cross if I call Roley's sister Cat. And his sister gets cross when he calls Kat . . . '

'I get the picture,' Alice said. 'I don't suppose they have middle names do they?'

'My sister doesn't,' John said after thinking for a moment and Alice sighed.

'It wouldn't work if only one of them changed. I think the only solution's for them both to be called something completely different.'

'I think so too,' John agreed. 'I wouldn't mind changing.

In fact I'd quite like it. What about you? Do you like your name, Alice?'

'Usually,' Alice said, uncomfortably. 'I mean, I don't usually think about it.' Changing the subject she asked: 'Where are we going now?'

John explained the attics and the double staircase as well as the connecting door between the two central rooms.

'This is my room,' he explained. 'And that's my bear and my binoculars and my wooden box puzzle that Harriet gave me. Catriona's room is through here.'

'Are you sure we should . . . ' Alice said as he opened the door and then cut herself off. The bed was covered with dolls.

They weren't soft toys like John's bear. They were naked, faceless, hairless imitation people, even their eyes were gone and only gaping holes remained. Spread out across the bed and the floor they looked like a miniature massacre, lying like puppets with their strings cut. In the middle of the bed, sitting cross-legged, was a single girl doll with long hair, china blue eyes, and smiling red lips.

John took a step backwards and then very slowly and carefully shut the door again. As Alice watched him in surprise, he pressed his ear against the door, his face intent as if he was listening. After a moment he beckoned her over and treading very softly as if the carpet was a litter of broken branches, Alice listened with him. It was a moment before she could hear anything but her and John's breathing. But then she became aware of a sound just on the very edge of the audible range: a mice-like scraping, the movement of tiny feet on floorboards. John met her eyes, nodding very slightly as he removed his head from the door and stepped back.

'They move by themselves,' he said, so softly that his lips barely moved. 'Daddy and Harriet didn't believe it and they sent Catriona to her room because they kept seeing the dolls. But it's not her doing it. Honestly.'

Alice stared at the closed door. She had a sudden wild urge to haul it open and see the scene on the other side again. But instead she stepped backwards, pointing back towards the staircase with eyebrows raised. John went willingly enough but as they went back down Alice couldn't shake the sight of those dolls gathered together in the teenage girl's room. There had been a real sense of menace in that room and she caught herself listening for the sound of tiny footsteps.

'So, basically, this house is haunted,' she said quietly.

'I don't think it's the house,' John said. 'I thought that too but then the mirror people came with us over the lake. And Fox can go anywhere he likes.'

'Fox is one of them.' Alice had half known it ever since she'd heard John and Katherine talking. 'He's a ghost or . . . or something.' She suddenly wished she'd spoken to Roley for longer. He'd wanted to talk to her, she realized, but he'd held back for fear of freaking her out. John was succeeding well enough at that and Alice felt desperate for answers.

'They don't haunt the house,' John said, pursuing his own line of thought. 'I think they haunt us, our family.'

'Then why is Fox following me?' Alice asked, the words spilling out.

'Maybe you're related to us?' John looked as if he wasn't

sure whether he approved of that idea and Alice felt bizarrely disappointed. She'd thought they were getting on well, given the peculiar circumstances.

'I think Roley knew something,' she said, realizing that she was talking to the little boy as if he were much older. 'But he didn't have time to explain.'

'I think he was in the magical land of Barnia,' John said. 'Maybe he left something there that would help.' Alice wondered if he really had flipped just before he gave her a quick grin. 'Katherine found it but Catriona named it,' he explained. 'Come and see.'

'All right.' Alice let him lead her through a bedroom but stopped him as he approached a cupboard door.

'There's not really a magical land through there, is there?' she said. 'Because I'm starting to believe anything's possible in this house.'

'No, it's all right.' John opened the door confidently. 'I think this is the safest place, actually.'

The weird thing was the fact she believed him. The barn room ahead was dimly lit and festooned with cobwebs. But as she followed John down the steps Alice felt the sense of oppression lighten somewhat. But perhaps that was only because John had relaxed. He looked almost cheerful as he skipped over to the pool table where a litter of objects were arranged in a way weirdly reminiscent of a science experiment.

'It looks more like a treasure hunt than a ghost hunt,' Alice said and John nodded as if she'd said something very clever.

'Yes,' he said. 'Maybe we'll find a map to where something is buried.'

14
Things that Sting

The sky was grey and the trees bracketing the road to the village stood out like black cut-outs. Katherine started off running but couldn't catch her breath and when she got a stitch in her side she slowed to a walk. It wasn't cold but she felt exposed and vulnerable in her jeans and T-shirt and wished she'd stopped to bring a coat.

Her head ached where Catriona had ripped at her hair and her wrist stung where she'd scratched her. She hoped her stepsister hurt even half as much but she doubted it. Catriona's tears were always fake—the result of not getting her own way. In contrast her violent outburst had felt very real. It was the first time their rows had erupted into a fully-fledged fight and Katherine wished for the hundredth time that her father hadn't remarried. She wanted to rip apart the pretence that they were a family and force her father to admit they couldn't go on like this. But would Peter listen?

Her footsteps faltered and finally stopped entirely as she stared down the dark road and wondered what his reaction would be to her bursting in on him and Harriet in the pub. He'd be embarrassed if she caused a scene and Harriet would take Catriona's side. They'd probably both be angry that she hadn't listened to Roley when he was supposed to be in charge. Katherine's mouth trembled and she felt the tears beginning again as she realized there was no one who would take her side. Her father was too invested in this idea that they could be one happy family to accept that it was never going to happen. The road blurred and through a veil of tears Katherine saw a shadow detach itself from the trees and step out ahead of her.

'Where are you going?' a voice asked lightly and she realized that it belonged to Fox.

'What do you care?' Katherine demanded. For a moment she'd been frightened as he'd appeared out of nowhere but her certainty that Fox wasn't a real person gave her the strength to recover herself. 'Why don't you mind your own business?'

'Perhaps I don't have any to mind,' he said and she snorted.

'Probably because you're not a real person,' she said, staring him down. 'Go on, tell the truth for once. My mother invented you, didn't she? You're the ghost, not her.'

'I'm no ghost,' Fox said quickly. He reached out a hand towards her and when Katherine flinched away he added: 'Touch me if you don't believe it. I'm as solid as you are.'

'Touch you? I'd rather touch a dog turd,' Katherine sneered at him. 'Go and find Catriona if you want someone to hold hands with. I'm not interested in your games.'

'Too late.' Fox dropped his hand and regarded her with cold green eyes. 'The game was begun long ago. All that remains to be seen is who the winners will be—and the losers.'

'And I suppose I'm one of the losers.' Katherine meant to say it angrily but her voice betrayed her, faltering fatally at the end of the sentence.

Fox's green eyes examined her critically, roving from her straggling hair across her tear-stained face and down over the rest of her body. Katherine wrapped her arms around herself defensively, trying to block out that stare. She knew she wasn't slathered in make-up like Catriona and her chest was still as flat as a boy's but she didn't care since she wasn't interested in boys—especially not in some bad-boy biker who thought he was just too cool for words. Even so, his unblinking stare unnerved her and she wished she'd never spoken to him in the first place.

His eyes returned to her face and when he finally spoke his words were anything but reassuring.

'You look like a loser,' he said. 'No one listens to you, no one sees you, perhaps you're the one who's a ghost, not me.'

'I'm real,' Katherine insisted but she felt dizzy, as if an abyss had opened at her feet.

'Oh yes?' Fox sounded faintly amused. 'Then what's your name?'

'My name?' It was an unexpected question and she was thrown by it, after all they'd been introduced only that day, he couldn't possibly have forgotten. 'You know what it is. I'm Kat. Katherine Brown.'

'Katherine was your mother's name,' Fox said, his voice strangely gentle, as if he was trying to politely remind her of an obvious fact. 'Brown's your father's name. And Cat's what your sister is called. Don't you have any name of your own? None at all?'

'I do!' Katherine found her voice and practically screamed the answer at him. 'It's Kat! *I'm* Kat, not her. It's *my* name. She tried to steal it but it's mine.'

Fox raised his eyebrows, as if he couldn't believe her capacity for self-delusion.

'It's not me you have to convince,' he said softly. 'It's not I who makes the rules.'

'What rules?' Kat demanded. 'What are you talking about?'

'The rules of the make-believe game,' Fox said, infinitely patient again, as if reminding her of something she should already know. 'The name-eater must be fed,' he said softly as Katherine felt the hairs on the back of her neck slowly rise. 'And since you don't have a name to call your own . . .'

'I do.' She was properly frightened now, of Fox and of his cryptic words that seemed to cloak horrors beyond imagination. But with the fear came anger, the same anger that had risen as she'd clawed and spat at Catriona, the horror of having her identity erased. 'I have a name,' she said again. 'And I'll prove it to whoever you like. Just tell me what I have to do.'

Fox smiled, it was not a pleasant expression. But, poised between fear and fury, Kat hardly cared.

'You have to make a sacrifice,' he said. 'But I don't think you'll mind very much. After all, your sister tried to steal your name, didn't she?'

'She's not my sister,' Katherine corrected him. 'And it's my whole life she's tried to steal, not just my name.'

'So take it back,' Fox said. 'And let her see how it feels for a change.'

'Why?' Katherine was still suspicious. 'I thought you liked her, fancied her, you know.'

'Then you were mistaken,' Fox said. 'I don't care about her at all. She's not the one I want to help.' He held out his hand for a second time. 'Come on,' he said. 'I'll show you what to do. Anne told me how it works.'

'Then you did know her.' Katherine was determined to make him admit it and this time Fox nodded.

'Yes,' he said. 'She invented me. If it helps you can think of me as a brother.'

'I have a brother,' Katherine told him. 'I don't need any more.' But she took his hand and felt his fingers tighten around hers, cold but real.

Together they began to walk along the road, not towards the village but uphill, to where the woods began.

It was muddy in the woods. Within minutes of leaving the house Catriona's trainers and the hems of her jeans were sodden with filth. Scrambling up a muddy bank and through the trees, she tried to put as much distance between herself and the house as she could. Roley was pathetic but in his new pose of 'responsible adult' he might follow her and have another go at telling her to go to her room.

That was one thing Catriona was determined not to do. It wasn't her room anyway, her room was back in London. Her room had a deep-pile purple carpet, instead of creaking old boards; double-glazed windows instead of a loose wooden frame that rattled and banged in the slightest wind; a TV and a dressing table and a walk-in wardrobe with its own light instead of a creepy old doll's house and a box of freaky dolls. She felt a fierce longing for her own room; to curl up in her duvet, instead of a scratchy old blanket that smelt of mothballs, and watch *The* OC and eat banoffee ice-cream out of the tub.

In her room she was in control. She could turn up the volume on her stereo and if her mother yelled up the stairs she'd pretend not to hear. She could take the cordless phone in there, saving money on mobile bills, and phone her friends. She could close the door and shut out everyone else. She could pretend that Peter and his children weren't there. That it was just her and her mum—and Roley, of course.

But in Fell Scar everything was out of control. Harriet had abandoned her, refusing to believe the honest truth even when Catriona swore it was true. Peter had as much as said her mother was sick of her. Roley was acting like some sort of tough guy and not taking her side. John kept watching her as if she was some kind of wild beast and the unspeakable Katherine had actually attacked her. Catriona really believed her stepsister had finally lost the plot. What sort of person started kicking and biting just because they ran into you when they weren't looking where they were going?

Catriona could feel the bruises rising on her wrists and when she looked at her hands she saw that her fingernails were torn. She felt the ragged edges gingerly and then shuddered violently when her fingers brushed against hair. Holding her shaking hands out into the grey light of evening filtering through the trees she saw that it hadn't been her imagination. Strands of light brown hair were wrapped around her wrist, caught in the bracelet of her watch strap. Katherine's hair, pulled out in the fight. Cat began to pick at it, feeling the tight strands cutting into her flesh as if they were wire. She'd seen enough of hair to last her a lifetime and this was a horrible reminder of how she was tied to Katherine in their new family.

Her frantic fingers slowed. She felt her own face harden as she looked at the strands of hair she'd pulled loose. This was all Katherine's fault. Her mother had lived here, that was the only reason they had to stay in that house of horrors. Her mother had made the dolls, given Delilah her tresses of stolen hair. And who else but Katherine would have woven Catriona's hair into those locks? Again Catriona's mind shuddered away from the idea that Delilah had done it herself. No, Katherine was responsible and John's claims Delilah moved by herself were just covering for his sister. He was only a little boy, maybe he did believe it was ghosts or something. But it was more likely that Katherine had finally fallen prey to whatever mental illness her mother had and she was the one doing this. There was nothing Katherine would like more than to drive her away, make Catriona go and live with her father or something so that she would be the only 'cat' in the family. And it was working; right now all Catriona wanted was to get *away*.

It was too dark under the trees to see what she was doing. Every minute the light seemed to thicken into darkness. Somewhere further up the hill she could hear the trickling sound of water and in the distance birds called with croaking voices. No one knew where she was. It seemed Roley hadn't even bothered to come after her and she suddenly wondered if he'd gone looking for Katherine instead. Perhaps he'd found her and they were all back at the house talking cosily about how Catriona was crazy, messing around with dolls and stealing things from shops.

Catriona hesitated, turning to look back down the hill. Through the tangle of trees she couldn't even see the lights of the house. The wood might as well go on for ever. *I could die out here*, she thought. *They wouldn't find my body for days and when they did* . . . She'd played this make-believe game before, imagining sorrowing relations gathered around her death-bed while she, pale and beautiful, forgave them nobly for their cruelty. But the fantasy was blotted out by the image of her body lying in a drift of leaves, putrefying with rot and mould and insects crawling out of her eyes. As if her thought had conjured it, there was a buzzing sound, a drone that carried through the still air. It came from below her, further down the hill, an angry buzz as if a hive of wasps had been roused into fury.

Walking through the woods at night, Roley was aware of his mood shifting from worry to anger and back again. He was worried about the girls and about the spirits they seemed to have stirred up, quite apart from the mundane accidents that could easily occur when you went walking around in woods without so much as a jacket. But he was also angry that, yet again, the two girls had built an unpleasant situation into a complete nightmare scenario—especially when something actually occult seemed to be happening.

They couldn't go on this way. No matter what else happened, Roley was quite certain of that. For better or for worse Harriet and Peter had been pretending that, with enough time, their children would get along. Well, they weren't completely off base with that idea. Roley had to admit that he'd miss John if their parents broke up. But right now he could willingly have drowned both cats in the next pond.

'I don't mean that,' he said out loud, crossing his fingers superstitiously. But as he panned the torch back and forth through the undergrowth he felt that it was absolutely typical of girls that they'd throw a hysterical fit just when everyone needed to be most calm.

Except for Alice. Meeting her again had almost made up for the rest of it. And she hadn't seemed fazed at all when he'd asked her to watch John. He only wished he could have explained better, that he'd had more time to explain, or knew the right words to use. Even now he still wasn't sure what was really happening. It wasn't ghosts, not exactly. But he'd only had time to scan through the book of the make-believe game and it had raised more questions than it answered. The biggest shock had been seeing the drawings of people halfway through. Fox, with his secretive smile; Mirror and Glass trapped in a square frame; Delilah with her loops of stolen hair coiled around the drones. And there were other drawings, figures he hadn't recognized: a twisted tree with groping limbs; children with black feathers sprouting from their shoulders; winged insects with human faces.

Roley remembered Peter saying lightly 'someone made a house of horrors' and thought his stepfather had spoken more truly than he knew. There were horrors hiding around Fell Scar and their family had stirred them up like an ant's nest. Roley had an image of himself with a kettle of boiling water and half-laughed, half-grimaced at the idea. But he knew that what was happening had to be stopped; exorcized or whatever it was that paranormal experts did to lay ghosts to rest. But, first things first, he had to find the girls and get them to calm down for long enough to let him explain the danger they were in.

Wet leaves squelched under his feet and his trainers were already soaked through, their grips failing against the sheer volume of mulch that seemed to have accumulated in the wood. Above him the trees cut out what little light remained in the sky and the torch showed him trunks twined with ivy and thickets of brambles and bracken. He'd given up shouting names into the blackness. There was something about the way the words fell echolessly into the depths of the wood that he didn't like. Now he just forged ahead, hoping that he'd find some sign or path to follow.

The beam of light showed a passage between the bramble thickets, opening out into a wider expanse, and he played the torch about, illuminating the scene ahead. He was at the edge of a clearing, one in which a tree had fallen down—or been chopped down. It lay on its side, branches snapped and broken and twigs turned into kindling. Snake-like roots had been torn out of the ground and gouged out a great hole in the muddy earth. Roley realized that an axe had been buried in its heart. He took a step forward to take a closer look and then paused, abruptly reminded of the drawing he'd seen in Katherine's book. Was this the twisted tree, which had had the words *The*

Knarl hand-written beneath it? Carefully he directed the beam of the torch across the length of it; spotting for the first time the black feathers that lay scattered all around as if, in falling, the tree had brought down an entire rookery of bird's nests. *Rookery* was another name from the book, the name for the bird children, and he viewed the tree more suspiciously than ever as the beam of light crept down the trunk towards the hole.

Squinting his eyes to see, it was a while before he noticed the noise: a low hum just on the edge of his hearing. Another age seemed to pass as he watched the shadows shift in the hole, as if the roots of the tree were rippling. No, not rippling, *crawling*. As the hum rose in pitch, winged shapes lifted up from the torn tree and he finally realized what he was seeing. It was a nest, but not of ants, or flies, or wasps. The winged figures that rose from the roots and hovered above them weren't shaped like any insect he'd ever seen. They were barely more than an inch long, with insect thoraxes, filmy wings, and a barbed stinger. But placed on those tiny insect bodies were arms and legs that looked human—although impossibly small. The heads atop those insect bodies had human hair, or something very like it, silvery grey filaments that moved like feelers, questing around.

Roley watched as the creatures turned to look towards him and saw, for the first time, the pinched faces. Mouths like a scar, noses that were mere dots, and eyes that all but filled the face: black and multi-faceted; insect eyes. He'd seen those faces before, a host of them filling a double page spread of the book, above a single word: *Vampiries.*

* * *

Alice considered the items laid out on the pool table, taking each one in turn as she tried to make sense of the puzzle. The empty china dish stood for Delilah and her drones, and Alice didn't allow herself to forget that they were still up there in the attics—at least she hoped they were, and hadn't moved out into the rest of the house. A couple of children's books lay face open on the table, each showing a mutilated page with the name of one or more characters crossed out. Next on the table were the photographs, several bundles of them, glued together with withered snakes of rubber bands. Finally there was a notebook, with the words *Make-Believe Game* written on the cover.

The photographs interested her the most, since it was her own area of expertise, but instead Alice picked up the notebook. It looked like the most likely to hold the answers, and Alice was very conscious that her ally in this search was a ten-year-old boy. A very strange boy, but still a child who didn't seem old enough to be hunting ghosts or searching for buried treasure or whatever Roley had set in motion here.

'Why don't you look through the photos?' she suggested. 'I want to take a look at this.'

As John obediently began to sort through the first batch, Alice opened the book. Her gaze skipped down past the weird poem to the names at the bottom and she felt suddenly cold as she read them: *Anne Katherine Stone, Charlotte Miranda Dean, Emily Jane Wheeler.*

'What's wrong?' John asked, looking across at her.

'My mother's name,' Alice said. 'It's in this book. Her and her friends, they wrote this.'

She wasn't looking at the book but at scenes from the past unfolding in her imagination, her life flashing before her eyes. All the times Emily had seemed frightened, her warnings about the wood, Charlotte's failed degree and Emily's pregnancy, her own birth. Alice was suddenly certain that she held in her hands the answer to the mysteries of her life and for the first time she didn't want to know.

An image floated before her clouded vision, one she *hadn't* seen before: three girls sitting on the edge of a stone fountain. Blonde, black-haired, and brunette. Two of those faces she recognized, the third she'd never seen before.

'That's my mother,' John said. Alice blinked and saw that he was holding a photograph in front of her. 'The one in the patchwork dress. Which one's yours?'

'This one.' Alice touched the photo with a fingertip, pointing to a young Emily dressed in blue velvet. 'At least, well, Emily's my mother but she and Charlotte brought me up together.' She pointed to the third girl, dressed like a boy, familiar dark eyes challenging the camera. Now she was looking properly she could see the same faces repeated in the first set of photographs spread across the table.

'Maybe that's why Fox is following you,' John said slowly. 'Not because you're related to us. But because you're related to *them*.' His face screwed up tightly, as if he was grasping for an explanation. 'What's the book about?'

'I'm not sure.' Alice picked it up and flicked through the pages, the paper dry in her hands like dead leaves. She stopped when she reached drawings and together they looked at the pages one by one: *Fox, Mirror and Glass, The Knarl, The Rookery, Vampiries.* The photographs must have been sixteen years old, which suggested the drawings were too. But Alice couldn't process that information. She couldn't make it add up to anything.

A whisper of sound called her attention to the second bundle of photographs. John had prised the rubber band loose and was spreading them out on the table as he had the first set. These photographs were darker, taken in poorer light conditions. Patterns of light and shade in a thicket of trees, a thin stream of water falling across a scree of tumbled rocks, a hilltop tarn surrounded by trees, the water almost black in their shadow, a blur of winged insects repeated in several shots.

'Stop there,' Alice said and John paused in laying out the photographs. The last three were all of winged shapes and as the two of them leaned closer, Alice made out tiny fairy-like figures, each with ephemeral gauze-like wings. 'Cottingley fairies,' she said out loud.

'What-ingley fairies?' John looked quizzical and she smiled, grateful for a breath of humour.

'It's a famous case of fake photographs,' she explained. 'In the early twentieth century two young girls from a place called Cottingley faked these photographs of themselves with fairies. All sorts of experts were fooled by them and thought the fairies were real.'

'These are all blurry,' John said. 'Does that mean they're fake?'

'Well, in theory something with wings might move too

fast for the shutter speed of a camera,' Alice explained. 'But fairies aren't real. The Cottingley girls drew them with pen and ink and attached them to the ground with hatpins. With all the techniques we have nowadays it's fairly obvious the photographs were faked but at the time people believed in them. I suppose, deep down, they wanted to believe that fairies existed.' She looked at the photographs again, frowning, then down to her own camera, still hanging around her neck.

'I think these ones are real,' John said quietly. 'Because they're in the book. But they're not fairies. They're vampiries.'

'Fairies that suck blood.' Alice was trying for another joke but the words fell flat. 'Oh lord, like fairy mosquitoes. That's . . . ' She made a face.

'They sound bad.'

John was looking at the picture with a worried expression and Alice could guess what he was thinking. The vampirie photos had been taken in the wood, the wood that Roley had gone into armed with nothing but a torch.

'How can they be real?' Alice asked. 'The book, it's the rules for a game. It says *The Make-Believe Game* on the cover. Make-believe isn't real, it's like "let's pretend". It's fantasy, not reality.'

'But none of the make-believe people are really real,' John said, looking surprised, as if she'd missed something obvious. 'Dolls are only pretend real, aren't they? But Delilah really does move by herself. And the mime people, Mirror and Glass, Roley thinks they're ghosts because they're not quite real either.'

'The others too,' Alice said, realizing what he was implying. 'I've seen black feathers lying around a lot recently, but I've not seen birds. If the Rookery is real, they're the ones dropping them. And the Knarl . . . ' She shuddered. 'That's real too, or it *was*.'

'And Fox,' John's voice was urgent, his golden-brown eyes meeting hers seriously. 'He's one of them. One of the make-believe people.'

'He doesn't seem like the rest of them.' Alice fought back a blush. 'He's flesh and blood, like us.'

'Not like us.' John shook his head. 'Like them. The make-believe ones. Because he doesn't grow older. He's the same as he ever was. See?'

He held out a photograph. The edges were smudged, the glossy print dulled with age. But Fox looked out of the picture, watching them with the same sly smile he'd given Alice that afternoon. And in sixteen years, he'd not changed at all.

15
Crossed Out

Katherine felt disconnected from herself as she walked into the shadow of the trees. It wasn't a new feeling. Ever since her dad had married Harriet she'd felt lost—as if she didn't know who she was any more.

When she'd changed schools she'd had to stand up in front of the class and introduce herself and she hadn't known what to say. Even simple questions had become difficult to answer like: 'do you have any brothers or sisters?' More and more she'd retreated into her books, losing herself in stories of other people's lives. Now, with Fox, she felt as if she'd stepped into the pages of a story and it was carrying her along without her control. Fox had talked about games and rules, but Katherine still didn't know what he expected to achieve, or even why he was helping her in the first place.

He kept hold of her hand as he led her along a zigzagging path through the trees, slowly moving higher up the hillside. The wood was dark and silent around them, even the bracken barely crunched beneath their feet. Fox seemed to know the smoothest paths over the mossy earth.

'What was she like?' she said, breaking the silence at last. 'My mother? When she was young.'

'She was angry,' Fox said.

Katherine blinked. She'd never seen Anne even raise her voice before she became ill. Her mother had always seemed the kindest gentlest person she knew.

'Angry and alone,' Fox added. 'Even after she met Emily and Charlotte she still spent most of her time alone. All the things she did were private. She'd read, or make jewellery, or play with her dolls in her room. She said her parents didn't care what she did.'

'Why?' Katherine had never known her grandparents on that side of the family. They'd never even sent so much as a birthday card to her or John. She'd have assumed they were dead if her dad hadn't told her they lived in the Channel Islands.

'They were dull,' Fox said casually. 'They did the same things every day in the same way. Anne said her father talked about the news at breakfast and went to work at the same time. When he came home he'd drink two gin and tonics and talk about his work. Her mother talked about housework and whist drives. Anne was different. She wasn't like them and they didn't care who she really was.'

'What about the others?' Katherine tried to imagine her mother as a young girl growing up in Fell Scar, feeling neglected and ignored by her parents. 'Her friends? What were they like?'

'They were angry as well.' Fox smiled sideways at her reaction. 'But they showed it differently. Charlotte was clever, everyone knew it. She said her teachers hated her because she was more clever than they were and she didn't try to hide it.'

'And Emily?'

'She had to pretend to be happy,' Fox said. 'Her father was the doctor, he had a position to keep up. If Emily didn't look happy he'd beat her with a leather strap until she was sorry.'

Katherine let go of Fox's hand, turning to look at him with shock. His expression hadn't changed at all, his voice still as level as before.

'That's horrible,' she said, shuddering. 'Especially if he was a doctor.'

'Then it wouldn't matter as much if he wasn't?' Fox asked, with a curious expression.

'No, I didn't mean that,' Katherine said. 'Just . . . don't you care? That her father beat her?'

'Naturally I cared,' Fox said, still as calm as ever. 'But it was a long time ago. They stopped playing the make-believe game. They can't see us any more —or they chose not to.'

'My mother didn't choose to leave,' Katherine said angrily. 'She died. Don't you care about that either?'

'She left me,' Fox said levelly. 'Long before she died, she forgot me. If she'd cared to remember, or cared to stay, wouldn't she have?'

Katherine fell silent. The questions he asked went too close to the bone. Secretly she'd always wondered if there was something wrong with her, that if she'd been different perhaps Anne wouldn't have forgotten who she was, wouldn't have died. Her dad had said 'don't blame yourself' but who else was there for her to blame? Perhaps Katherine had really been as much of a disappointment to Anne as she was to her own parents.

Fox pointed ahead. The ground was levelling out again and ahead the trees didn't look as thickly clustered as they had lower down. She could see the sun setting through them, setting the sky on fire with crimson and gold flames.

'We're almost there,' Fox said softly. 'It's nearly time.'

'Time for what?' Katherine looked at him doubtfully. The shadows were closing in around him and she wondered again why he was helping her. Was it because of who her mother had been, or some other private reason of his own.

'Time for the ritual,' Fox said. 'They always came here for it. To Shystone Tarn.'

'The ritual . . . ' Kat remembered the book she'd found, the one she'd left behind in the house. It had described rituals with pens and paperknives, slaughtering books. 'I don't have a pen with me,' she said, thinking out loud. 'Or paper. I didn't have time to get my bag or anything.' For once Fox did look worried.

'You have to write it down!' he said, green eyes wide with alarm. 'Otherwise the blight won't know . . . '

'Write what down?' Katherine was frustrated by the way he never explained anything, even his answers to her questions were evasive, raising more questions still. 'Won't know what?'

'The *name*,' Fox said insistently. 'The name of your enemy. You have to give it to the blight. That's what it wants, it's an eater of names. That's where it gets its power and in return for a name it'll share the power with you.'

So there it was. Katherine felt the answers clicking into place. The words of the poem she'd read on the very first page of the notebook, the crossed out names in the novels, the rituals involving pens and paperknives, even Fox himself—it all made sense now.

'That's how they invented you,' she said. 'Anne and the others. It's about the power of belief, isn't it? Characters in books aren't real but reading and talking about them makes them seem as if they are . . . It makes them powerful—even if it's only in your head.'

She thought about the characters from her favourite books and the characters that people talked about at school and thought how strange it was that a fictional character could seem more real than the people you actually knew.

'They used that power,' she said. 'They crossed out the names and swore never to talk about those characters again. They sacrificed them just as if they were real people—that's what the poem means. They gave them to the name-eater and used the power to make you up instead.'

'That was the idea,' Fox agreed. 'Death for life. Or perhaps you could call it a deal with a devil.'

'They really did invent you . . . ' Katherine was awed, looking at Fox in a new light as if he'd just stepped out of the pages of the secret notebook. Something in the back of her mind suggested that he made an unlikely hero.

'But then they became frightened,' Fox said, his words ominous in the light of the sinking sun. 'The name-eater couldn't be stopped, only sated for a time. It's always hungry and it'll take any name it can get. It's been feeding from all of you since you got here. And if you don't give it what it wants somebody else will.'

'Catriona.' Katherine thought of her stepsister taking Delilah everywhere she went, the doll always smiling the same perfect smile. Catriona had been trying to steal her name since the first moment they'd met. She wouldn't hesitate to use any mean trick she could think of to put Katherine down, why would she stop at black magic?

It was black magic, Katherine was in no doubt about that. But for once in her life she'd been offered power, the power to do what *she* wanted. And her mother had given it to her; had invented Fox and the ritual. They were her inheritance. 'I don't need a pen,' she said. 'Find me a stick, or something sharp.'

'Allow me.' Fox stepped aside and there was quick rustle and a snapping noise. Then he moved back out of the shadows, holding a thin branch, broken at one end to form a jagged point. He bowed as he offered it to her and Katherine smiled. She could imagine him treating her mother the same way, carrying out her wishes with respect.

'Come on then,' she said. 'What are we waiting for?'

Catriona's feet slipped and slid over wet stones. The trees hemmed her in on either side as she scrambled upwards over boulders, worming her way between monoliths of rock. Moss tore beneath her fingers, wet from the trickle of water falling from somewhere higher up. Her hands were bruised now and she'd torn her jeans and scraped her leg painfully against a jagged edge of rock. But beneath her in the wood the drone of insects was accompanied by a crashing through the trees. Something large was coming her way and she'd no intention of waiting around for it to find her. The only way up was over the rocks and she forced herself to keep climbing, even as the light faded around her and the sunset turned the water red and yellow as it gushed past.

She couldn't have done it if she hadn't been half wild with fear. The further she climbed the wider and steeper the rivulet of water became so that she was pulling herself up one side of a stepped waterfall, splashing and pooling its way down the hill even as she climbed upwards. Behind her, bird calls suddenly rang out, screaming wails that reverberated across the wood, ringing from stone to stone as the trees rustled with sound. Putting on a last desperate burst of speed Catriona threw herself onwards, clawing her way up the steep trail.

Scrambling over the top of a jumble of huge rugged stones she finally crested the hill and saw a sheet of water ahead of her, burning with the light of the reflected sunset. It was a tarn, a hilltop lake. The wood surrounded it, leaving only a short expanse of dark moss as a shore. At the far end the tarn narrowed and the trees on either side slanted inwards, their branches reaching over the water to twin together into a matted tangle of darkness that merged with the wood behind. At the top of the waterfall a great stone lay across the other rocks, blocking the cascade. It was flat on top, black with lichen, the water lapping almost to the top.

Catriona came to a halt before the stone, stumbling over the smaller rocks as she turned to look back behind her. All around the wood formed a black sea, the lights of the house and the village lost somewhere in the swell of branches and twigs. Across the horizon loomed black shapes of hills, fuzzy edges with distant trees, or craggy with rocks. There was no sound other than the slow gurgle of the water trickling downhill. The insect swarm and the sounds of pursuit had vanished. She was alone.

Horror film visions flickered through her mind again. She'd been crazy to run into the woods. That was the last thing you should do. Everyone knew that when the hero and heroine left the town or the house or whatever, the monster would come for them. Hugging her arms around herself, Catriona looked up at the sky. The last embers of the sun were dimming now, red and gold fading to streaks of pink and orange as the sun dipped below the horizon. Soon it would be night—and not the safe street-lit night of her London suburb but the absolute black of night in the countryside.

Catriona had always thought she was a night person. She loved being out in the West End with her friends with twenty minutes to go until her curfew and no chance of making it in time. What did it matter if she'd run out of money for the night bus? There were always taxis and her mum kept emergency cab fare in the front hall just in case. Sometimes Catriona would stand with her mates outside the club for half an hour, letting the ringing of the music die back in her head, smoking cigarettes and flirting with the bouncers. But this was something else entirely.

A rustle from the wood had her heart leaping in her chest and she whirled, fists tightening defensively and then opening just as convulsively when one of them touched the hair still caught on her watch strap. Something was coming out of the wood.

It was Fox. For a moment she started to smile with relief, already framing a flirtatious comment in her head, something casual that would make it seem she was here by her own choice. But then she saw who was behind him.

'You?' Her gaze flew from Fox to his companion, with a sense of betrayal. 'What are *you* doing here?'

'Me?' Katherine smiled. A small mad smile, and Catriona's nerves tightened as she thought she'd never seen her stepsister look like this.

She looked half-crazed, her hair tangled around her face and her eyes shining lambently in the last of the light. In one hand she held a sharply pointed stick and she looked down at it, testing the point with her free hand as she added: 'I've come to cross you out.'

When the vampiries had swarmed, Roley had turned and run. His feet pounded against the earth, the torch beam swerving crazily from side to side as his arms pumped, bracken and twigs breaking and crashing all around him as he tried to evade the menacing drone of the hive.

Stupid, stupid, stupid. His thought rang inside his head like beats of a drum. He'd known something was alive in these woods, he'd known it was dangerous, he'd even been hunting for ghosts, and yet he'd come out here without anything to protect himself. *For Christ's sake*, he almost laughed at himself as he realized, *even his* mother *would have brought bug repellent.* He'd been trying to play the hero, that was what it was. Trying to impress Alice by showing off how brave he was, going out to rescue his sisters like a big stupid cowboy, and leaving her to mind the homestead. Well, what good was dumb muscle against a hive of fairy-wasps?

His lungs were burning with each quick gasp of air he took, drawn in as desperate rasps, gasped out as *oufs* of sound as he tripped or staggered on the treacherous ground. The light faltered and faded with every stride he took and he knew he couldn't keep running for long. The wood was slanting upwards and even on level ground he didn't have a hope of outrunning the swarm.

He tore himself through another thicket, wrenching free of the sharp twigs only to jar himself against a boulder and fall sideways, hands grasping for purchase against stones slimy with algae and mould. It wasn't falling so much as a sliding stumble that brought him to his knees and then his hands against a stinging gravel submersed in a puddle of stagnant water. The drone built angrily behind him and he rolled over to look back.

Then the livid sky was blotted out as all around him huge black bird-shapes erupted from the trees and shrieked their fury to the night. It was a flock of black-winged creatures with the bodies and faces of children and eyes rounded and blank. They screamed with human mouths but their voices were wordless bird calls.

Roley found himself standing with no recollection of how he'd managed it. Whether the bird-children were rescuing him or attacking the vampires for reasons of their own, he had no intention of waiting around to find out. He left at a run, forcing himself to breathe regularly, despite the noises behind him. Bird calls and the insect hum mingled and it sounded as if, for the time being, he was clear of the hive. As the ground slanted more steeply uphill he considered going back to the house but Catriona and Katherine were still out here somewhere—unless they'd come to their senses and gone back.

Roley slowed, and then stopped. As the crunching of leaves and his own breathing died down he realized the sound of conflict behind him was gone, replaced by an ominous silence. The sun had finally set and the patches of sky he could see through the densely clustered leaves were deep indigo. Reaching into his jacket, Roley pulled out his mobile phone and watched the screen light up. He only had one bar of signal and he watched it as he dialled the number, worried it would drop back entirely to the black line of no connection. The screen read *dialling* and then *ringing* for so long that he had almost given up when it finally switched to *connected* and he brought it to his ear.

'Hello?' a voice gasped suddenly into the phone. 'Fell Scar House?'

'Alice?' he said and there was another intake of breath and then the voice sharpened suspiciously.

'Yes, who is this?'

'It's Roley,' he said. 'I'm calling from the wood, I don't have much signal.'

'Oh, Roley, sorry, I thought you might be someone else. Did you find your . . . your sisters?'

'No, not yet. I was hoping they might have come back.'

He knew already they hadn't and when she confirmed it, he sighed, wondering if he should just turn round and come back.

'Look,' she said, 'John showed me the things you'd found. The book and the photographs. I don't know if you realize, but there are things in the wood . . . '

'Like the vampiries?' he said. 'Yes, I've met them. I don't

think there's any point pretending there's not something really weird going on here—however mad it sounds.'

'Maybe you should come back?' Alice suggested. 'It's not just the wood. There's . . . You're right, it sounds insane. But there's an army of dolls in the attic and I'm not sure what to do about them.'

'Hell.' Anything Roley could say seemed inadequate. 'Um . . . for what it's worth the bird-creatures might be on our side. I think they chased off the vampiries—which are most definitely unfriendly. Look, I don't see how I can come back. I'm sure Catriona came this way, and I don't think Katherine can have gone to the village. If she had our parents would have come back by now—or phoned or something.'

'What should I say to your parents if they get back before you do?' Alice asked. 'It's getting late.'

'You can tell them the girls had a big fight,' Roley said. 'That's true enough. But anything about doll armies and vampires and they'll think you've lost it. That or we've been re-enacting *The Blair Witch Project* or something.'

'I can try talking to my parents,' Alice said slowly. 'I think they're involved in this. My mother's name is in that book and she's in the photographs as well. With Charlotte and Anne.'

'OK, look, I'll just stay another half hour,' Roley said. 'There's a lake at the top of the hill and from up there I might be able to see something. And if the vampiries come back I can always jump in the lake.'

'Don't stay too long,' Alice said. 'I don't know what good it does to say the creatures aren't real. But they're not. They're part of this make-believe game that's written in the book.'

'They seem very real,' Roley said. 'I think they're a kind of ghost. Perhaps they can be exorcized . . . '

'That's a job for a priest,' Alice said. 'Don't stay out too long, please. Your brother's worried about you.'

'Tell him I'll be careful,' Roley said. 'And you be careful too.'

'I will.'

There was an awkward silence and then the line went dead. Roley put the phone in his jacket and began to walk up hill.

Katherine took another step forward and smiled as Catriona took one back. Her stepsister had moved on to the lichen-covered flat stone at the edge of the lake and if she moved any further back she'd be into the water.

'You're crazy,' Catriona said, her face pale and her eyes very wide as she stared at them.

'Perhaps I am,' Katherine said. 'You've tried hard enough to make me think so, haven't you?'

'I don't know what you mean.' Catriona shook her head. 'It's not my fault you've lost it.'

'I haven't lost anything!' Katherine said, her voice rising angrily. 'Everything I have you steal . . . My father, my family, my *name*.'

'It was my name first,' Catriona said instantly. 'I'm older. And besides—'

'SHUT UP!' Katherine screamed. 'I'm sick of hearing it. I'm sick of you and your lies and your manipulations and everything about you.' Her grip tightened on the stick and she lunged forward, feeling a sense of power as her stepsister cringed away, crouching down at the very edge of the stone with her hands raised to protect herself.

'Fox?' Catriona's voice was a pathetic whimper. 'Why are you helping her? I thought you liked me . . .'

'You were wrong,' Fox said. 'Katherine, we don't have much time.'

Katherine raised the stick, but before she could use it, she heard a noise behind her and Fox said warningly, 'Delilah.'

'What?' Katherine turned to look behind her. Across the jumble of rocks at the top of the waterfall were the drones. They were perfectly still, standing or sitting on the rocks. Hands and arms used to brace themselves as if someone had carefully arranged them there. In the middle, her hair trailing on the ground, was Delilah.

'What's she doing here?' Katherine murmured to Fox and the boy frowned.

'She wants something,' Fox said. 'I don't know what.'

'I do.'

Katherine turned to see Catriona had inched back from the edge. She was fiddling with something, clawing at her own wrist. The tears had dried on her face and for once she didn't look immaculate and untouchable. Her clothes were grimy and torn and her hair a tangled mess.

'I know what Delilah wants,' she said savagely. 'And if you don't back off I'm going to give it to her!'

Frightened, Katherine glanced back at the dolls and froze when she saw they'd moved closer. They were almost to the flat rock now.

'Delilah can't move while you're watching her,' Fox said softly. 'But when you look away . . . '

'Then I don't have much time.'

Moving so she could see the dolls Katherine took the stick and gouged it into the lichen on the top of the flat rock, scraping out the shapes of letters: C A T R I O N A. Catriona's frenzied fingers stopped tugging at her wrist as she watched the movements of the stick as if it were a snake.

'What are you *doing*?' she asked, her voice a frightened whisper.

'You'll see.' Katherine took ... p breath and began to speak the words of the poem. 'Names crossed out cannot be spoken—a character dead is a story broken. Every sacrifice must cost, you can't recover what's been lost.' Her voice shook as she spoke and she wondered if it would matter. She knew what she was doing was wrong, but didn't Catriona deserve it?

There was a scraping noise behind her and Katherine flicked her eyes that way to see that at her end of the rock Catriona was tearing at the lichen with broken fingernails. In her free hand she held something like a friendship bracelet, a circle of light brown hair.

'Hurry up!' Fox warned and Katherine turned back to see Delilah was at the edge of the rock now, her hands stretched out and reaching.

'Stolen words must be spent; borrowed power can't be lent,' Katherine said quickly. 'The name-eater must be fed . . . by the living . . . ' As she spoke she bent one final time and stabbed the stick into the ground in front of the first letter.

'Delilah! Catch!' Catriona threw the loop of hair like a lasso and Fox made a sound like a snarl as it caught on one of the doll's outstretched hands.

'. . . or the dead!' Katherine spoke the final line of the poem like a curse and sliced the stick across her stepsister's name. Then, like an echo, she heard the sound of tearing moss and looked to see Catriona's fingernails complete their own sweep across another name, written in jagged uneven letters on the rock: K̶A̶T̶H̶E̶R̶I̶N̶E̶.

Her heart thumped hard in her body and she swayed, the letters blurring before her, and she wondered if she was going to faint. At the end of the rock Catriona was a huddled dark shape, shaking convulsively as if she was having a fit. Above them the sky was indigo black and the tarn a flat mirror of the darkness, even the riffled waves stilled into a glassy smoothness.

'It comes,' Fox whispered. Even Delilah was still now, she'd got both hands on the loop of hair while Katherine wasn't looking and the drones had moved up to surround her.

'What will it do?' Katherine whispered, wondering too late if it would make any difference that she wasn't fictional, hoping that might protect her name from the fate she'd wished on her stepsister.

'It devours . . . ' Fox said. He was moving away from the shore; stepping carefully around the dolls, as fastidiously as a cat walking across a crowded mantelpiece.

'But what about me?' Katherine pleaded, like an echo of Catriona's earlier question. 'I thought you cared about me?' She knew before he said it how he would answer.

'You were wrong.'

Then, from the trees around them, birds began to scream. No, not birds, the Rookery. Like children in a playground they had gathered in the trees above them, clinging with human hands to the branches, their naked bodies half hidden by the sweep of huge black wings. Their mouths opened, jeering wordlessly, and Katherine realized she was shaking only when she could no longer stand; her legs folded beneath her and she collapsed on the rock. Catriona raised her head, still trembling violently, and opened her mouth to speak. But then her lips drew back, exposing her white teeth as she *hissed*.

Katherine's skin seemed to tighten all over her body at once, like pins and needles and cramp all together. It felt as if she was being stabbed by tiny invisible swords and she heard herself make a sound like a snarl and she fell on her side against the hard rock, lying over her stepsister's mutilated name. She clawed at the ground, not even thinking, too caught in knots of agony, sensing rather than seeing Catriona thrashing around beside her. For one last moment she saw the names beneath her, crossed and sliced with savage lines.

There was a splash and a cry and even as Katherine registered the sound her body contracted with cramp, and she twisted and fell. Icy water closed over her head and she sank into blackness and knew nothing more.

16
Deep Water

Roley heard the birds calling as he reached the top of the hill and slowed down, wondering how they'd got ahead of him. But in the darkness of the night above, it wasn't that unlikely they might have circled around silently. He smiled grimly to himself. It seemed that no matter how strange things had got he still needed to explain things.

He reminded himself of that as he approached the edge of the trees and looked out across a dark open space. It was the tarn at the top of the hill. But if he hadn't known it was there he might not have spotted it. The sky was dark enough now that the sheet of water was a black void ahead. The trees grew around and even over it, stretching across the water to cut out even more of the sky. The bird calls had ended and nothing moved. He played the torch across the water, seeing it shine like wet tarmac. There was something moving on the other side of the lake. He heard splashing even though here the water seemed still.

'Catriona?' he called. 'Cat? Is that you?' Silence answered him and he began to make his way around the lake, listening intently. The splashing noise wasn't repeated but little ruffles of waves disturbed the smooth surface of the lake now, coming towards him and away from whatever the disturbance had been.

'Katherine?' he tried, just in case. And then, uncertainly: 'Kat? Are you here?' Again, no answer.

With a sigh he gave it up, skirting the lake until he reached the point he judged the sound had come from. There was a wide flat rock lying half in and half out of the water and, as he got closer, he could see that the mossy lichen that covered it had been torn up. Torn in what looked like patterns or letters. Narrowing the torch beam he studied them, frowning. There were two names written on the rock, both crossed out.

'CATRIONA!' Roley shouted loudly this time, hearing his shout ring out across the lake. 'KATHERINE!' He took a deep breath. 'Please come back! It's dangerous out here!' His voice cracked on 'dangerous', and he listened to the night. No answer but the lapping of the water.

He opened his mouth again to shout and heard a sudden splash and turned sharply towards it, his torch catching a glimpse of something dark and animal erupting out of the tarn and scattering droplets of water as it made for the trees. The splashing noise continued and as the first creature raced out of the torchlight another moved through it. Slick fur gleaming wetly, wild animal eyes reflecting the light for an instant before it too disappeared into the dark. Otters perhaps? Maybe his shouting had disturbed them.

They were gone before he had time to move and Roley was left at the edge of the lake, the torch swinging backwards and forwards across the black water. He couldn't escape the feeling that he was on the brink of the mystery. Just five minutes sooner and he might have caught up with the girls, found out why they'd crossed out their names and where they'd gone afterwards—or stopped them from leaving.

He should go back. There was nothing here. But still he hesitated. And as the last of the ripples died away and the water smoothed over again he saw two white shapes floating out of the blackness.

'Of course.' Roley grinned with sheer relief. What he needed were witnesses who'd seen whatever had happened here. He'd had to travel through the wood alone—nothing there for the twin reflections to use. But now, when he needed them most, Mirror and Glass had appeared.

Here, in the water, they appeared quite differently from on the flat planes of glass and mirrors in the house, or from when he'd first seen them over the side of the boat. Here they looked as if they were underwater swimmers in the black tarn. The girl was floating on her back, her drifting hair like seaweed fanning around her head as she gazed up at him, white clothes clinging to her body as if they were really wet. The boy looked as if he was holding on to the rocky edge of the tarn, head turned up to look at Roley as the rest of his body was lost further down in the blackness.

'Did you see what happened?' Roley asked, kneeling down on the edge of the stone. 'Did you see Catriona or Katherine?'

Yes. The girl shaped the word carefully and nodded. The boy nodded as well, counting off on his fingers. *Yes, both.*

'When? Just now? What happened?' Roley leaned forward eagerly and was disappointed when the two reflections shrugged in unison. Perhaps that had been too many questions at once. 'Are they still here?'

No. They seemed definite about it.

'Are they OK?'

Yes. No. Shrug. They were undecided and Roley was not reassured.

'What happened?'

The reflections looked at each other and then, while the boy remained still at the edge of the rock, the girl shifted in the water and stretched out a hand. It took Roley a moment to realize that she was pretending to write, with her forefinger, on the under surface of the water then sliced her finger across where the word had been and looked at her twin.

He mimicked her action of writing and her slash at the space where the word had been and they both turned back to Roley, gesturing that the pantomime had ended.

'They crossed out their names.' Roley looked again at the torn lichen, scarred and crossed with lines and claw-marks. 'But why? Why did they do it? Where did they go?'

The reflective twins hesitated and then leaned closer with renewed enthusiasm, coming right up to the water's edge.

Come here. They beckoned together, so there could be no mistake. *Here. In the water. Come in.*

'You must be kidding. In there? I'll get hypothermia!'

Idiot. Coward. Their gazes were equally despising. *Goodbye.* They were sinking down in the water and Roley called out quickly:

'Wait!' He stared down at their faces. 'Please, wait. Just tell me why. How will it help?'

Sigh. They rolled their eyes, and then surged up towards the surface again to stage a pantomime charade. Mirror spoke silently, gesticulating, explaining something as Glass

221

watched with exaggerated incomprehension—his face a parody of dimwittedness. Then Glass dived away from the rock, somersaulting in the water and coming up next to his twin. They clasped hands and Mirror spoke again. This time Glass nodded along, acting enlightenment, and speaking silently back.

'If I come in, I'll be able to understand you? You'll show me what happened?' Roley wasn't sure about this idea. The twins had certainly been helpful so far but the water looked very cold and black.

Wait. Glass raised a hand in warning. *First . . .* He pantomimed writing again and then struck a hand across the word.

Roley looked down at the stone again and the crossed-out names. The girls had crossed out their names and gone— somewhere. Now Mirror and Glass were suggesting he do the same. They were waiting, and not patiently either, swirling around in the tarn like ghosts, white shapes lost in the black water.

'Wait,' he said again. 'Let me think.' He took the phone from his pocket and looked at it. No signal. He was already later than he'd promised to be. John would be worrying, maybe Alice too. The longer he hesitated the further away the reflections moved. What they were suggesting sounded dangerous. On the plus side, he *could* swim. And what did it really matter if he wrote his name down and crossed it out? It wasn't as if he was that attached to his name anyway. Suddenly Roley wondered if that was the solution. Names had torn their family apart, cross out the names and what did you get?

Roley stood on the brink of the tarn. He could still turn back. But if he did he'd be a coward, abandoning his sisters because he was too afraid to find out the truth. To hesitate now might be the mistake that finally split their fragmented family apart.

'All right,' he said, hearing himself make the decision. 'OK, I'll do it.'

The reflections moved back towards him, swirling around and about beneath the flat surface of the lake. They waited, watching him with water-coloured eyes in which he could read nothing.

'Just a minute.' The lichen was too torn for any words to be written there. Instead, Roley fumbled in his jacket pockets, finding a piece of paper with an old shopping list written on one side and a chewed biro. Testing the biro he scribbled at the bottom of the list to make it run, holding the torch awkwardly to light the paper.

Impatience. Mirror and Glass were waiting at the water's edge, beckoning him in. Roley wanted to trust them although the idea of the crossed-out names disturbed him Still, he couldn't escape the feeling he was running out of time. The girls might be getting further and further away every second he delayed—and the twin reflections had helped him once before.

His hand moved across the paper, writing ROLEY in careful capitals. It wasn't as if he cared about his name. It was one he'd grown to despise and with it the image it conjured of someone who was dim-witted, overweight, and slow.

'Here goes nothing,' Roley muttered and put the paper down at the edge of the rock, weighting it with the torch.

Then, with the biro, he drew a straight black line through the name on the page.

He had a sense of finality, a decision made for better or worse. But nothing else happened and he realized he'd been tensed up for some drama. But at the edge of the water, Mirror and Glass reached up to him, the girl with her right hand, the boy with his left; fingertips brushing the surface from beneath. It was hard to tell with the torch on the ground but perhaps the smooth surface of the water had rippled a bit, as if they were reaching *through* the barrier. Bending down over the edge of the rock, Roley leaned forward and thrust both his hands into the water.

It was ice cold. He flinched with the shock of it and then, impossibly, felt his hands clasped and held. He saw for an instant his own, wide-eyed reflection between the boy and the girl. Then the hands on his tightened and *pulled*, and he overbalanced on the stone, falling head first into the black water.

Something awful had happened. John knew it for certain, even if he couldn't have explained why. As the others had disappeared into the darkness he'd felt a sense of dread. Ever since the sun had set he'd felt a bone-deep certainty that the darkness had swallowed them entirely.

After the phone call from Roley Alice had suggested they move to the kitchen where they'd be able to hear the telephone better if it rang again. She'd tried Roley's line twice but there was no reply. She'd made a pot of tea, giving John his with extra sugar, for energy, she said, since neither of them had eaten anything. She stirred the teaspoon round and round in the brown liquid, staring into the middle distance, her grey eyes troubled. John watched the whirlpool swirling in her cup and wondered if she liked Roley. If she did that was good—but it made it harder to tell her the truth.

'I don't think Roley's coming back,' he said quietly.

'You don't?' Alice dropped the spoon and it disappeared beneath the surface of the tea. She looked at her watch and said uncertainly, 'He's been gone longer than he said he would be but . . . '

'I don't think he can come back,' John tried again. 'I think something happened. Something bad.'

'You're sure?' Alice looked gravely at John and then nodded herself. 'Yes, you are.'

'I'm sorry,' John said. Even though he was sorry, he was pleased at the way Alice didn't question him. Sometimes it seemed as if people didn't listen when he told them things. Katherine said that no one ever listened to children but even she didn't always pay attention. John thought it was because people heard what they expected to hear, not what you actually said.

Standing up, Alice crossed to the telephone extension on the kitchen counter. Her expression was serious as she picked up the phonebook next to it and looked up a number. It wasn't until she'd found it that she looked back at him.

'I'm going to call the police,' she said.

'What for?' He was surprised. 'They won't be able to help. Not against people who don't really exist.'

'Maybe not,' Alice said. 'But I'm not going to tell them about that. Roley said not to tell your parents either. What do you think? Will they believe us if we tell them what we think has happened?'

'No,' John said. 'Harriet will be too cross and frightened to listen. And Daddy will try to listen but he won't understand.'

'That's what I think too,' Alice said. 'And, John, one of the reasons I'm calling the police is so your parents don't blame me. They don't know me, you see. I don't want them to think I was to blame somehow for all this. Even if the police can't help, it looks better to call them.'

John nodded. As Alice dialled the number he took a sip of the lukewarm tea, hearing the spoon clink in the bottom like sunken treasure. In an emergency you were supposed to dial 999. Katherine had taught him that when he was still very little. But Alice had called another number and as it rang, told him she was calling the local police station.

'That's where they'd send someone from,' she said. 'And remember we don't *know* anything awful's happened . . . '

'I do,' John began but Alice waved him silent.

' . . . hello,' she was saying. 'I need to report some missing people. Yes, I'll hold.' There was a pause and then she continued, 'My name's Alice Wheeler. I live in Stirkley village and I'm calling from Fell Scar House, a holiday home in the north of the village next to Blyght Wood . . . Yes, that's right, three missing people. A friend of mine and his two sisters . . . Just a minute . . . ' She turned to John. 'How old are they, John?'

'Roley's sixteen, Catriona's fifteen, and Katherine's thirteen,' John told her and listened as she relayed the information to the police person on the other end of the line.

'The two girls had an argument and they both ran away from the house about two and a half hours ago,' Alice continued. 'Their brother went out to find them, taking his mobile phone. He called about an hour ago to say that he'd found no sign of them and he was going to come back to the house. Since then I haven't heard from him and his phone goes straight to voicemail. I know it's early to report them as missing but their parents aren't here and seeing as they all went into the wood . . . '

There was another pause and Alice filled the gap by taking a pen from a pot near the phone and scribbling down the times she'd told the police and passing it to John.

'Does that look right to you?' she said and he nodded. 'Good, it's important to get the times right . . . yes, officer, I'm here.' She nodded along as the voice spoke tinnily and then said: 'Yes, I'm sure that's true but it's bad ground up towards Shystone tarn. No, I'm here with the youngest of the family he's . . . '

'Ten,' John supplied. 'And three quarters.'

'He's ten, Roley asked me to look after him . . . The parents are out. No, I live locally. I only met the family this week . . . Wheeler, Alice Wheeler. Twenty-seven Mill Road, Stirkley. Oh, would you? Thank you so much. It's Fell Scar, on the slopes of the fell.' She began giving directions, ones that were a lot better than the ones the family had been sent. When she finally hung up the phone she turned back to John and said, 'They're sending someone. I think they're taking it seriously, thank goodness.'

'Should I tell them about the fight?' John said. 'The cat fight?'

'Yes,' Alice said. 'Tell them everything that happened since your parents left. But . . . ' She hesitated. 'I'm not sure about the evidence table. If the police see it they might, I don't know . . . They might think we were up to something occult.'

'No,' John said. 'They won't even look in the barn, will they? And if they do it's just old books and photographs. I can say they're things that belonged to my mother, if they ask. But I don't think they'll ask.'

'You're right,' Alice nodded. 'At least, not until they've searched the woods. But if they don't find anything . . . ' She sighed. 'I guess we cross that bridge when we come to it.'

The police came quickly. Alice had said they would and she was right. It was a man and a woman, both smiling and friendly and saying this was just routine. But underneath they were worried and the first question they asked was if Alice was sure Roley and the girls had gone into the wood.

'Quite sure,' Alice said. 'Roley called from the wood and he said he thought Catriona had gone that way, didn't he, John?'

'She did go that way,' John said. 'Katherine ran off towards the village and Catriona left just seconds after. She wouldn't have gone the same way and she didn't. I saw her go round the side of the house towards the path that leads into the woods.'

'And what was this fight about?' the policeman asked, kneeling down to look John in the eye.

'I think it was about a lot of things,' John said honestly. 'Catriona and Katherine don't like each other very much, you see. But none of us saw it start. When we came in they were fighting on the ground.' He pointed to the place.

'John threw water over them,' Alice added. 'I think the carpet's still a bit damp.'

It was while the police were inspecting the carpet thoughtfully that John heard the crunch of another car on the gravel. The front door was still open, left that way by the police, and he saw their family car come to an abrupt halt. Harriet had opened the passenger door before it even stopped moving and came running towards the stairs. In the circle of light from the house John could see her face was a white mask of fear.

She didn't even seem to see him at first, her eyes tracking towards the police constables. But when she did she reached out, putting an arm around his shoulder protectively as she faced the police.

'What's happened? What's going on?'

'No need to worry yet, madam,' the policeman said smoothly. 'It seems a few of the young people here haven't come back yet from an excursion. Why don't you have a seat and we'll get you up to speed?'

'Who's missing?' Peter had come to join them and he too reached out to touch John's shoulder, as if touch was the only way he could reassure himself of his son's presence. He frowned at Alice. 'What's been going on here?'

'The young lady called us,' the policewoman said. 'Perhaps she can tell you what she told us?'

Alice began her explanation of the fight, Roley leaving and his later phone call; John saw the adults' faces tighten as if they were waiting for worse revelations to follow. When she finished they looked almost relieved.

'Well,' Peter said cautiously. 'It sounds like a bad argument but I'm not sure we should be worrying quite yet.'

'That's my opinion too,' the policeman said. 'What we'll do, if that's all right with you, is to have a look around and see if we can spot any of the young people.'

'And if you can't find them?' Harriet asked, sharply. 'What happens then?'

'Well, let's not get ahead of ourselves,' the policewoman replied. 'It's very likely they'll come back of their own accord. Now, if we can just check their descriptions with you, we'll be able to start looking.'

The adults had found photographs of the three missing teenagers. The one of Roley wasn't very good, his eyes were squinted up against the sunshine of the photographed day and he looked much fatter than he was now. Catriona smiled sweetly at the camera posing in a white tennis dress, teeth gleaming like a toothpaste advert. Katherine by contrast was on the edge of her own photo, scowling at the lens and hiding behind her hair.

Taking the photographs carefully, the policewoman suggested that she and her colleague give Alice a lift back home. Harriet frowned, as if she was only just now beginning to wonder who Alice was and what she was doing there.

'Thank you for looking after me, Alice,' John said quickly. 'Um . . . perhaps you should leave your number in case we need to call you?'

'OK.' Alice nodded. 'Let me know if anything happens, OK?'

'Bye,' Peter said distractedly. 'Thanks for helping out.'

John watched as Alice and the police left. He was relieved she'd been offered a lift. Even just the short walk to the village seemed dangerous when it was through the night. But it wasn't so safe inside the house either. Looking across the gravel drive, John saw the pattern of yellow rectangles, light from the windows laid out across the lawn, separated by a cage of black bars. The police car moved from shadow to light to shadow, barred alternately with black and gold, and vanished into the night.

Alice sat in the back of the police car, watching the hedges slip by in a blur of darkness. Halfway through the journey it had started to rain and the police constables murmured quietly to each other, their voices low and concerned. She guessed they were worried about looking for the missing teenagers in the worsening weather. The woman peered through the dripping windscreen, wipers sweeping back and forth showering arcs of spray, while the man radioed the station, calling in the description of Roley, Catriona, and Katherine. At least they were taking it seriously, Alice thought, although she was afraid John had been right when he'd said police couldn't help.

The lights of the houses in the village seemed weak and watery through the rain and it wasn't until the police car pulled up outside number 27 she realized her own house was dark. The police glanced at each other.

'Your folks not in, love?' the man asked.

'I suppose not,' Alice said, hearing water gushing through the gutters as the car engine sound stopped. 'They took the dog to the vet.' She tried to remember what Emily and Charlotte had said when they'd left. She'd been half-dazed at the time, not taking the information in properly. 'I think they were going to visit friends in Bowness while they were out.'

'We could come in with you,' the policewoman said and Alice shook her head.

'No, I'll be fine,' she said. 'You need to look for Roley and the girls. I'm fine. I have a key. I'm sure my parents will be back soon.'

'If you're sure.'

Alice got out of the car and swung the door shut with a thump, dashing across the pavement and jiggling the tricky latch of the gate and hunching her shoulders against the rain. The police car waited as she hurried up the path, and when she'd unlocked the door she turned and waved and saw a blurred hand raised behind the windscreen.

Turning the hall light on, she shut the door slowly, watching the tail-lights of the police car vanish into the night. There was no sign of life in the house, and it took Alice a moment to remember the answerphone; bought by Charlotte so she could call-screen tricky calls from editors about deadlines. Its little light was blinking softly from across the dark kitchen and Alice went to it and pressed the button, hearing Charlotte's voice crackle from the speaker.

'Alice, it's Charlotte calling at six. I'll try again later. We've been held up at the vet's; nothing serious but Baskerville does need a few stitches and they're short-staffed

232

here. Give me a call on my mobile when you get back.' The message cut off with a click and the machine whirred to itself before producing the next message.

'Alice, it's Emily. We're finished at the vet, Baskerville's going to be fine. It's . . . um . . . seven-ish now. We're going to stop for some dinner and then come on home. You can reach us on Charlotte's mobile.'

The machine whirred again and the next message was shorter.

'Alice, Charlotte again, calling at eight. I hope this damned thing's not broken. We're held up in traffic and won't be back before dark now. Please call me when you get this message.'

The machine clunked to a stop and Alice left it as it was, resisting the urge to play back the tape just to hear another human voice. She thought they'd sounded worried and wondered how she could explain to them they were right to be. She'd not even thought to call home herself, too focused on the revelations in Fell Scar. She'd come home expecting to confront them, intending to demand an explanation.

Her hand hesitated over the receiver of the phone. She should call, she knew. They'd obviously been expecting her to call for the past hour or more. But explanations of where she'd been would lead to those questions she wanted to ask in person. A blatter of rain at the window made her jump with a sudden fright and realize she was still standing in the dark. She felt for the switch and as the kitchen was flooded with light the windows turned black and she pulled the curtains across them hastily, trying to shut out the drumming of the rain.

Her hand stilled with the curtain half across the window. Had something moved in the back garden? She thought for a second she'd seen the light glisten oddly, reflecting back from the darkness as sharp pinpoints. She stood there, tensed for the slightest sound, and heard the hiss of the rain and gurgling gutters, a rattle of slates on the roof. The rattle came again and a scraping sound; wind whistled in the kitchen chimney and brought with it the voice of birds.

A flash of white in the corner of her vision and Alice turned her head quickly and saw a face pressed up to the window. A child's face, blank of any intention, head cocked sideways and black bird-eyes watching her. Her heart thumped alarmingly and she pressed a fist to her chest, forcing herself to breathe. As quickly as it had appeared the rook-child vanished but now she could clearly hear movement above on the roof, thumping and scrabbling sounds, impossible to ignore.

Roley had said the Rookery might be on their side. And Fox claimed to have sent them to rescue her from the Knarl. But she wasn't inclined to take anything on trust. She glanced at the phone, considering calling the police. They might not believe her about the Rookery but they would probably send someone if she said she was afraid to wait alone in the house after all. Or she could call Emily and Charlotte, tell them she was being followed by the make-believe creatures they'd invented, and ask them for help. But she couldn't imagine doing that; couldn't imagine how they'd respond.

Alice walked slowly across the room and opened the door to the attached greenhouse, the smell of earth and plants surrounding her. The rain was drumming heavily on the plastic roof and coating the windows with a second liquid pane. There was no light in here, the whole room was a Perspex bubble attached to the side of the house and with her night vision gradually returning Alice craned her neck to look up through the curtain of rain.

The roof of number 27 was covered with black bird-shapes, perched like gargoyles around the chimneys and gutters. Between the darkness and the rain Alice couldn't tell how many of them there were, only that she was sur-rounded. They'd helped her before, but now the watching shapes seemed menacing in the stormy night. At the far end of the greenhouse the external door rattled in its hinges, blasted by a sudden squall of rain, and she felt sud-denly fragile in her clear bubble, only separated by the thin plastic windows from the violence of the storm.

It really was a storm now. Thunder was crunching in the distance, drowned out by the wind-whipped rain against the sides of the house. There was nothing to suggest the weather was anything but natural, nothing but her own growing superstition and her fear for Roley and his sisters, and Emily and Charlotte, all beyond the fragile protection of even these thin walls. The roof frame shook, rain bouncing off it like hail with the sheer force with which it was falling, and a sweep of black feathers passed by outside the window. Then, abruptly, the curtain of darkness was torn aside by a bright crack of lightning right overhead. The garden was lit up in sudden white light and as Alice blinked instinctively she was left with the impression of a dark figure burned on to her retina, standing in the middle of the wet grass.

Forcing her eyes open again she stared out into the night once more, the plastic walls cold and shaking beneath her clammy hands as the shadow strode out of the darkness and resolved into shape on the other side of the window.

'Alice,' he said, his mouth moving silently. His fur coat was drenched and his hair a dripping mass from which water ran across his face. Circling around the greenhouse he moved towards the back door and, as he put his hand on the handle, Alice realized that the bolts were drawn, rattled out of their housing by the shaking of the A-frame.

The door opened, framing Fox in hissing streaks of silver as the rain lit the darkness with slivers and shards of broken light.

'What are you doing here?' Alice demanded, looking left and right for any sign of a weapon, spotting pruning shears and weeding forks, all out of reach.

'Alice,' he said again softly. 'You don't need to be afraid of me. I've come to protect you.' And in three long strides he crossed the distance between them to take her in his arms.

17

Shadows Beneath the Skin

Roley started to panic when he felt the waters close over his head. He hadn't had time to take a breath and he'd closed his eyes instinctively when the reflections pulled him into the tarn. Their grip on his wrists hadn't lessened as they dragged him further down. The water was freezing, enclosing his body in an icy cage and driving a cold spike into his head. Behind his eyelids, squeezed tightly shut, the blurred blackness was sparkled with gold: the flashing lights of a migraine headache.

Still they dragged him down. His lungs were burning now with the desperate need to breathe. The water seemed to be solidifying like treacle, so that he could barely move, only let himself be drawn ever further down into unfathomable depths. His head pounded, pressure building between his temples; his chest compressed by a tight band of pain; light and dark strobing behind his eyes. His mouth gasped open, and he felt coldness rushing in and down his throat into his lungs, ice water streaming through his veins. His eyes opened wide and he was surrounded by white light.

He gasped again and felt the sting of it. It wasn't air or water he was breathing but something cool and liquid. He was no longer falling, he was standing and the sensation of ground beneath his feet made him dizzy with confusion as he turned in a slow circle, staring into the bright emptiness.

He stood on a smooth sheet of mirrored glass. Beneath his feet blurred images shifted and swirled in a chaos of colour and light that made his eyes ache to watch it. Above him and around him sheets of the same substance glittered from the edges of the expanse, reflecting shards and slices of images back and forth across an impossibility of planes and angles. He could see himself in the reflections, his body chopped up into sections, waved into immensity and vanishing into smallness all at once, as if in a carnival hall of mirrors. Curiously that comparison calmed him, even as a thin wail of sound escaped from his mouth. After all, where else would reflections live but in a world of fragmented images?

They were there, of course, although he hadn't seen them before looking for them. Here in the carnival funhouse of their reflection world, they were more real than he'd ever seen them in windows and picture frames. Their white clothes were skin-tight, their feet encased in white boots on metal blades that it took him a moment to identify as ice skates. He realized it only when they moved, gripping him by the wrists and spinning him with them as they skated over the glassy surface of the bright ground.

The grip on his wrists slackened and he staggered around in another rotation before finding his feet again and coming to a halt. Mirror and Glass still circled him but from further away. Streaks of silver followed their skating feet across the glass ballroom floor like vapour trails, fading back into the mirrored surface and vanishing there. They spun and turned and flipped like acrobats—each mirroring the other's movements with liquid ease. And all around them more reflections in the walls, in the floor, in the shining sky flipped and turned and spun, in an infinite series of echoes vanishing into the distance.

Roley took another breath that burned with cold and shouted, hearing his own voice ring back and forth across the ice.

'STOP IT!' His head thrummed with reverberations and he was forced to drop his voice to a whisper to ease the pain. 'You said you'd speak to me.'

'*You said you'd speak, you said you'd speak, you said you'd speak, speak, speak, speak . . .* ' It wasn't an echo. The voice was cool and thin, brittle like ice, liquid like water, falling into his ears like a jangle of broken glass or a glissando of cymbals.

'That *hurts*.' Roley clamped his hands over his ears. 'Can't you talk sense?'

'*Talk sense, can't that hurts, sense hurts, can't talk, talk sense, hurts, hurts, hurts.*' The crystal voice rang mockingly from the walls and floor and ceiling of the mirror world and Roley glared uselessly at his tormentors, covering his ears with his hands as he tried to block out the sound that jangled through his head.

Ice sliced and scraped as the figures swooped in towards him. Words jangled through his mind, repeating and recurring, meaning and sense jumbled into an inanity. He couldn't feel the surface beneath his feet and as he realized that he was falling again, through the spinning images into the liquid glass of the mirror world.

* * *

The tortoiseshell cat spat at the policewoman from the corner of the bus shelter, hackles rising and tail fluffing up to twice its natural size. Its eyes reflected the light of her torch as she swept the beam around the small concrete box and turned to look back at her colleague.

'Nothing in here but a stray cat,' she said and he nodded, hunching his shoulders against the squalls of water blown in by the wind.

'Tortie, isn't it,' he said glancing at the hissing animal with a passing interest. 'They've got a mean streak in them. Female equivalent of gingers, so my sister-in-law says.'

The cat wasn't collared and it was skinny enough for a stray; the thick coat disguised its size and matted into clumps where the wet fur was plastered with mud. It glared at them as if prepared to protect this pathetic shelter against all comers, eyes wide and pupils dilated.

'I'm a dog person myself,' the policewoman replied. 'That's the last of the local hangouts anyway, not that any kid with sense is going to be out on a night like this.'

'And since when did kids have any sense?' her colleague said, peering out through the rain. 'Reckon we're wasting our time here. Search and rescue's been called out to search the woods. They'll be the ones to find those kids, one way or another.'

The policewoman nodded, pulling the hood of her mac up as she followed her partner back to the car. Inside, they could hear the rain beat an unrelenting tattoo on the metal roof.

'They'll have their work cut out for them,' she said. 'Filthy weather for finding one missing kid, let alone three. You've got to feel sorry for the parents.'

'Reckon this is one holiday they'll try to forget,' her colleague agreed.

'That's if we find them.' The policewoman frowned. 'Otherwise they'll be remembering it for ever, won't they?' She reached out and turned the engine on.

For an instant after turning the headlights on the police-woman saw the cat staring out of the shelter, then the engine startled it into flight. As the car pulled away it streaked back into the shadows.

John had allowed his father to put him to bed. He didn't see much point to it when surely Peter knew that he wouldn't be able to sleep. But after the second visit of the police neither of the adults seemed to know what to do with themselves.

Harriet had let herself be cross while the police were out searching. She'd criticized Peter for not questioning Alice further and then demanded John tell her every last detail of what had happened while they were out. He'd been worried about how to describe their research in the barn but he hadn't even got that far. Recounting the fight again had started an argument.

'Roley's completely irresponsible, letting them run off like that,' Harriet had said irritably. 'And leaving John with some popsy he only met today.'

'Alice seemed like a sensible girl,' Peter had argued.

'And I don't think we can blame Roley for the girls running off. I just wish they'd come to us. Katherine's usually so sensible.'

'I haven't seen much sign of it,' Harriet contradicted. 'If she didn't always rise to Cat's snipes.'

'My Kat's a gentle soul,' Peter said angrily. 'She takes things to heart. Catriona's been making her life a misery ever since they first met. Ours too, if you're honest . . . '

'If you want my honest opinion,' Harriet began dangerously but then she'd remembered John still sitting there.

Up in his bedroom he waited until Peter was gone before turning on his torch and taking the book from beneath his pillow. He'd gone back to the barn to get it when he was supposed to be brushing his teeth. He'd propped his bear up on the end of the bed, facing the connecting door to Catriona's room. He'd already looked there when Harriet was searching it earlier, checking to see what clothes were gone, and there had been no sign of Delilah. John opened the door again and looked inside once more before propping it open with the chair from his bedroom.

'You watch out to see if she comes back,' he told his bear, reasoning to himself that he'd rather see Delilah coming than imagine her in there creeping back to the doll's house.

Sitting cross-legged on the bed he opened the book and began to read. He didn't read as quickly as Katherine but he had plenty of time and it wasn't all words anyway. After the poetry and the rules of the rituals there were maps and then drawings of the make-believe people. The pieces of writing that followed were all short fragments, brief descriptions, and one line entries that read almost like a journal.

The Rookery nest together in a tangle of trees, branches woven around each other to wall out the night. They're a mob, not a company, damaged children in search of a ringleader.

Mirror and Glass went with me in the train, I saw them watching in every window of the city. I meant them to be companions but more and more they seem to mock me from their cold reflective world.

Fox is always waiting in the wood. Does he say the same things to each of us? Sometimes I think he knows more than he pretends to. That he's more real than we imagined him.

The winter pantomime makes no sense, full of references to books and people I can't remember. I can't claim I didn't know the price I was paying but I never expected it to cost me so much.

John wondered if Katherine or Roley had got this far in the book. Alice had read it cover to cover. Unlike a storybook it didn't end neatly on the last page. Instead the last third of the book was blank. The last words were a single line of handwriting.

I don't know what's real any more.

Any one of the three girls could have written that, John thought, but somehow he was certain it had been his mother. Katherine thought he couldn't remember her, but he could. He just didn't like talking about her with his sister. Katherine's memories were so fierce and passionate they seemed to blot other people's out. John guarded his as carefully as the secret name he'd chosen for himself. They weren't the sort of things you told other people, anyway. He remembered his mother's smell, like apples and soap;

the way she'd hug him goodnight, wrapping her arms around him so that they were locked together in the hug. They were small memories but they were all his.

Reading the book was like doing a puzzle, moving the pieces of what he knew around in his head until they fitted together. He thought his mother must have known she was doing something wrong when she crossed the names out of books but she couldn't have thought it mattered. It wasn't like murder; everyone knew people in books weren't real. But it was the sort of thing you wouldn't do unless you were very unhappy. And when you were unhappy sometimes you remembered the bad things you'd done and they made you feel worse. Perhaps his mother had tried to forget the past and ended up losing the present instead. People's brains were complicated, the doctor had told them that, and no one completely understood them yet.

John put the book back under his pillow and lay down on the bed, looking up at the cracked ceiling. He'd never thought Roley was right about the make-believe people being ghosts haunting the house. It wasn't the house that was haunted, it was them—their family. The make-believe people had come after them for a reason, and not just because of who their parents were. John, Katherine, and Alice might be related to the girls who'd invented the game but that didn't explain why Roley or Catriona had been targeted. A piece of the puzzle was missing and John couldn't make the pattern come right without it.

It had to do with names. He was certain that was the key to the mystery. Names had been their family's trouble from the beginning. Something about names and naming had made the make-believe people notice them—and perhaps something else had been watching as well. Something more sinister, hovering on the edge of reality, something that wanted them gone.

The tabby cat shivered by the side of the road as it watched the group of dark shapes milling around the van. Its paws hurt, bruised by the hard surface of the tarmac, the result of a long walk along empty road.

It was a small cat, only half-grown. It managed to make itself smaller still as it crouched under the hedge and sniffed the air anxiously. The search and rescue team didn't notice it, as they clustered by the open doors of the van consulting plastic-sheathed maps by the light of their torches. Their clothes steamed in the rain, water-slicked jackets spraying raindrops as they stamped muddied boots against the cold.

'. . . couldn't get much further than that,' one of them was saying. 'The whole tarn's spilling over and channelling left and right through the woods. Half the hill's a mudslide and the other half's a waterfall.'

'Forestry have really screwed up on this one,' another voice agreed. 'Some of those trees look as if they could come down any minute and with the branches that tangled they'll bring down more with them.'

'We can't hope to find those kids under these conditions,' another agreed. 'I hope to hell the little bastards have found themselves a shelter and are waiting it out.'

There were more mutters and flapping of maps, frowning

faces occasionally glancing back out of the circle to peer angrily through the dark. The tabby cat eased itself back slowly under the hedge, crouched into the smallest space it could occupy, fur twitching as rain scattered through the leaves to spatter on its bedraggled fur.

The radio in the van crackled into life and feet stamped round the side of the van, followed by a blurred exchange of voices inside the driver's cab. The rest of the team waited wearily, until the stamping feet came back.

'Got to keep at it,' a commanding voice announced. 'Uniformed division have got their knickers in a twist right and proper. Apparently there's another kid gone missing and heads may be about to roll.' A confusion of enquiries was drowned out as he continued. 'It's only the girl who called in the three we're looking for as missing. Cops say they dropped her back at her house and an hour later her parents call them and log *her* as missing. No sign of the girl in the house and the back door's wide open. Seems she walked in the front and walked straight out again. And get this, her folks seem to think there's a chance she's gone searching for the first lot.'

'So now we're looking for four of them?' the voice was incredulous. 'All running off in different directions in the middle of the bloody night.'

'In a bloody gale with half the fell sliding sideways,' the commanding voice agreed. 'That's about the size of it. Come on, lads, we'll skirt round by the southern road and try to make a better approach from the leeside. I don't see we've got any option but to keep trying.'

Boots clanged on metal as the team climbed back into

the van, thumping the doors shut behind them. The wind whipped a scourge of rain after them as the headlights blazed out across the road and were lost almost immediately in the choking darkness. The engine chugged slowly into life and the van set off, sending a spray of water from the wheels into the hedge. The tabby cat sneezed and huddled tighter into itself, a little ball of misery alone in the dark.

Alice saw the lights of the village fall far away beneath her as she rose on a carpet of black wings. Small grasping hands held her arms and legs, clawed fingers digging in through her clothes and adding a sharp pinching pain to the bruises the Knarl had left. Her stomach lurched violently as the wing beats rose and fell through a flurry of raindrops.

She hadn't even tried to struggle after the first instinctive movements when she was lifted off the ground. To free herself would be to fall through the vast blackness to smash on the stony fell. She could feel the black wings beating above her as if they were part of her body, muscles lifting and pulling to raise her dead weight up through the clouds.

Her left wrist was held in a vice of fingers, and through a blur of beating wings she could see the children's blank faces strung out across the shape of the figure beside her as they lifted him with her into the night. His fur coat flapped in the storm like bat wings. *Or a flying fox*, she thought giddily.

She hadn't had time to struggle, she thought. She thought she'd known what he was capable of; even as she looked for weapons she hadn't really believed he might harm her. She'd been thinking of him as only half real but his tightly muscled arms had felt real enough as he'd lifted her up and carried her bodily into the garden and whistled the bird children down from the roof. Their screams of victory hadn't shaken her as much as his dazzling smile.

It was too late now to regret all the things she should have done but her mind rang with 'if onlys'. If only she'd asked the police to stay with her, if only she hadn't gone into the greenhouse. If only she'd returned the calls on the answerphone. If only she'd realized what he intended when he said he'd come to protect her. The Rookery wheeled in the sky, dipping with a suddenness that forced a thin scream from Alice's throat as they dropped low enough for her to see the dark sea of the wood rising up beneath her, branches rolling like waves in the wind.

Then beneath her a black void opened, spilling darkness from its edges with a rushing sound she could hear as they fell down towards it. Alice saw her own face, suddenly, leaping out at her from a black surface. She recognized the onyx sheet as water only when the bird children holding her skimmed across the surface in a sickening dive. Then they were rising abruptly again, as a scribble of branches enclosed them in a wooden cage. Her body swung from her captors' hands as they hauled her into a dark cavern, the smell of wet wood giving way to a musty cloistered darkness. Her feet stumbled on something and she realized she was standing only as she fell, finally released from the prisoning hands.

Fox caught her easily and she didn't have the strength to fight as he held her to him. In the distance the sound of the rain had dropped away, cocooning them in a feathered silence. Her heart thumped out the rhythm of her fear as his arms closed around her and she heard him whisper softly.

'You'll be safe now, Alice. I won't let anything hurt you.'

Something inside her told her she shouldn't give in to this. This wasn't protection, whatever he wanted her to make-believe. This was capture and he was the predator in the woods she should have had the sense to fear.

'Why me?' she asked now as she had then. 'Why do you think you need to protect *me*?'

'Alice.' Fox shook his head gently, looking down at her with tender eyes, filled with a terrifying possessiveness that she realized was the love he'd sworn to her. 'Haven't you guessed yet? You're one of us.'

18
Then There Was One

Dawn brought mist and an interminable drizzle of rain that rattled against the windows of Fell Scar and trickled from the trees. The day didn't lighten so much as pale, the world outside the house a palette of shades of grey. The first of the police cars arrived with a sluice of wet gravel and the two police constables from the day before emerged slowly, looking as bleak as the weather.

'It's not good news, I'm afraid,' the policeman confessed at the door. 'We've had search and rescue out across the fell half the night and we've not found any sign of your children. And the storm last night was a stroke of bad luck.'

The adults stood in the doorway, their faces grey in the cold light of dawn. The policeman looked past them and saw the boy standing on the stairs and met his eyes uncomfortably before looking at the ground. His colleague took up the tale awkwardly.

'There's a tarn on the top of the fell. We've got police divers ready to search it when the floods dry up enough for them to get close. But it's quite possible they never got that far.' The policewoman chose not to mention the black mud that had turned the fell into a virtual swamp, choked with dead leaves, fallen branches blocking the few solid paths through the dripping wood. 'We won't stop looking until we find them. There's a good chance they found some- where to shelter when the storm began.'

It was impossible to know what to say in these circum- stances. Did you encourage the parents to hope for the best or try to brace them for the worst? With the little lad watching her from the stairs she found herself at a loss for words and her partner supplied them.

'It's early days yet,' he said. 'And we'll keep you posted of any developments.'

'Thank you,' the man said. 'We did try Roley's mobile this morning but . . . '

'The storm might have interfered with the signal,' the policewoman suggested. 'I wouldn't put too much weight on that. But we've got the number ourselves and we'll keep trying it, of course.'

'Was there anything else?' the woman interrupted, her anxious eyes searching their faces with sudden suspicion. 'You'd tell us if you'd found anything?'

The policewoman tried to smile reassuringly but gave it up as a bad job. It took her a moment to work out how to phrase her next question.

'Actually there is something, but it may not be con- nected. I was wondering if your lad could tell us about the young lady who was watching him. What was her mood like while they were waiting for the others to come back?'

'John?' Both adults looked puzzled and the father called the lad forward before suddenly looking sharply at the police constables. 'Why? What do you need to know?'

'We took the young lady home,' the policeman explained, the words sounding tired as the result of too many repetitions. 'But it seems she didn't stay there. We're concerned she may have taken it into her head to go looking for your three.'

'We don't even know her,' the woman said sharply before her husband added:

'She's the gardener's daughter. John said he and Roley met her earlier in the week.'

'Something of a Good Samaritan act then, her staying with your lad last night,' the policeman suggested. 'And calling the older three in as missing, too.' He sighed. 'She *seemed* to have her head screwed on all right then.'

'Perhaps she was worried about Roley.' The boy spoke for the first time. 'I think she liked him, a bit.' His golden brown eyes were guileless as he looked at the police.

'That might explain it,' the policeman said. 'Well, just in case she shows up here, please call us. Her mother's frantic and I can't say any of us are feeling too happy about it.'

'I shouldn't think you would,' the woman said sharply. 'I thought you were supposed to be finding our children, not losing someone else's.'

The policeman nodded uncomfortably, making allowances for her worry, and left with promises to call if anything changed. To be honest, this couple had taken it rather better than the two village women. They'd had to leave Emily Wheeler to the care of her friend when she'd had hysterics at the suggestion her daughter might have gone into the wood.

John tried to slip away as another argument began but for once both Peter and Harriet noticed and broke off their row to demand where he thought he was going.

'Just into the garden,' he said and they both frowned.

'Stay at the front of the house, where we can see you,' Peter told him.

'I don't think he should be going out at all,' Harriet objected and Peter bent down to speak quietly to John.

'Look, old chap, you know how worried we are about Kat, Roley, and Catriona, don't you? Promise on your honour you won't go anywhere on your own—or with a stranger.'

'I promise,' John said and felt disappointed when Harriet looked quickly at his hands to see if his fingers were crossed. 'I don't lie,' he told her and saw her eyes fill suddenly with tears.

'I know you don't, John,' she said, hugging him suddenly and tightly. 'But you're all we have left . . .'

'I promise,' John said again. 'Honestly.' He hesitated and then said definitely: 'They're not dead, you know. Roley and the cats. They're not.'

'Of course they're not,' Peter said with a fake smile and John knew his father didn't believe him. But he hadn't said it for Peter, but for Harriet, whose bleak eyes lightened with a faint glimmer of hope.

John walked across the wet grass to the broken fountain. The empty basin was filled now with inches of rain, wetly reflecting the grey sky. John stared into the pool of water, and for the first time in days saw only his own reflection. Mirror and Glass seemed to have vanished as mysteriously as Delilah. Fox hadn't shown himself since yesterday afternoon and none of the other make-believe people were haunting the garden.

'Where did they go?' John asked aloud, his voice vanishing into the thin morning air. 'How do I bring them back?'

The grey sky seemed light years away as Roley swam towards it, forcing himself through the liquid glass of the mirror sea. John's face looked over the edge of a stone parapet, his lips moving silently and his golden eyes troubled.

Then as Roley's palms touched the cold surface of another barrier, John's face retreated, vanishing somewhere out of sight and leaving only the grey sky framed with dripping trees. Roley swore to himself, as he found himself sliding down a tilting surface, the empty sky sliding away and being replaced with a different view. He recognized the perspective only because it was one he'd found himself returning to again and again through the long hours he'd spent in the mirror maze, the big mirror in the hallway of Fell Scar. The room seemed empty until a shadow shifted in the doorway and he saw a tortoiseshell cat eeling over the sill and padding surreptitiously into the room.

It wasn't the first time he'd seen it. As he ran and hid amidst a funhouse of twisted mirrors, tortoiseshell and tabby cats twitched in and out of sight, Alice vanished behind a cloak of black feathers, Fox laughed and bared white teeth, and John looked solemn and small.

Everywhere he ran the images appeared, as if Mirror and Glass were taunting him with visions of the real world—knowing he couldn't reach it.

Sharp angles surrounded him, a forest of prisms, reflecting views of trees, hedges, and stones. The reflections had hunted him through this maze, playing hide and seek behind the refracted images. Now it was himself he saw in the prisms, his own moon face gaping moronically, blubbery arms and legs windmilling as he steadied himself. Lumpy and useless Roley, too stupid to see when he was being made a game of, fool enough to believe that Mirror and Glass were on his side. Lumbering through the sharp crystals he saw his own clumsy and shambling shape reflected everywhere, scowling at him from every surface.

A fat ugly tear bloomed on the face of the lumpen figure in the mirror and Roley saw its mouth distort in a grimace of misery. Like a rat in a trap he had no choice but to run through the maze, hoping that somewhere in the world of reflections he could find the way out.

The tortoiseshell cat was being hunted. Each step it took through the dusty house was more slow and careful than the last. The smell of the enemy was tannic and chemical, swathes of it lay across the dust in the stairs in trails like mouse footprints.

The tortoiseshell cat's ears flicked back, hearing a skittering behind the walls. The hunters were everywhere. The cat had tried to hide from them in the woods but had been followed. The wood was no escape, not from the hunters and not from the Other One. The Other One was there too, always there. The tortoiseshell's fur twitched with confused memories of unfairness. The Other One had set the hunters on its tail. The Other One was to blame.

Paws padded softly around the turn of the stairs. Somewhere in the house were the people but the people couldn't be trusted. They hadn't protected the cat from the hunters, they hadn't got rid of the Other One. The cat wanted to be with the people but that wasn't the safe place.

The safe place was far away and soft and warm. The safe place had lights and smelt nice, not of dust and hunters and of the Really Bad Thing that the cat's mind shied away from. The tortoiseshell wanted the safe place but it didn't know the way there.

But here, at the top of the house, in a room that reeked of the hunters, there was a big wooden box. A part of it was open and inside were soft things that smelt of the safe place and of itself. Treading a firm circle on to the soft things, the cat curled itself up into a tight furry ball, tucked its head between its paws and tried to forget its fears in the softness of sleep.

Grey light filtered into Alice's prison cell as she stared through the cage of branches to see the Rookery wheeling and diving over a vast lake of water. As she watched one of the bird children alighted on a nearby tree, a girl with filthy hands and feet, her naked body covered with a light plumage of black down, vast wings sprouting from her skinny shoulders. She snapped her mouth shut over a worm, tilting her head to swallow it down her gullet.

Sickened, Alice turned away and looked at her jailer, lying comfortably in his feathered nest. Fox reclined on a drift of black feathers, piled up in the centre of the round room. Around him, scattered on the floor or hung on the walls of knotted branches was a rubble of items, trinkets that glittered but were anything and everything but gold. If this was the Rookery's nest then they were like magpies, stealing shiny items for no reason but their glitziness. Or perhaps they really were the feral children they looked like and these were their toys. Broken torches, binoculars with scratched lenses, glass bottles, the face of an alarm clock, a weather vane and a TV aerial: they all lay scattered in the mess of feathers. She supposed she should be grateful that they had kept their nest clean; the only smell was from the black lichen that filled the gaps between the tangled branches.

'You have to talk to me at some point, you know,' Fox said casually, a faint smile playing across his lips as he observed her from his seat in the heart of the feather pile. 'Is there anything you want? Food, perhaps? A book to read?'

Alice gave him a long look. He was a chameleon, she'd decided. Changing his mood and his tone as his situation demanded. *A leopard never changes its spots*, her mind whispered. *He's a predator. Don't trust him.*

She couldn't trust herself to speak. The words he'd whispered to her in the night were the stuff of nightmares. Every time she tried to think her way out of this prison her intellect faltered against the huge question Fox had raised over her whole existence. She was a coward, she knew that now. Too afraid to ask her jailer the reasons for her capture, already starting to believe that she might deserve it. It was safer to stay silent, when any random word might open a wound.

'I want you to let me go,' she said eventually. They were the only words she'd said to him for hours and she saw a flicker of irritation cross his face as she said them again.

'I can't do that, Alice,' he told her. 'It's not safe out there.'

He stood abruptly and when she froze in place he growled suddenly, frightening her again with ferocity just as she'd been in danger of accepting the light mocking tone of his earlier words as real.

'I'm not going to *hurt* you!' he said, real desperation in it. 'Alice, Alice, why don't you believe me? I *love* you.' That too bore the hallmarks of repetition. All through the night they'd gone round this little circle, the words getting sharper and tighter each time, Fox pacing as if he were the one in the cage.

'Then let me go.' The words had worn a groove in her mind. They were utterly useless and yet they were all she could think of. The shred of dignity she possessed compelled her not to plead. If she begged him she'd be accepting his power over her. Even now, she couldn't do that.

Fox sighed and slumped back into the feathers, pouting like a sulky teenage boy. There was that about him too, she reminded herself. Unlike the rest of the make-believe people, he really did look human, even with the fox fur coat. *If he can look human,* her mind screamed silently, *what am I?*

The tabby cat wanted to get into the house but the house was dangerous. It wanted to get inside because the outside was dangerous. Outside stank of Fox and Fox was dangerous. Inside reeked of something else, the something that rustled the hedges and crept on tiny feet when the tabby wasn't watching out for it.

The cat shivered and sneezed, its fur bristling uncomfortably in the drizzle of the garden. It was cold and hungry and frightened and something had brought it to this place but now its instincts were confused by the fear and it didn't know what to do.

Each step a torture of indecision it inched its way towards the stone steps, eyes fixed on the open door. The sudden sound of footsteps cast it into an agony of fright and it flattened itself across the steps as a person emerged from the house and shouted suddenly across the garden.

The voice was high-pitched and set the cat's ears flicking despite itself. From across the garden another voice floated back, a kinder voice, one the tabby recognized as one of its people. It curled around itself to look and only realized its mistake when the first voice rose in surprise.

The noises meant something; the tabby cat knew that. But it couldn't remember what they meant. It watched the person as it knelt in the doorway and stretched out a hand that smelt almost familiar.

'Are you a stray, little one? What are you doing here, kitkat?'

The words meant nothing, but the voice was gentle. The tabby cat watched the hand as it came close, hunching itself back in preparation for a blow.

'You're shivering.' The voice roughened and the cat flinched as the hand extended a finger and held it in front of its nose. 'Little cat, are you lost? Come on, little one, it's all right . . .'

The cat shivered again convulsively, panting shallowly as it eased itself an inch forward and the tip of its nose dabbed the finger. Its resistance collapsed as a gentle touch smoothed over its head and across the fur of its back. Collapsing into the hand, it allowed itself to be lifted and carried into the house.

John saw Harriet pick up the cat and take it inside. He'd been watching her since she'd called out to him across the lawn and had seen her bend and stretch out a hand towards the steps. It wasn't until then he'd seen the cat and he watched her speak to it with a sense of surprise. He hadn't known she liked animals.

Looking down at his footprints in the wet grass John wondered what to do. The one thing he was certain of was that he was in danger. Ever since they'd arrived in the Lake District, something had been stalking them. It wasn't just the make-believe people; it was something worse. Unlike them you couldn't see it, or describe it, but John could feel its presence all around him. A black tide had poured

260

out of the woods and crashed over the house and the quiet garden was full of invisible wreckage from last night's storm.

There was a darkness at the heart of the make-believe game. Whatever the three friends had believed when they'd written the poem and performed their rituals in the wood, they'd stirred up something. Their anger and unhappiness had fed that darkness, and brought it to life. It hadn't been a game when his mother died. It wasn't a game when his brother and sisters vanished. It wasn't a game that had persuaded Alice out of her house and into the night.

But perhaps it was safer to pretend it was a game, and that he couldn't feel the darkness waiting, hungry to consume him as it had consumed the others. John thought about the games that Roley played on his computer: maps of areas, names of pieces, and lists of equipment. War games, Harriet said disapprovingly, but Roley had told John all games were about strategy.

At the door of the house John stopped and looked at the door knocker with its wicked curved beak and the heavy iron lock he'd helped Catriona open. Everything had started when their family had arrived here. Alice had lived in the village for sixteen years without anything weird happening. They'd started it. It was something his family had done which had awakened the make-believe people. Perhaps they'd been sleeping or hiding here ever since the three girls stopped visiting them. They were sort of ghosts, ghosts of dreams and fears and fairytales. Maybe they needed to be believed in.

John felt a bit sorry for them. But he felt sorrier for everyone else. For Katherine and Catriona, Roley and Alice. For Anne, Emily, and Charlotte. For Peter and Harriet. For everyone who'd been hurt by the make-believe game. John had read the rules on the first page of the book and he'd read to the end of the book last night. He had all the puzzle pieces, even if he didn't yet know how they were supposed to fit together.

'All right,' he said to the bird-beaked door knocker. 'I'll play.' Stepping carefully across the doorway, he walked into the house and whispered: 'Ready or not, here I come.'

19
Ready or Not

Roley saw John step into the hallway from the other side of the mirror. He banged on the glass to attract his attention and groaned when his hands pounded silently on the invisible wall. A glissando of laughter surrounded him. Mirror and Glass were back and it was John they were watching, their water-coloured eyes gleaming with a mixture of curiosity and covetousness.

John was the only one left, Roley realized. In his glimpses of the real world the little boy was alone with their parents in Fell Scar. In the house he guessed was Alice's, two women sat silently at a kitchen table, watching each other with grief-stricken eyes. In the wet woods police and rescue people combed wearily through a muddy flood of dead leaves. The other glimpses he'd had of Alice and the two cats were anything but encouraging.

John was the only one of them left in the real world and Roley feared he knew what was about to happen. One or other of the ghosts would trick him into crossing out his name. And there was nothing Roley could do about it because he was completely and utterly useless. He slumped down against the invisible pane, feeling it chilling his forehead. He was truly pathetic. Catriona despised him, Katherine hated him, Alice had only felt sorry for him. He was a complete waste of space. All his clever scientific theories and his trying to take charge had been worse than useless. It was completely appropriate that he end up trapped in an invisible box, since he'd never actually done anything with his life.

'Roley?'

He'd be here for ever, running up and down the mirror maze to amuse two completely cracked ghost people. He'd have to spend the rest of his life looking on as everyone he knew grew old and died.

'Roley!'

Of course he might starve to death first, watching his blubbery blundering body thin down to a skeleton. Perhaps he'd end up as dust blown around the mirror world.

'ROLAND! It's me!'

He jerked upright and stared straight ahead. On the other side of the mirror John's golden eyes were staring up into his, grave with worry that melted into smiling relief when Roley looked up.

'What are you doing in there?' he asked. 'Come out!'

'John . . . ' For an instant Roley believed the nightmare might be over, but the invisible wall bruised his hands as he tried to reach out to his brother and he slammed his fists furiously into the glass. 'I can't!' he said, panicking all over again. 'I can't get out.' Then he remembered that John couldn't hear him and his shoulders sagged. 'Oh, this is hopeless.'

'Don't panic,' John said quietly. Climbing up on a chair he brought his face close to the glass and looked seriously at Roley. 'I'm sorry, I should have guessed you couldn't get out. Do you know why?'

'No.' Roley saw John wait patiently and then remembered to shake his head. 'No, sorry.' He spread his hands wide and clenched his fingers, trying to think of how to mime what he wanted to say, and John smiled at him.

'I'm waiting,' he said kindly. 'Take your time.'

Roley felt warm inside. He'd never understood that expression before now. His liking for the little boy seemed to bubble up like a hot spring. John was a fantastic kid. Roley promised himself that if he ever got out of this mess he'd be the best brother ever. Dinosaur Lego, trips to the zoo, midnight feasts—whatever a little boy could possibly want.

'I did something,' he said. 'They told me to do it, Mirror and Glass.' How did you mime mimes? Oh, right, the old trapped-in-a-box gag. Roley stopped in confusion, wondering if John would get it.

'Mirror and Glass put you there?' John said helpfully and Roley heaved another sigh of relief.

'Yes.' Remember to nod. 'Yes. I was in the wood . . . '

It took a while. Roley cheered himself up with the thought that if, *when*, he got out of this he would be bloody brilliant at charades. He acted himself wandering through the woods, and the swarm of vampiries, then the bird creatures. He must look like a complete fool, making mean insect faces and buzzing noises and then flapping about like a big bird, but John didn't laugh. His small face was serious all through it.

Roley had trouble with acting the tarn; water ripples wasn't the best way to describe it when it had been so flat but John seemed to get the idea. When it came to the stone with the crossed out writing, Roley was actually able to improve on the reflection's mime. He wrote with a finger on the invisible wall so the words were backwards from his perspective, forwards for John.

'Written on the water? By the water,' John said, out loud. 'Catriona and Katherine. Both crossed out.'

'Yes.' Roley nodded. However good he was getting at charades his brother was some kind of genius. Catriona would still be shouting 'say the number of syllables' and Katherine would be complaining 'I only know books'.

He'd got to the tricky bit. It was embarrassing to admit how stupid he'd been. But he got some amusement out of imitating Mirror floating around in the water and shaking out her long hair and beckoning like a siren. Then he did Glass's promise to explain and followed it up with himself, stupid old Roley, writing his name and crossing it out— only to find himself falling into the lake and ending up in looking-glass land. He finished up with the trapped-in-the-box routine, feeling it appropriately underlined his own stupidity.

'You're not stupid.' John's eyes were kind. 'Anyone can make a mistake. It's not your fault Mirror and Glass lied to you. I think it was brave to do what you did.'

'I didn't want to be a coward, so I was a fool instead,' Roley contradicted, sketching his thoughts simplistically. Crossed out my own name. What an idiot.

'You should stop doing that,' John said seriously. 'I think it's the mirror world making you feel stupid. If you were out here then you'd feel differently. You wouldn't blame yourself so much.'

'I can't *get* out!' Roley cried, acting trapped-in-a-box again with angry frustration.

'I think you can,' John said quietly. 'But not as Roley.' He looked troubled, as he came closer to the glass, meeting Roley's eyes. 'I liked Roley. He was a good brother. But you crossed him out so you can't be him any more.'

'I have to be someone else?' Roley felt naked, as if John's words had stripped his personality away, leaving an echoing void. 'How? Who?' He didn't have to act incomprehension.

John reached out to the glass, but this time he didn't speak. Instead he directed his hand in slow careful movements, writing a name in mirror writing so that one by one the letters appeared on the other side of the glass: R O L A N D.

'I think that's the way out,' he said quietly, not quite whispering but keeping his voice low 'I think that's who you need to be.'

'How? I'm still trapped . . . ' Roley touched the invisible wall again and John reached out his own hand and placed it on the other side of the mirror glass, matching it up to Roley's.

'You have to believe it,' he said. 'Leave everything else behind and come back through the mirror glass.'

'I can try. But I don't even know where to begin.' Somehow Roley knew John's answer was the right one. Roley was all too familiar: dim-witted, overweight, and slow—everything he'd been running from. But Roland was a stranger to him, someone he didn't even know. How was he supposed to transform into this stranger capable of walking through an invisible wall?

'You'll work it out.' John smiled at him encouragingly. 'I know you will.' He paused. 'I have to find the others now. Will you be OK?'

'I guess.' Roley pulled himself together. 'Yeah, I'll be fine. Thanks. You're brilliant.' He mimed two thumbs up.

'Do you know what happened to them?' John asked. 'Katherine and Catriona never came back. And Alice, she vanished too.'

Roley frowned. Alice was in a dark place. She was there with Fox. He'd seen them embracing and had run away. He'd been too ashamed to let her see him. But that really was stupid. He should look for her. And for—

'Cats!' Now he didn't care if he looked ridiculous, miming cat ears and a tail and then pretending to lick a paw. 'They're cats. Tabby and tortoiseshell.' How did you mime tortoiseshell? Oh, right of course.

'They're cats! Tortoises!' John laughed suddenly at Roley's expression. 'Definitely *not* tortoises. Two cats, they're both cats. First cat, striped cat, tabby cat. Second cat . . . Oh, right. Tortoise*shell*. I get it now.'

Roley grinned at him and John grinned back. Then the boy took his hand from the mirror and climbed back off the chair.

'I'll find them,' he said. 'What about you? What are you going to do?'

'I'm going to look for Alice,' Roland told him.

Alice watched the black water beneath her cage in the trees. Fox had finally wearied of her silence and left her, whistling to the Rookery whose child-sized hands with long-blackened fingernails opened up a part of the cage for him to step out on to their platform of wings. She had tensed then, eyes fixed on the opening as he turned back to look at her.

'I wouldn't,' he said warningly, barring the aperture with his body. 'If you fall—and you would fall, Alice, without me to catch you—you'll be falling into the heart of the darkness. The blight is powerful here.' He paused and smiled, the tender smile that frightened her. 'And so am I.'

She had watched him go, lifted on borrowed wings, across the floodwater and into the shadows of the wood. Once he was out of sight she'd looked out through the barred branches and shouted. She'd called 'Hello?' and 'Help!', and 'Can anyone hear me?' Her voice deadened and sank into the silence, leaving her feeling more hopeless than before.

Testing the weave of branches, her hands slipped on the lichen and it felt slimy beneath her hands. Twigs cracked and snapped in her fingers, enough for her to tear a window in the round nest. But the largest branches defeated her and as she strove to pull them away the trees creaked and ground ominously, stilling her movements as she was reminded of the Knarl.

Eventually she turned away and began to comb through the drift of feathers. She had no plan, her mind felt coated in cotton wool, cocooned in its own fragile protection. If she'd been looking for a weapon, her search seemed doomed to failure. The few heavy items might have knocked Fox out but she was doubtful if she could take him by surprise. Perhaps if she pretended to have given in to him, but even the thought of pretending was unpleasant.

'You have to face it,' she said to herself quietly, sifting through the rubble of trinkets strewn among the feathers. 'Come on, Alice, think.'

Her mind refused to focus, like a misaligned camera lens. Everything was mixed up together. Fox's insistence that he was protecting her, Roley's last phone call, the evidence table in the barn, her attack on the Knarl and its attack on her. Then further back to a distant past before all of this had begun, when she was just Alice Wheeler.

Who is Alice? The girl she had been seemed like a distant memory and she watched that remembered figure weeding vegetables, walking the dog, developing camera films, and leading her quiet unremarkable life.

'If I'm a make-believe person, I'm not a very interesting one,' she said to herself, testing the idea gently inside her woolly head. 'No wings, no stings, no army of dolls, not even a motorbike.' In fact, for all that they might be considered unconventional parents, Emily and Charlotte had brought her up in a very conventional way. They'd taught her to cook, reminded her to do her homework, and encouraged her to get a summer job. But, now she thought about it, they'd never played games of let's-pretend or make-believe with her. They'd never even read her fairy stories. Christmas presents were labelled with their names—she'd not been the first of her school friends to learn Santa Claus wasn't real, she'd never believed it in the first place. Their house was stuffed with gardening books and political exposés but the only novels were gifts that neither of her parents displayed much interest in and there was no poetry or books of myths and legends.

She reviewed the facts with a growing sense of betrayal. In no way had they ever warned her that she was peculiarly at risk from the land of make-believe. The closest they'd come was to warn her against going into the wood. And Emily had always discouraged her from coming to Fell Scar, although Alice had helped out in other gardens. But they'd kept their secrets locked so tightly inside their heads that Alice had never tried to question them. She'd never felt she had the right to demand the answers and what did it matter how she'd come to be born when the important thing was she had parents who loved her?

They'd be frantic now, Alice guessed. They'd have come home to find an empty house. Would they have spotted her camera in the kitchen? Would they think to use her equipment to develop the film and find the photographs in the wood of Alice and the Knarl—and Fox? What would they think when they saw their secrets surround her like shadows?

In the drift of feathers Alice's hands snagged on something sharp and she snatched her hand back, seeing blood bloom on the side of her forefinger. Brushing the plumes carefully away she saw she'd found a broken mirror, long shards lying like glass daggers against the edge of the frame.

'Seven years' bad luck,' she said to herself, testing the weight of it in her hand. Light gleamed on the silver edge of the blade and she looked down and met her own grey eyes, their expression frightening her with its hopelessness. But as she watched the eyes changed colour, shifting from grey to brown. The face in the mirror wasn't hers any more, it was Roley's.

He looked worried, his eyes screwed up to peer searchingly out of the mirror glass. Alice wasn't sure if he could see her. But then his mouth moved, and she read her own name on his lips.

'You're in the mirror?' she couldn't quite believe it until she saw his bleak nod of admission. He began to gesture, and in the broken pieces of glass at her feet she saw his arms and hands flicker across the rest of the mirror.

'I don't understand,' she admitted. 'I don't know what you're trying to say.'

His face fell and he watched her silently through the glass, embarrassing her with the intensity in his gaze. She hadn't realized until now that he liked her but something about the way he looked was comforting. For all its intensity, it was nothing like the powerful possessiveness of Fox's green stare.

'Don't,' she said. 'Don't look at me.' She bowed her head, feeling ashamed to admit what had happened to her. 'I'm trapped too—in Fox's cage—and he won't let me go. He says he loves me.' Her voice stumbled on that and she risked a glance at the glass to see Roley's start of surprise covered by a sudden black frown. He glared at her out of the glass and she laughed brokenly. 'I don't believe it. But it's no good, he says I belong with him. He says . . . ' She forced the words out. 'He says I'm one of them.'

No! Roley shook his head fiercely, mouthing an angry denial. *No. It's not true.*

272

'It *feels* true,' Alice whispered, not sure if it was herself or Roley she was really speaking to. 'My parents are two of the girls in the make-believe book. I never did know who my father was . . . '

She stopped. Roley's face was a mask of horror, mirroring her own freezing certainty. Her veins seemed to have turned to ice water as she listened to the echoes of her own words ring back and forth through her head.

'I never knew who my father was,' she said again. And then: 'He said he loved me.' The shard of glass fell back on to the feathers as her fingers lacked the strength to hold it and she saw Roley's hand reach out towards the glass as if trying to catch hold of something—even as the broken shard dropped from her hands.

It all fell into place now. She knew now why Fox had called her one of them, she knew what had happened to Emily in the wood, she knew why they'd tried so hard to give her a normal upbringing. There was blood on her hands; she'd gripped the shard of glass too tightly.

'Blood's thicker than water,' she said, looking at it, and as she spoke she began to shake.

Alice crouched on the knotted floor, burying her head in her hands as her shaking shook the cage. The branches creaked and through the gaps between them she saw the black water, higher than it had been, only a few metres beneath her swinging prison. It was rising to meet her, she was sure. The darkness would come to claim her, to devour the last traces of the girl who'd been Alice.

'No.' Something gripped her shoulder with abrupt force. She flinched, turning to see a square hand, freckled across the knuckles, fingernails bitten down to the quick. 'You're going to get out of this,' a voice said firmly. 'We all are.'

She couldn't quite believe it until he pulled her to her feet and she found herself looking at a face that was stronger and more confident than she'd remembered it. She glanced down at the broken pieces of the mirror, empty now, and then back at him; opened her mouth to say his name.

'It's Roland,' he said quickly, before she could speak. 'From now on, it has to be.'

The fight began when the tortoiseshell cat padded softly into the kitchen, tempted out of its warm nest by the smell of cooking fish. None of the family had felt like eating but Harriet had broiled up some pieces of fish in milk and as the tortoiseshell entered she was placing the plate tenderly in front of the bedraggled tabby stray.

The tortoiseshell let out a metallic screech of rage, hurling itself at the other cat with a powerful fury and boxing its ears. The suddenness of the attack frightened Harriet into screaming herself. Peter came running in time to see the tabby fly up his wife's jumper and cling to her shoulder, doubling in size as it hissed at its antagonist. Grabbing his jacket from the back of a chair he dropped it over the tortoiseshell and wrapped the cat in the fabric, wrestling with the furious squirming bundle.

'What on earth's going on?' he asked.

'I was feeding this stray,' Harriet said, reaching up to attempt to disengage the quivering tabby from her shoulders.

'I suppose the smell must have attracted that other cat. Can you put it outside?'

'Why don't we put them both outside?' Peter said, eyeing the tabby doubtfully. 'Darling, it's scratched you. You could get tetanus. Do put it down.'

'Peter, it's terrified!' Harriet reproved him. 'And it's barely more than a kitten. Poor baby, did that other cat frighten you, then?' She crooned softly to the tabby and Peter watched her gently.

'All right then,' he said, carrying the wriggling bundle of jacket back out to the front door and then shaking it out on to the drive.

He watched the tortoiseshell land on its feet and curl around to make a beeline for the open door.

'Oh no you don't, girl,' Peter said, blocking its way. 'We've had enough of cat fights in this family to last us a lifetime . . .' He stopped and bit his lips, sending up a silent prayer that his words wouldn't be taken literally. Give him a hundred years of cat fights if that was the price of getting their children back.

'You're barely more than a kitten yourself, aren't you?' he addressed the cat more gently, running his hands over its matted fur as it tried to force its way back in. 'Hungry too, aren't you? Seems unfair you shouldn't get any fish.' He sighed at himself. It was amazing what sheer bloody terror could do for you. He'd become suddenly superstitious and the idea of turning the cat away was distasteful.

'All right then, you scrounger,' he said, picking the tortoiseshell up firmly by the scruff of its neck. 'Watch your claws, you little devil.' Taking the cat back inside, he took it through to the living room and closed the door on it. 'I'll see if Harriet can spare some fish,' he said through the closed door and then shook his head at himself.

He'd expected his wife to object violently when he told her what he'd done. But instead she dealt out the remainder of the fish on to a clean plate and filled a bowl with water.

'We've had plenty of practice, haven't we?' she said, looking down at the tabby, gorging itself on its meal. 'Not that we've made a very good job of it. Taking care of cats . . . '

'We'll do better in the future,' Peter said firmly. 'When the girls get back we'll damn well sit them down and sort this out once and for all. Poor old Roley, left in charge of those little hellions.'

'Poor old John,' Harriet returned. 'God, it's taken this disaster for me to really see him and it breaks my heart. We don't pay him nearly enough attention.'

'It's always too damned noisy to hear yourself think, isn't it?' Peter said. He paused. 'Do you sometimes wonder . . . '

'No.' Harriet shook her head. 'We didn't make a mistake. Every single day I tell myself that. The mistake would be giving up.'

'Then we won't give up.'

Peter brushed a kiss against her cheek and then took the tortoiseshell its lunch. Sitting on the sofa, he watched it eat, and found himself reading it a lesson on manners. Ridiculous to talk to a cat but somehow comforting. But when it had finished its meal and lapped up half the water it walked towards him on determined paws and leapt into his lap. Stroking it absent-mindedly and beginning to tease out the burrs from its fur, Peter felt marginally less miserable.

'We won't give up,' he told the cat firmly. 'This family is going to survive. It has to.'

John had seen the tortoiseshell cat padding carefully down from the attics. At the top of the stairs it had flicked its ears and looked anxiously back behind it, not in John's direction but back up the stairs. Its hackles had risen and it had rabbited down the rest of the flight and along the shadowy corridor towards the main staircase.

Instead of following John looked back and in the dim light he saw the small doll sitting halfway down the steps from the right hand attic, as carefully as if someone had placed it there. Behind her, three of the drones lay in the angle of the wall, like puppets with their strings cut. Only Delilah sat comfortably, her legs dangling over the stair lip. She was the first of the make-believe people he'd seen since last night and John thought she was probably the one most attached to the house. Her doll's house was in the attic after all and he'd expect a doll to feel attached to those doll-sized rooms. But she wasn't in the doll's house now.

John sat two stairs below and considered the doll. When he'd first seen her standing on the breakfast table her long hair had been divided into three distinct sections: black, brown, and blonde. Since then she'd acquired two more slender brunette stripes. One was a deep chestnut brown, the other a mid brown that almost matched one of the larger sections. John remembered Catriona's terror that Delilah had cut her hair and he remembered how she'd been pulling Katherine's hair in the interrupted fight.

'It's girls you like to play with, isn't it?' he said, looking up at Delilah. 'You never bothered Roley, the mirror people got him. And Alice was a bit too grown-up for you, I expect.'

Delilah said nothing but he hadn't expected her to. Her smile was malevolent and satisfied, but perhaps also a bit curious. She wasn't interested in him but if he tried to cause problems for her perhaps she would be.

'But it wasn't you who turned them into cats,' he continued. 'You took their hair and you're still hunting Catriona, maybe both of them, but hunting's what you do—you don't change people.'

Delilah's smile didn't alter. She didn't seem to consider that the change was that important. Maybe, to her, it wasn't.

John stood up. He'd been considering trying to make a deal with Delilah but now he realized it was pointless. He didn't have anything she wanted, and if he did he wouldn't have given it to her. He could try and look big by doing something to annoy her, kicking her down the stairs, for example. But he didn't think that would be a very good idea. Catriona knew the doll better than anyone else, perhaps she would have an idea how to handle her.

'You're not very nice, Delilah,' he said finally. Her painted eyes looked bored but he didn't mind. It was better if she thought he wasn't dangerous. But as his gaze travelled to the drones he looked at them more gently. 'It's *you* I feel sorry for,' he said. 'Do you even have minds of your own? Wouldn't you like to be free?'

The drones didn't move and John shrugged. Walking carefully down the stairs, in case there were more of them, he went to find the cats.

The police came again that afternoon but there was still no sign of the missing teenagers. Peter went out to talk to some of the search and rescue people and returned with the news that the woods were almost impassable. Allthough helicopters had been out over the area they'd spotted nothing.

As the afternoon wore on towards evening Peter and Harriet were increasingly quiet. She had made several phone calls to her ex-husband and they'd left her tired and red-eyed. She sat on the living room sofa, trying and failing to read a book with the tabby cat tucked up beside her. Peter had made cheese sandwiches and brought them in on a plate, the tortoiseshell following him hopefully. In the end the cats had got most of the food. Peter had fidgeted around the room for a while before piling up logs in the hearth and starting a fire.

John had watched the cats curiously. He'd tried whispering to them and petting them and although they'd accepted it, they'd not shown any response. The tortoiseshell lay on the hearthrug, grooming its fur to a silky smoothness. The tabby kept a wary eye on it from the sofa, twitching at every snap and crackle from the dry wood. John thought he could guess which of them was which and it was interesting that the adults didn't seem to have reached the same conclusion. It was a bit disappointing that they didn't recognize their own children, even if they were so transformed, but John hadn't really expected that they would.

The trouble came when Peter eventually sat down next to Harriet and put his arm around her. She rested her head on his shoulder and the tabby took this opportunity to worm its way across her lap and put a paw on Peter's knee.

'Hello, princess,' he said, pleased at the attention and the tortoiseshell sat up abruptly, tail twitching angrily.

'Watch out, your cat's getting jealous,' Harriet said lightly. Then she looked bleak and put down her book with elaborate care, hiding her face as she turned aside to reach out to a cluttered tabletop. The tabby, uncomfortable with her shift in position, squirmed away, retreating along the back of the sofa.

'Can I have the cats in my room tonight?' John asked and the adults looked grateful for another voice in the room.

'If you like,' Peter said. 'But I don't know if they'll go with you.'

'Why don't you take the cheese sandwiches?' Harriet suggested. 'I'm not going to eat any more but you should. And I think you'll get the cats to come with you if you do.'

'That's a good idea,' John agreed. 'Thank you.' She smiled at him, weakly, and his father said he'd come up to tuck him in later. Carrying the sandwich plate, John looked at the cats. 'Come on, cats,' he said, moving slowly towards the door and holding the plate low so they could smell it. 'Lovely cheese.'

The cats didn't follow at once. They were cats, after all, John thought, not exactly inclined to do as someone else suggested. Then, quite unexpectedly, he had a stroke of luck. Harriet had reached out for her book and suddenly there was a clatter as she recoiled from the table.

'It's that horrible little doll,' she exclaimed with revulsion. 'What the hell is that doing there?'

'Come *on*, cats,' John whispered quickly and two furry shapes streaked towards him as he hurried out of the room. He trotted quickly up the stairs but instead of going all the way to the attic he turned instead towards the door into Barnia. 'Come on, cats,' he encouraged. 'It's safe this way, Delilah never comes here.'

They blurred past his ankles and down into the barn, taking up opposite positions on either side of the room as he shut the door and turned on the light. He carried the remaining sandwiches over to the pool table, which was still covered with Roley's collection of evidence, and crumbled the bits of bread and cheese into cat sized bites.

'Come on, cats,' he urged. 'I bet you're still hungry.' They looked at him snootily and John sighed. He hadn't expected them to be quite this contrary.

'Look,' he said, eventually, 'you might only have little cat brains now but I know who you really are. And maybe it doesn't make much difference to you whether or not you spend the rest of your lives that way, but it'll matter a lot to our parents.'

The tabby jumped on to the pool table and approached the cheese gingerly. It was impossible to know whether or not it was understanding him but it was certainly listening—its ears twitched whenever he spoke.

'I'm beginning to understand how the game works,' John continued. 'There's something in the woods that feeds on names. I know you crossed each other's names out and I think the make-believe people made you do it so the thing could be fed. And when it ate your names it changed you, made you less real and more make-believe.'

The tortoiseshell jumped on to the pool table and began to prowl forward, tail lashing warningly as it approached the plate.

'It doesn't have to be this way,' John told the cats. 'You don't have to be cats. But if you want to be real again you have to make a sacrifice. That's what the book says.'

Perhaps they were listening; they faced each other down over the sandwich plate but neither of them had sprung— yet. John sighed. He'd hoped they would be able to understand, as Roland had, but perhaps little cat brains were just too small. He'd have to make the decision for them and hope that if he believed in it enough, it would make it real.

'You have to trust me,' he said. 'Because it's really better this way.' Reaching out over the table he put one hand on the tabby and the other on the tortoiseshell, feeling the soft fur prickle. 'You're not to be cats any more,' he said. 'However you spell it. You have to be people.'

He looked at the tabby, trying to cringe out from under his touch. He'd liked his sister's name but that wasn't the only thing he liked about her.

'You're my sister,' he said. 'You're kind and thoughtful and you're always looking out for me. It wasn't your fault

Mum died. Sometimes bad things just happen. But good things do too—if you'll let them.'

The tortoiseshell was bigger and harder to keep hold of. He didn't know it as well but there were some things he'd guessed.

'You're my sister too,' he said. 'You're pretty and clever and a lot of the things you say are funny—even when you're being mean. You can't be angry at your mum for ever. All she wants is to have a happy family.'

The cats had stopped moving. He could feel little shivers crossing their flesh under the fur and he knew they were frightened. But he was sure he was doing the right thing. Under the glow of the hanging bulb, he could almost feel the darkness lifting.

'Don't be cats,' he said again. 'Be people. Be Erin and Iona.'

John didn't close his eyes. He wanted to see what was happening. But the change, when it came, wasn't something you could see. Between one heartbeat and another they shifted. Instead of two cats, two tired muddy girls, bodies freckled with minor scratches and bruises, were sitting on the pool table. They stared at each other with wide eyes, shocked speechless. Then, one girl reached out across the table to the other.

'I'm sorry,' she said. 'I didn't mean it.'

'Me too . . . and me neither,' the other girl whispered. 'I'm sorry too.'

20
The Waiting Game

Erin sat in the darkness of the barn. Only a little grey light filtered through the skylight. John had turned out the light when he left. He'd convinced her they couldn't let their parents know the girls were back, not when Roland and Alice were still lost.

'We have to finish it,' he'd said, his clear gaze forcing them to take him seriously. 'The make-believe game has to end tonight. Until then we have to keep this a secret.'

It seemed cruel, Erin thought, looking at the splintered floor. More than that she wanted to run up the stairs of the barn and into the house and fling herself into her father's arms. But she felt too guilty about what she'd already done to break her promise to her brother. She was the one who'd deliberately used the words of the poem against someone. She'd crossed out someone's name and hadn't cared what the result would be. *A character dead is a story broken.* Only now did she think about what could have happened to her stepsister, what still might happen to Roland, who had only tried to take charge.

It was cold in the barn. John had made one hasty trip back into the main house before rejoining the adults and that had been to bring out a bundle of clothes. He'd not been able to bring their own, not sure if the adults would

284

check their rooms again, so instead he'd brought Anne's. Erin had always wanted to wear one of those beautiful dresses but the thin fabric wasn't much protection against the night air.

Just a metre away sat her stepsister. She was a stranger and always had been, for all that they had been joined together in the same family. But with her new name she seemed like a complete question mark. In a grey silk dress she looked utterly unlike herself and her eyes were haunted with the memories they'd both have for ever. As Erin watched, Iona turned her head to look at her.

'Can we whisper?' she asked, the words barely more than a breath of air.

'What?' Erin asked. 'What is it?'

'I just wanted to say, there was one thing I liked. You know, when we were . . . ' She found the word difficult to say, Erin guessed, because she felt the same way.

'What was it?' she asked, moving closer to keep her voice low. 'What did you like?'

'Your dad,' Iona said; she shifted, looking a bit embarrassed. 'I mean, my dad's great but he's not into . . . He likes dogs. I don't think he'd have hesitated about booting me out of the door. That's kind of . . . yeah, well. I just wanted to say, he's OK, your dad.'

'Yeah.' Erin looked at the ground. 'Your mum too,' she said after a moment. 'I never liked the way she always treated me like a little kid but it was good to be looked after.'

There was a pause and then finally Iona spoke again. She wasn't looking at Erin, but at her own hands, picking at the ragged edges of her torn fingernails.

'When I'm sick,' she whispered, the words floating over the space between them, 'she makes me hot chocolate with marshmallows and puts this special blanket on my bed. I know it's lame . . . but sometimes I pretend to be ill just so she'll do those things.'

'I understand,' Erin said after a moment. 'I miss my mum. And, even before she died, she wasn't really able to look after us. Mostly I feel like I don't need to be looked after because of that but I suppose I want it more than I realized.' Trying to lighten the mood she added: 'Hot chocolate would be nice about now.' Iona glanced at her, with a glimmer of a smile.

'Mmm,' she agreed. 'Whipped cream too.' She glanced up at the skylight and added: 'How much longer do you think?'

'A while yet,' Erin said. 'John said he'd come back at eleven, right? It's not that late. I can still hear them moving around in the house.'

'How can you be so calm?' Iona's voice rose slightly before dropping again. 'You know he wants us to go out there. Go back through the wood . . . '

'I know,' Erin said, wishing she was as calm as her sister believed she was. 'It scares me too. But crazy as it sounds, I think he's right. And John, well, I know it's weird, but when he's that certain about something, people should listen.'

'I'm not saying he's wrong,' Iona mumbled. 'But . . . I'm going to be completely useless out there. Just the thought of those things . . . in the house, in the woods . . . ' She shivered. 'Seriously, I don't think I can do this.'

'You can,' Erin said. 'Besides, don't you want to give them a taste of their own medicine? John said he had a plan.'

286

'I'd like to kick Fox right where it hurts,' Iona admitted. 'But I still can't think of him like the rest of them. Like,' she swallowed and her voice dropped almost out of hearing, 'Delilah.'

'Remember she can't do anything while we watch her,' Erin reminded her. She'd not been hunted by Delilah for long, but it had been long enough to appreciate her stepsister's fear of the tiny doll. 'Just keep your eyes on her and she's powerless.'

They were silent for a while but Erin knew Iona wasn't convinced yet and it was hard to keep sounding certain when she didn't even know what John's plan was. All he'd said was that the game had to end.

'I still don't understand though,' the other girl said eventually. 'Fox and Delilah and the crossed out names. I believe it, I have to, don't I? But I still don't understand it.'

'It all began with the make-believe game,' Erin said. John still had the book but she didn't need it to tell the story. 'Three girls invented their own imaginary world but that wasn't enough for them—so they tried to make it real . . . '

When he'd considered their position, Roland wondered if he'd made a mistake breaking out of the world of mirrors. Initially Alice's cage hadn't looked so impregnable. If they could break apart the branches they ought to be able to climb out into the trees. But the branches were resistant to his efforts; they twisted out of his hands and sprang back into place as if they were half-alive. And the cage hung from the tangled branches of the grove of trees he'd seen at the end of the tarn. Even if he could force a way out, they were hanging over the black water and Roland wasn't anxious to take a second dive into that.

But when he'd seen Alice's face in the mirror, all he'd thought about was how alone she'd seemed and how frightened. He hadn't even consciously tried to escape his own prison; he'd simply reached out to her and found himself here. Even now she stood frozen when his efforts with the branches made the cage swing and creak.

'I'm not sure if this is the kind of thing you can just smash out of,' he said, abandoning his attempts for the time being. 'For me, the key was my name. But you never crossed your name out, did you?'

'No,' Alice said, shaking her head. 'And I don't really understand why you did.'

'It was a leap of faith,' Roland said a bit stiffly. Then he shrugged. 'But it was pretty stupid. I just didn't see what else to do. I wanted to find the girls and Mirror and Glass tricked me into thinking it would help to cross my name out.'

'Anyway,' Alice said, 'if changing my name will get us out of this, I'll do that. Any suggestions?'

'Uh . . . ' Roland's head flooded with girls' names but he couldn't fit any of them to Alice. Her name seemed to suit her and he couldn't just summon up an alternative and expect it to fit. 'I'm not sure it would help,' he said thoughtfully. 'You didn't cross your name out. In a way each of the rest of us chose to play the game. You didn't.'

'I was kidnapped,' Alice said, looking out over the still water.

The sky was shading towards evening now. A whole day had passed since the make-believe game had sucked them in. Roland clung to the fact that people were looking for them. He'd even seen the search and rescue helicopters buzzing over the fell, although too far away to see them in their eyrie.

'Perhaps the choice was made when I was born,' Alice said. 'The girls all made sacrifices, didn't they? Perhaps I'm one of them.'

'I don't buy that,' Roland told her. 'In fact, I think the last thing you should do is consider changing your name. One of the books in the house was *Alice's Adventures in Wonderland*, did you see it?'

'It was on the pool table with the rest of your evidence,' Alice said. 'Lots of names crossed out.'

'Pretty much every character,' Roland insisted. 'Every character but one. I think your parents named you after the girl who survived. The one they couldn't bear to cross out. After all, what's wonderland without Alice?'

Her grave grey eyes lifted to his and Roland blushed. He hadn't meant his remark to sound romantic. He'd guessed that would be the last thing she wanted right now but some of the feeling he had for her had escaped just a bit then and he hoped she'd be willing to ignore it.

'The way I see it,' he went on quickly, 'the girls tried to stop playing the game but it wasn't so willing to let them go. Anne, John's mother, she had some kind of mental illness, and she died in hospital.'

'Charlotte failed her degree,' Alice said. 'And she wanted to be a writer, one of the village gossips told me. I mean to write stories. But all her journalism is factual and sometimes I think she hates doing it. I've been wondering if it's because she can't remember those characters she crossed out and doesn't dare invent any more make-believe people.'

'And Emily,' Roland hesitated.

'The game blighted her life,' Alice said. 'Didn't it? Getting pregnant at sixteen and her parents blaming her. There's no way she could have explained the truth to them, who'd believe it?'

'Come on.' Roland knew he needed to shake her out of this bleak vision. 'Your mum loves you, both your parents do. The way you talk about them it's clear they do. Whatever sacrifices they made, they made for you.'

'Then why didn't they tell me anything about all this? Warn me, somehow?' Alice's voice was less despondent, more demanding.

'Who wants to know their biological dad's a motorbike riding bad-boy with the emotional maturity of a teenager? No, not even a teenager. My brother John's more grown-up than Fox and he's *ten*.'

Alice didn't answer and Roland was disappointed. He'd hoped to make her smile at least. But she wasn't looking at him. She was looking through the bars of the cage to where the Rookery had dropped silently out of the sky and now surrounded a slim male figure, leaning casually against the trunk of a close-by tree.

'You can't be expected to understand the appeal,' Fox said to Roland.

He was smiling but it didn't reach his eyes. Roland could

see that he was very angry and only just keeping it under control.

'So you're back,' Roland said, trying to sound casual. 'We were getting tired of waiting.'

'You were trying to break out,' Fox corrected, looking at the section of torn twigs in the globe of the cage. 'Don't you know yet how dangerous that is? If Alice were to fall . . . '

'What would happen?' Roland wasn't sure if he was doing the right thing by taking on their side of the conversation. But Alice had told him about her self-enforced silence and he thought she might be compromising herself if she tried to talk now. 'She wouldn't turn into a cat, or be trapped in mirror world. Even if she fell she wouldn't be crossed out.'

'Then she'd drown,' Fox said sharply. 'It isn't safe for her. You people, you roused the blight. You woke it and fed it and made it stronger. You're the ones who should pay the price. Not my Alice.'

Alice shuddered and Roland put his arm around her. Bad idea, he realized when he saw the queer green light of Fox's eyes. Still, perhaps it wasn't such a mistake to get the make-believe boy angry. Everyone knew that was the way to make a villain say more than he meant to.

'She's not *your* Alice,' Roland told him. 'Not after sixteen years. You don't get to have a say now.'

'You're wrong,' Fox said. 'Now is precisely when I get my way. Emily and Charlotte had her all that time. Now it's my turn.'

'She's not a toy!' Roland was disgusted. 'She's a person, for God's sake. You don't get a bloody turn!'

'Oh really?' Fox spoke very softly. 'And what about you? Trying to claim her for your side. You want her to be yours as much as I do. The difference is my claim is of longer standing. You barely know her.'

Roland let his arm fall away from Alice's, suddenly riddled with doubt. Fox saw his advantage and continued quickly.

'We're not so different, you and me. We both want to protect her.'

'No.' Roland knew he was faltering. 'That's not fair. Alice wants you to let her go.'

'Alice.' Fox's voice was as soft as fur, rippling across the distance between them. His voice was very different when he spoke to her to the one he used to Roland. 'Alice, you understand now, don't you. You know I was telling the truth. Do you believe now that I love you?'

Alice raised her head and looked Fox in the eyes.

'Yes,' she said. 'I do.'

John had promised he wouldn't go anywhere on his own. He knew what the adults meant by that and he knew that he was going to be breaking the spirit of his promise even if not the actual words. But Peter and Harriet didn't, couldn't, understand and with each hour that went past John was more worried that he might have left it too late.

When the adults went to bed John got dressed again and, carrying his shoes and rucksack, padded softly down the stairs. There was no sign of Delilah but he knew she would be watching. Nothing went by in this house without her noticing. He didn't mind, the more of the make-believe creatures who noticed him the better chance he had to finish the game.

When he opened the cupboard door he saw the two girls stare up at him from the darkness of the barn.

'It's time,' he whispered. 'Come quietly.'

They crept softly downstairs, stopping in the hall for long enough for the girls to collect heavy coats and wellington boots from the miscellaneous collection lying around in the cupboard. John took a large torch but he didn't turn it on as they turned the key in the lock and tiptoed out of the house.

He'd expected it to be dark but the rain had finally stopped and the clouds had cleared away so that the night sky was speckled with stars and a half moon shone brightly above them, supplying easily enough light to see by. Instead of going around to the back of the house John led the way towards the five-barred gate and the road.

'We'll have to watch out for the rescue people,' he said. 'But I think we should get as far up the fell as we can before going into the wood.'

'I came this way with Fox,' Erin said softly. 'I think I can remember how to get to the tarn.'

'But what about the mud?' Iona asked. She'd found woolly gloves and a beanie hat in the pocket of the coat she'd borrowed. The combination of those and the wellingtons and the silky dress John had found for her made her look a bit ridiculous but she didn't seem to care. Like all of them she had better things to worry about now. 'If the search and rescue people couldn't get through, how can we?'

'I think it'll let us through,' John told them. 'You see, I have something it wants.'

'It?' Katherine looked doubtful. 'What do you mean?'

'The name-eater,' John told her quietly. 'The thing at the centre of the make-believe game. It must be pretty angry with me now, because I changed you back and because of the things I told Roland. But it has to let us reach the tarn so we can work the magic. And, like I said, I've got something it wants.'

The girls exchanged worried glances over his head. John knew it without seeing them do it. He would have liked to tell them more but he thought it was better to sound as if he was certain even though he still didn't know exactly what he was going to do. He had to finish the game—he was certain of that. The only thing he didn't know was how.

The road ahead forked. One side led into the wood and a bright yellow barrier lay across the road, police tape attaching it on either side to the fences. CAUTION, it read, ROAD CLOSED. The tarmac surface of the road was covered in thick black mud, pitted and cracked in places where it had partially dried, deeper puddles of it oozing up through the cracks. Ahead, the tree-covered hillside closed out the sky and from the deeper darkness John could hear an insectile hum.

'I don't think I can do this,' a voice stammered and he turned to look at the dark-haired sister he'd named Iona. She was staring into the darkness and shaking her head. 'It's too much.'

'Does she have to?' his other sister asked. It had to be Erin speaking because the girl she used to be would never have been so sympathetic to her sister's feelings. 'Do we all need to go?'

'I think . . . ' John hesitated and looked back down the road. He'd expected to see it empty, the thin grey line snaking down the hill towards the house. But he'd been wrong.

The dolls had followed them. They stood just at the curve of the road, Delilah at the head of her army watching with a sweet unchanging smile. In her tiny hands she held a pair of delicate silver scissors.

'She's come for me.' Iona swayed and looked as if she might faint and Erin had to help her stand up straight.

'They're not moving,' she said. 'I don't think they *can* move. Not while we're looking at them.'

'If we go on we'll have to turn our backs on them,' Iona said, shakily.

'If we go back, we'll have to go *through* them,' Erin pointed out.

'We can't go back,' John said firmly. 'Here, take this.' Reaching back into his bag he pulled out two heavy cylinders. The first was the torch and he gave it to Erin, watching as she clicked it on and a beam of white light shone ahead of them into the wood. Only then did he pass the second to Iona. It was a can of bug spray, emblazoned with the image of a winged insect crossed out.

'What's this for?' Iona asked, giving a quick glance at the can before looking back to where the dolls waited.

'Vampiries are like insects,' John said. 'Look at the logo. It will work, believe me.'

'OK then.' Iona nodded. 'Let's go before I lose my nerve.'

Facing forward, Iona stepped out into the mud, her leg sinking down into it until the black tide reached almost to the top of her wellington.

'Urgh,' she said, but she didn't stop, taking another step and wading onwards as fast as she could. Erin followed her, shining the torch to make a path for them.

'We're being watched,' Erin said quietly, as they forged their way through the mud. She wasn't looking back but down.

'Mirror and Glass,' she said. The reflections played across the shiny puddles of the mud, mocking them with imitations of their clumsy wading stride.

'Ignore them,' John said. 'They only imitate us because they don't have proper minds of their own. They're reflections, that's what they do.'

'Wannabes,' Iona said unexpectedly, rolling her eyes at the two mimes. 'That is so *sad*.' Her voice was scathing and Erin picked up on her tone.

'Pathetic,' she agreed.

John didn't contradict them. After all, he agreed. Mirror and Glass were sad and pathetic. He just didn't mean the same thing by it that the girls did. All the make-believe people were trapped by the story they'd been woven into. They didn't have a choice about how to be. But he forgot the reflections when the humming insect noise began to gain volume, becoming a buzz that seemed to reverberate through his head. John had been afraid when he'd first seen insects in the wood, sensing the rot that seemed to lie beneath the landscape. But he wasn't afraid now.

The torch beam tunnelled into the darkness and shone on a blur of flickering gauze wings. The vampiries were massing in the wood ahead. Iona raised the bug spray and the buzz built to a dull roar as the insect fairies swarmed towards the light.

'Hey, vampiries,' Iona said, pressing the trigger. 'Bug *off*!' With a hiss the spray misted out in front of them into a cloud.

'Nicely done,' Erin said and then as the swarm headed in her direction she ducked and shouted: 'I *don't* believe in fairies!' Her expression was one of sudden realization. Like John, she'd found a key to understanding the world of make-believe. 'I don't *believe* in fairies.'

The insect buzz was frantic as the tiny bodies twisted and writhed in the light of the torch. Arms, legs, and wings fluttered desperately as they tried to avoid the deadly mist of bug spray. Insect bodies pattered on to the mud like rain, falling all around them.

When the air cleared they stood in a haze of chemical mist, covering their mouths with their free hands as the torch shone on a litter of fairy bodies, already sinking into the dark ooze. John pointed the way and Erin shone the torch up the fell, across the chaos of brambles and fallen trees.

'How are we going to get through that?' she asked. John hesitated and heard Iona answer, suddenly sounding a lot more confident.

'I have an idea,' she said.

The torch beam swept right as she and Erin aimed it together across a twisted tree, uprooted and lying in a rough clearing swamped with mud. In the heart of the tree metal glinted, the head of an axe, buried deep in the wood. Dropping the empty can of bug spray, Iona crossed the clearing and put her hands on the shaft of the axe.

'It's buried really deep,' she said, pulling at it.

'Think King Arthur,' Erin suggested, juggling the torch awkwardly so the light bobbed and ducked as she added her efforts to Iona's.

'Let me see,' John said, reaching between them and giving the axe a hard tug. It sprang loose from the wood as he touched it and the girls cheered softly.

'Way to go,' Iona said and John smiled at her.

'It was a group effort,' he said.

'If you say so,' Erin said, holding the torchlight straight again as they set off for the tangle of branches.

Roland felt his heart lurch with an emotion that was half jealousy and half fear. Alice's eyes were shining in the moonlight, very cool and clear.

'I believe you,' she said again, looking straight at Fox. 'I know you've been trying to protect me. You were right when you said I'm like you. It's true, I am. I know that now and I know you love me.'

'You do?' Fox sounded hesitant for once, his expression wavering between delight and suspicion.

'I do,' Alice said, her voice clear with conviction. 'I believe it. I believe you.'

Fox smiled. He was good-looking, Roland thought bitterly. Even while he hated the boy, he had to admit that he was every inch the romantic hero as his eyes searched Alice's looking for any trace of doubt and she smiled back at him. Roland saw that smile and felt jarred by it. It wasn't an expression that belonged on Alice's face: cruel and tender at the same time. Like Fox.

'But I don't love you,' she said.

Fox's face froze, his eyes turning blank as if he'd been hit. Alice's smile had dropped off her face and now she fixed him with cold hard eyes.

'You're a pretty fantasy,' she said. 'A shell of mannerisms and witticisms around an empty core. You don't have feelings, you have *hungers*. You *want*—something, anything to make you less empty inside.' She took a breath before continuing. 'Well, you've got what you wanted. I believe that you love me—as far as a thing like you is capable of love. But that's your fantasy, not mine. Love isn't possession, it isn't *having* and keeping and wrapping someone up in a cage of your desires. If you really loved me you'd accept that. You'd do something human for once in your make-believe life and watch me walk away—and be *happy* for me because I know what I want.'

The tide of words were like blows of an axe, biting into Fox and with each one he shuddered.

'Alice . . . ' he said, the word a plea.

'No,' she said, shaking her head. 'I'm not yours. Humans can't live in wonderland. And I might be make-believe but I'm real too. I didn't choose this, I don't choose you. I choose me. Alice. My name was never crossed out.'

The cage rocked as all around them winged-children screamed suddenly, shaking the branches and cawing with their bird voices, expressing the distress that shone from Fox's wild eyes. Roland planted his feet more firmly and stretched out an arm and felt Alice take his hand in hers. Perhaps her words had broken Fox and he'd lash out but right now Roland didn't care. It wasn't pride he felt but awe. Alice had struck right at the heart of the make-believe game and as the Rookery screamed wordlessly around them he felt sure the blow had gone home.

21
Nameless Fears

The Rookery screamed from the trees as John and his sisters crested the fell and saw the smooth black surface of the tarn ahead of them. Stars floated in the depths of space reflected in the water and he saw it as a void, a hole in the earth, a tear in reality.

On either side of him the girls drew closer together, closing ranks against the unreality of it. The whole wood was shaking and creaking in an invisible wind but the surface of the water was deathly still.

'Oh, hell,' Iona said flatly behind him and without looking he knew the dolls had followed them.

'Remember what we talked about,' Erin reminded her quickly and he heard them move behind him.

John didn't look back. It was time for him to speak to the spirit of the make-believe game, the dark presence that had blighted the lives of the people he loved.

'I'm here,' he said and heard the screams of the Rookery silenced so that he spoke into a vast waiting emptiness. 'I'm here to play the game and I'll play it by your rules.'

Iona felt Erin grab her hand as John spoke. Her sister was shaking as much as she was now. The memory of what had happened here before had gripped her when she'd seen the dolls at the edge of the wood and when John spoke again she felt the hairs rise on the back of her neck.

'Names crossed out cannot be spoken.

A character dead is a story broken.

Every sacrifice must cost:

You can't recover what's been lost.

Stolen words must be spent,

Borrowed power can't be lent.

The name-eater must be fed

By the living or the dead.'

Children had written those words, conjuring up a monstrous spirit capable of blurring the boundaries of reality and make-believe. They'd sacrificed fictional characters and broken apart stories in order to breathe life into their own fantasies.

Kneeling on the black altar stone John spread open the pages of the make-believe book to the empty part at the back. He had brought a thick black marker with him and he wrote the four simple letters of the name across the blank page: J O H N. Then, with a slice of the marker, he crossed it out.

Transfixed in horror, the girls stared at the ten-year-old boy as he stood up on the altar stone.

'John . . . no.' Erin was horrified, reaching out towards him to try and grab him back from the brink.

'What are you *doing*?' Iona's voice rose to a shriek of alarm.

'It's OK.' The boy turned to smile at them. 'That's not my name.' Then he stepped forward into the void.

* * *

Branches whipped and creaked and Roland saw the walls of the cage fall away as the roots sprang open beneath his feet. He and Alice were falling together towards the black water. He saw the shiny surface come up to meet him and with it the faces of Mirror and Glass.

Throwing out his hands to protect himself as he had in their crazy mirror world he hit the surface of the water hard. No longer liquid—it was suddenly smooth and glassy, like a sheet of ice. Next to him Alice had fallen to her hands and knees and was staring down into the black void beneath them. Dim stars floated in the distant depths.

Roland got to his feet gingerly, taking Alice's hand as they helped each other stand on the impossibly smooth surface. As they gained a slippery balance they looked back and saw Fox standing in a litter of wood and feathers, his face feral, fixed in an animal snarl.

On the other side of the tarn, a small figure stepped out from the altar stone. Distance seemed to swell and retreat, magnifying the size of the void between them while focusing on a pair of golden eyes. A boy was walking towards them across the surface of the still water. Watching him, Roland realized he was right when he'd credited his little brother with more maturity than Fox. He walked with supreme confidence, across a darkness that was spangled with stars.

Fox saw it too, looking past them at the approaching figure with something that might have been fear.

'Who are you?' he demanded.

'You don't know me,' the boy said quietly, coming to a stop at the centre of the tarn. 'None of you do.'

'John?' Roland asked carefully. 'What's going on?'

'That's not my name,' the boy told him. 'I said you didn't know me. But it's not your fault because I never told you who I really was. Catriona was right, John is a waste of a name. So I crossed it out.'

'So who are you?' Alice asked and then frowned, realizing that her question had been an echo of Fox's. Deliberately she reached for Roland's hand as she added: 'And what are you doing?'

The boy smiled at her. He liked Alice, and here at the centre of the make-believe game he could see her for who she was.

'I'm the magician,' he said. 'I'm the giver of names. I'm the one who's come to finish the game.' He was holding a book in his hand and all three of them recognized the battered cover that read: THE MAKE-BELIEVE GAME.

'You're here to destroy us,' Fox said, his eyes narrowing.

'No.' The boy shook his head. 'I've come to set you free.' He frowned. 'If you'll let me,' he added, with an uncertainty that actually relieved Roland.

His brother had always been a little uncanny but this was positively unearthly. He was grateful for Alice's hand in his as the boy continued.

'I couldn't save the vampiries,' he said. 'They're not really people, just paper cut outs. And Delilah.' He shook his head. 'I think she could have been a person but she's dark inside. There's nothing of her to save.'

'Like the Knarl,' Alice said and shuddered.

'The Knarl was rotten inside,' Fox said unexpectedly. He looked at Alice, and added bitterly, 'That's how you think of me, isn't it? Like the Knarl.'

'No, Fox,' Alice said sadly. 'You're beautiful. That makes it worse, somehow. I don't know why.'

'Alice . . . '

There was desperation in Fox's voice and Roland realized with shock that he was actually sorry for him. They had Fox cornered like an animal. He was just waiting for John to deliver the death blow and Alice was still ripping at him. Roland couldn't understand that and while half of him thanked God for it, the other half was reminding him of an overweight geek, trapped in a maze of reflections that showed him nothing but worthlessness.

'That's not entirely fair,' he said. 'You can't judge him by our standards. John's right, the make-believe people really aren't human.' He glanced up into the branches of the surrounding trees and saw the Rookery. 'Like them,' he said. 'They follow Fox, don't they? Because he's a ringleader and they know it. But they're like those feral children you read about who never got socialized. They're more animals than people.'

'They have what every human dreams of,' Fox said softly. 'The gift of flight. But they don't have words to tell us how it feels.' He hadn't taken his eyes from Alice.

It took everything she'd got to meet his eyes. She thought she'd vanquished him when she'd told him what she really thought of his love. But Roland had opened her eyes to something she found harder to accept. She didn't want to pity him, but she did.

'It's not me who's trapped, Fox.' She used his name the way he'd used hers, trying to convey everything she was feeling in it. 'It's you. You're an adolescent fantasy. You're my father, and you don't even know what that means.'

On the altar stone the two girls stood back to back, one facing the tarn, the other facing the wood.

'They're talking,' Erin said, her voice edgy with worry. 'I can see Roland and Alice and . . .'

'They're watching me.' Iona's voice rose with panic. 'They're just standing there, watching me. What do I do?'

'Just keep looking at them,' Erin repeated. 'They can't do anything while you're looking at them.'

'They can.' Iona sounded desperate. 'They're scaring the crap out of me.' She took a long shaky breath. 'I can't wait for whatever he's doing out there. Look, I don't know if you need closure, or whatever, and the names thing, that's fine. That's cool. We can even do the high school makeover scene thing if you want to but would you please unleash your inner geek or whatever it is your brother gets and I don't to sort them out? Because I don't get it and I really could use some help right now. Erin, *please?*'

'You said the magic word.' Erin turned around and faced the dolls.

It felt good to be the strong one for once. Delilah was frightening but she was also impotent. She was just a little doll. Her strength lay in her hair, the mingled strands she'd stolen from the teenage girls who'd believed in her. It was in her drones, the army of faceless, eyeless creatures who followed her mindlessly. And, more than that, it was in the fear she inspired.

Katherine had spent her life being afraid. She'd seen her mother disappear into darkness and ever since then she'd lived in fear. That was over now. Erin had seen her brother step into a darkness beyond imagining and walk across a path of stars into a world he created step by step.

'All right then,' she said. She was looking at Delilah but it was herself she spoke to. And, reaching out, she picked up the doll.

'Ohmigod.' Her sister was actually shaking. Iona was more vulnerable than Catriona had ever been, honestly at a loss when it came to mapping this make-believe world of myths and magic. But Erin knew how stories ended and that you had to cast out fear to vanquish the monster. She held Delilah by her hair, the doll dangling from her hand as she raised it up before Iona's face.

'Take the scissors,' she said.

'She made me steal them.' Iona's eyes were fixed on the doll. 'In the house, I found a box of blunted scissors. I had a dream and, in it, I imagined how your mother made the drones. She let Delilah hold the scissors when she cut off their hair. And then . . . '

'Take the scissors,' Erin said. She felt sick. Her mother had invented this and now there was only one way it could end. 'Come on, Iona. You have to.'

Iona took them from the doll's hand and held them between shaking fingers. Erin watched her frightened face and realized something about herself. *I'm more dangerous,* she thought. *When she's frightened she lashes out but she's never brooded over revenge the way I did. I need to watch out for that.*

'This is no time for doubts,' she said out loud. 'You know what you have to do. Come on. It's just like the vampiries. You have the weapon, use it.'

Iona sliced the sharp scissors through Delilah's hair and they watched as the body of the doll fell through the two metres of air and into the mass of drones. Beside it the scissors glittered as Iona let them fall and Erin was left holding the strands of hair.

'Don't watch,' Erin said softly and they turned their back on the drones, leaving Delilah's fate to their imagination. The silence was deafening before Iona spoke.

'She really scared me,' she said brokenly. 'She *hunted* me.'

'I know,' Erin said, trying not to think about the images her mind cast behind her. 'It's their revenge, really, not yours. No one likes being a puppet on a string, dancing to someone else's tune.'

'Erin?' Iona didn't look at her as she said in a small voice, 'Please remind me never to piss you off again.'

'Iona?' Erin was very serious when she said, 'Sometimes we'll fight. But not because we're enemies—because we're sisters.'

At the centre of the dark water the boy with golden eyes looked down at the book.

'It's time,' he said. 'To choose who we'll be, for now and for ever. Because the game ends tonight.'

'I've chosen,' Roland said. 'But I don't want to forget who I was even if I become the person I want to be.'

'I know who I am,' Alice said. She looked at Fox and said sadly, 'You invented me too, you know. I wish you could believe that.'

Fox's expression was grave and he dropped his eyes beneath her look of compassion.

'I think you invented me too,' he said. 'Reinvented me. Those things you said? About loving you enough to let you go? You're right, I don't understand. But perhaps I'm human enough to wish I did.' He looked away from her towards the boy. 'It hurts,' he said. 'Choosing.'

He looked down at the black surface beneath them and Roland saw Mirror and Glass beneath the still water, frozen in the same waiting attitude.

'Yes.' The boy's voice was gentle. 'But in the end, all that matters is how you want to be remembered. Because this is the end.' And he tore the book in half.

He'd opened it to the first page and it was that he tore across, the break opening across the poem and slicing through the words. Roland saw the break as if in slow motion, separating at the word *name-eater*, as the rotten pages behind separated like snowflakes and fell into the lake. Then he was falling too, the surface collapsing beneath his feet and sending him sprawling into freezing cold water.

Alice felt the ground open beneath her and took a breath. Her eyes stayed open and her left hand gripped tightly around Roland's. In the black water she saw Fox falling past her and for the last time he looked at her and opened his mouth. The syllables were bubbles but she recognized them and with a bubble of her own breath she said goodbye. He had loved her and she couldn't hate him any more. She watched him go and the reflections went with him, falling into the depths and lost there. But not forgotten.

She thrashed her free arm and her legs and rose to the surface with a splash, pulling Roland up with her.

'The game's over!' she shouted to him, as he blinked away water and released her hand to keep himself afloat. 'Your brother, he finished it.' She took another breath, trying to kick her boots off as she realized they were pulling her down. Above her in the sky birds wheeled against the stars, but they were only birds. The water that surrounded them was icy cold and very real. With the shock of it came realization of what it meant. 'Can he swim?'

'I don't know.' Roland looked wildly about and then swore suddenly and dived beneath the water, arms and legs powering into a crawl.

Alice dived with him and together they saw the floating body, head down in the murky water, golden eyes open and staring when they turned him over. Together they dragged him back to the surface and across the lake. It was impossible to tell if he was breathing, and his hands were chilled in theirs beneath the water.

From the shore the two girls waded forward, water sinking into their wellington boots and silky dresses plastering to their bodies as they hurled their coats back on to the bank. Together all four of them hauled the ten-year-old boy on to the smooth grey stone from which the black lichen had fallen away.

'Get the coats, Iona,' Erin ordered. 'We've got to keep him warm!'

'Here.' Iona piled the coats around the boy's body. 'Erin, Roland, do either of you know first aid?'

'I never took the class,' Roland said, shaking, and his sister didn't wait, turning the limp body on its back and leaning down to listen to his chest.

'He's not breathing,' Iona said and then knelt beside the boy and slammed two hands down on his chest, hard. She waited for a second and then covered his mouth with hers, breathing air into his lungs before sitting up. 'I only know this from TV,' she said. 'But I heard . . . ' she pumped his chest again up and down with one hand, 'if you don't know what to do . . . it's better to do something than nothing . . . '

'You're doing well,' Alice said, moving up next to her and laying a hand against the boy's neck. 'Keep on with the chest compressions, I'll count for you.'

'You did first aid?' Roland asked and Alice nodded quickly before counting aloud.

'Fifteen, sixteen, seventeen . . . ' The count was slightly faster than seconds and when she reached thirty she said, 'Two breaths, not one.'

They watched as Iona leant over to do as she said and Erin spoke quickly and urgently.

'Names . . . He told us he had a different name. What is it?'

'I don't know . . . ' Roland paused. He didn't know if it

would help even if he did. The boy had ended the game. Did that mean the rules didn't apply?

There was a choking spluttering noise and they all tensed as the boy spat up a mess of muddy water. The golden eyes had clenched shut as he choked but when they opened again they were alive, seeing them rather than staring blankly into nothing.

'Orlando,' he said, struggling to sit up. 'I forgot to tell you. My name's Orlando.'

The End

They came down the hill cautiously, for all the mood of jubilation that made them slightly crazy at the end. Orlando insisted that he could walk but he'd scared them all so thoroughly that they took turns to carry him on their backs or in an arm lift as they picked their way back down the hill.

Roland had tried to orientate the way back to the house but when he saw the lights of their rescuers ahead he accepted the inevitable. He and Alice had done their best to construct a halfway believable story, voices overlapping as they filled in the gaps with Erin and Iona occasionally contributing their own inspirations.

'Trapped in a sort of treehouse.'

'I guessed where they might have gone.'

'It was a sort of a game.'

'And then there was the storm.'

'Stupid not to leave a message.'

'It all went wrong but we were lucky.'

'Our parents are going to kill us.'

None of it seemed to matter all that much as they were bundled into a van and wrapped with blankets and driven down the moonlit road. Voices crackled over the radio and at one point they all heard cheers as people they'd never met sounded relieved that they'd been found.

Alice's hand found Roland's again between the fumble of blankets. Without looking at him she said:

'Was he right? Um . . . my . . . father. About you wanting to protect me?'

'I don't think you need protecting,' Roland admitted. 'I on the other hand . . . It's a jungle out there, you know. Parents, university entrance, anything could happen.'

'You're right.' She turned to smile at him. 'You're obviously going to need a lot of looking after. And protecting from them.'

The girls on the other side of the bench looked up with indignant expressions.

'Hey, we can't help overhearing,' Iona pointed out. 'Honestly, you two, get a room.'

'She's right,' said Erin supportively. 'Well, about that she is. Everyone gets to be right *once*.'

'Don't worry, Erin,' Iona said sweetly. 'You'll be right too someday.' They elbowed each other, giggling, and Roland rolled his eyes.

He looked towards the fifth occupant of the van. Golden eyes blinked sleepily back at him as the van slowed to pass between the five-barred gate and move up to take a place on the gravel between a police van and a battered Land Rover.

Outside the sun was rising, spearing the night with rays of amber and rose. The door of the house was open and four adults and a dog stood on the gravel, waiting impatiently for the van to stop.

'Orlando,' Roland said quietly. 'When did you choose that name?'

'It was after the very first cat fight,' Orlando said, leaning against him as Roland helped him out of his seat. 'When I said I wouldn't mind changing. I chose it because it was like yours.'

'Only one letter different,' Alice said softly. As the engine stopped she added, 'Will your parents be OK with it, you think?'

'You must be kidding,' Iona grinned.

'They'll be ecstatic,' Erin told her as the van doors opened and they stumbled out into the golden light of dawn.

Acknowledgements

In writing this book I was helped by many people. Firstly, my thanks go to John Nicoll, who lent my family his house in the Lake District where I found a secret room and the inspiration for this story. The house, the village, and the wood are real places but all names have been changed except for Windermere, Bowness, and Lake Windermere.

Thanks are also due to my writing partners, Frances Hardinge and Deirdre Ruane, whose constructive criticism continues to be invaluable. And to my mother, Mary Hoffman, without whose wisdom, experience, and support I'd be lost.

About the author

Rhiannon Lassiter was born in 1977 and is the eldest daughter of childrens' author Mary Hoffman. Her first novel, *Hex*, was accepted by Macmillan while she was still a teenager. Since then she has published nine further novels, a non-fiction book about the supernatural, and co-edited an anthology of war poetry and prose, in addition to several short stories.

Rhiannon lives and works in Oxford, where she attended university, reading English Literature at Corpus Christi College. In addition to writing, Rhiannon maintains her own website and web-edits Armadillo Magazine, an online quarterly children's books review publication. She has also worked as a journalist, web designer, and marketing administrator. Rhiannon's books have been widely reviewed and translated into more than ten foreign languages.

For more about Rhiannon Lassiter and her other published titles visit her official website at www.rhiannonlassiter.com